Praise for Michelle M. Pillow's
Realm Immortal: King of the Unblessed

5 Crystal Tattoos! *"In Realm Immortal: King of the Unblessed, Ms. Pillow has crafted an emotionally gripping story of love and desire, deception and betrayal, all set against the backdrop of a war between good, evil and all that lies between. ...From page one I was spellbound by the vivid imagery, engaging plot and believable characters. You are transported immediately into the two worlds... Ms. Pillow's rich words and sumptuous phrases bring both to life with a startling clarity...*

While Juliana and Merrick's relationship is the main focus of the book, several other characters have their chance to play in the sun. The result is love scenes that rate from sensual to lusty to a slight hint of kink; all of them sizzling.

I can only hope Ms. Pillow will take pity on us mortals and gift us with further adventures in the Realm Immortal." ~ Aislinn James, Erotic-Escapades

4 Blue Ribbons! *" REALM IMMORTAL is not your ordinary tale of romance and adventure. This story definitely has a dark side that will intrigue readers and keep them turning the pages... Michelle M. Pillow knows how to create a story that leaves readers breathless and wanting more."* ~ Angel, Romance Junkies

Realm Immortal: King of the Unblessed

By Michelle M. Pillow

A Samhain Publishing, Ltd. publication

Realm Immortal: King of the Unblessed
Copyright © 2006 by Michelle M. Pillow
Cover by Scott Carpenter
Print ISBN: 1-59998-054-1
Digital ISBN: 1-59998-008-8
www.samhainpublishing.com

Samhain Publishing, Ltd.
PO Box 2206
Stow OH 44224

First Samhain Publishing, Ltd. electronic publication: January 2006
First Samhain Publishing, Ltd. print publication:

Realm Immortal:
King of the Unblessed

By Michelle M. Pillow

Dedication

To my father, because you support me no matter what I do, because you instilled values and a hard work ethic in me by example, and because you are one of the most honorable, giving, kind-hearted men I know. I love you.

Prologue

Black Palace of the Unblessed, Kingdom of Valdis, 1406 AD

Immortality had a way of changing fate. None knew this as well as Merrick, dark elfin King of Valdis, ruler of all that was unblessed. Once, long ago in a time he did not like to remember, he'd been heir Prince to the Tegwen throne, future King of the Blessed. Happiness and pleasure had been his, as had love—love of a family, of his people. He'd been light and good. Now he was ruler of all that was dark and feared.

Well, not all that was dark. King Lucien of the Damned did have rule over the demons.

As Merrick gazed upon the narrow basin of water before him, the liquid was still. It reflected his eyes—eyes so brown they looked to be black. When he was angry, the whites would fill in with the dark color. Those who saw the change often claimed to see the demon lurking beneath his surface. His eyes were a strange contrast to his long blond hair. They were a reflection of what he'd become, changed the day of his Unblessed Coronation. The hair was a reminder of what he'd once been.

The divining basin was perched atop a tall column, which in turn was lifted up on a platform in the center of the dark garden. It had been a gift from King Lucien upon Merrick's coronation. His powers were somewhat connected to the Demon King, even though his coronation had been the first and last time he'd spoken directly with the man. The gray stone base was carved with images of demons sucking the souls from mortals. Within the shallow pool, the moonlight reflected on water to reveal to him all he would see, always the present, but sometimes the future and past. King Merrick didn't look to the future, for the images were blurred and often misread, and he refused to dwell on the past.

Silver moonlight shone over the expansive black garden. The plants were withered and neglected, and yet did not die. Dark stone paths led up from his castle palace, twisting about the grounds in a seemingly endless pattern. They were surrounded by thick walls covered in vines. The walls formed a labyrinth from which trespassers could never escape. Thorns, as sharp as blades, edged the vines. Amongst the thorns, crimson flowers blossomed, but they only did so for him. The flowers looked almost liquid, as if the petals would drip like blood to the ground. They were the only flowers in the immortal realm that would bloom when he was near.

Repeatedly, Merrick watched his presence suck the life from the world around him. He was necessary, as necessary as light and spring. He was fall, winter, death to the land. Without him, the immortal world would not rest. Without him, good would not be. And for this he was hated by those he'd once called friends.

"Show me that which I seek," Merrick ordered the water softly. He tapped a finger against the surface, rippling it. He knew what was to come. It tortured him as it soothed him. It filled him with longing and frustration. From the frustration came anger, and from the anger a bitterness he didn't try to hide.

Then there she was, sitting and staring at a fire, a look of longing in her eyes. He later discovered that she did that often. The human woman captured his notice one night as he flew around the mortal realm masquerading as a falcon. Unless magick favored it, which wasn't often, the falcon disguise was the only way he could go to the mortal realm in solid form for long periods of time. Otherwise he could only project a glamour of himself or send his minions in his place.

Merrick didn't think, had just watched her like he would a play. He loved her, or at least thought he could love her, as much as any being with a dark heart could love. Love was not so lofty an emotion and was wrongly thought exclusive to the blessed. However, as with all things, the emotion was more complicated than that, for love could be as dark as the underworld, as enslaving as death, as vengeful as a righteous cause. Beings killed in the name of love, died for it, lusted after it, greedily kept it locked away, withheld it, exploited it. This was not an emotion the King of the Unblessed sought to possess.

"I, Lady Juliana of Bellemare," she'd said that first evening he saw her, "have come here to slay your village dragon in return for my weight in gold."

Her voice had been low and soft, like a lullaby, but such voices he'd heard many times before her. Nymphs had been brought to his castle to sing and they were renowned for the sounds they made. Right away, he knew she spoke only to herself, imagining a world beyond that with which she was acquainted with. Dragons didn't exist in her world. Then again, he didn't exist in her world. Immortals preferred to keep the humans unaware, for they were uninteresting creatures who lacked power and magic. Mortals were ruled by fear and ignorance and King Merrick was amused to watch where that ignorance would lead them. But Lady Juliana was different than other mortal women, for she'd captured his notice. That alone marked her as special.

Why it should be so, he didn't understand. She was beautiful with long dark hair and wide blue eyes, but Merrick had seen too much of beauty to be swayed easily by it. For if beauty could conquer him, then just the sight of the Golden Palace at Tegwen would have done him in long ago.

No, there was no reason for it. All he knew is that night after night he was drawn to the garden basin to watch her. At first he'd hoped to find fault with her, thus losing interest. But the more he watched, the more he longed for her, wanted her, until she entered his thoughts when he was away from the garden.

Merrick knew obsession only led to madness. The creatures of Valdis wouldn't be pleased with an obsessed king, not when they struggled constantly with Tegwen, and with each other. There were many who wanted his throne. Only death would relinquish him of it and no matter how he tired of life, he didn't wish for death.

The water rippled over the vision. Juliana stood, stretching her arms above her head. Though fine by human standards, her russet gown was woolen and plain. The long trailing sleeves touched the floor, sweeping up over her elbows. The bodice was high and the skirts hung loose, hiding her figure beneath the padded underskirts. She didn't cover her dark locks, but let them hang freely to her waist.

Merrick frowned. There was only one option left to him. He'd go to her and offer her a choice. Either she would come with him until he tired of her or he would have her killed. If he possessed her, had her locked away in his castle, then he wouldn't be so obsessed. Lady Juliana would be under his complete control. If she chose death, then he'd no longer be able to gaze upon her face, unless it was to see it rotting in the ground. The spell would be broken and he would be free of her.

Merrick watched her for a moment longer, then waved his hand over the basin. Her image disappeared. He stared at the water a moment longer, contemplating his decision. It was for the best. He did not like the distraction she caused him.

Soon. He would offer his bargain to her soon. Death or enslavement. Balling his hand into a fist, Merrick really hoped she chose death.

Chapter One
Bellemare Castle, England, Mortal Realm

"She's been seen right here in this very castle, looking for her next husband in the guise of an old woman. Then, when she finds him, she'll come back for him as a young, fair maiden to lure him away with her. After their marriage vows are spoken, she'll take him to the sea where she'll lead him to his watery death beneath the waves!" Lady Juliana kept her voice low and her eyes wide. "The only way to tell if a woman is a Nixie is to lift her skirts and see whether or not she has fins instead of legs."

The children giggled, looking up at Lady Juliana from their place on the ground. Their dirty faces were rapt with attention. The noblewoman loved telling them stories.

"What of you?" a child called, pointing at her legs. "Have you fins?"

"Aye, my lady!"

"Have you fins?"

A few knights listened nearby, making light comments amongst themselves and smiling at Lady Juliana. The noblewoman knew the men well, for they served under her father before his death, and now owed allegiance to her oldest brother, Hugh, the Earl of Bellemare. Juliana kept a straight face until the children quieted once more. Seeing the boy who first yelled, she took a step toward him. Lowering her lids over her eyes, she said, "Methinks you'll make a fine husband."

The girls screamed. The boys eyed her, cautious. Juliana lifted her skirt and let them peek at her shoes. The children started laughing.

"Now be observant and watch the ground for a trail of water. If you find it and are truly brave, you may follow the trail and find a Nixie. Only beware, for she might just set her sights on marrying you." Juliana nodded seriously. The boys instantly boasted that they were unafraid. The girls continued to giggle. "Off with you my noble knights and gentle ladies! I'll tell you another story tomorrow about a valiant warrior and how he conquered the beast that was eating the King's men."

Lady Juliana waved her hand, watching as the children ran to the tents of the marketplace. She shaded her eyes, smiling at them. The marketplace was set up outside the castle walls, for Bellemare's keep was small. Merchants from all over the country came to sell their wares at market and all the neighboring households came to buy. Bellemare was blessed with good soil and fair weather, but was best known for its fine breed of horses. It was a reputation the family had taken pride in for generations.

"Honestly, Juliana," a voice drawled. "Do you think it wise to send them to the marketplace to lift ladies' skirts?"

Juliana spun around in excitement. Her face brightened as she looked into eyes as blue as her own. "Thomas! How long have you been standing there? I can't believe King Henry let you come home to us. When did you arrive? Why wasn't I told you were coming?"

"You should know I wouldn't miss your wedding vows." Thomas laughed. The warm spring air blew his dark hair over his face. "Come, I've been away for nearly five months. Have you a better greeting than that for your brother?"

"I'm sorry, Thomas, of course I'm happy to see you." Juliana rushed to him, throwing her arms about his neck.

"That's better." Thomas returned her hug, kissing her forehead. "You're as lovely as ever—a true gem on Bellemare's crown."

"Oh, I've missed you. Your last letter was so dull me thought you were sure to die of boredom afore coming back to us." Juliana pulled back, studying him. She patted her hand on his chest, smoothing down his green tunic.

Thomas was handsome, but all in her family had been graced with beauty. They were truly blessed in many ways. All of them had dark brown hair that gleamed in the sunlight, high cheekbones and proud features. The oldest, Hugh, and the youngest, William, both had brown eyes as dark as sin. Juliana and Thomas had blue eyes the color of the night sky, taking after their long passed mother. Juliana took her brother's arm and led him toward the gatehouse to go within the bailey walls. "Now, Sir Thomas, you must tell me all that happened whilst you were away. And please do make something up. I should hate it if all you had for me was the dismal truth. I know, tell me how all the Spanish knights at court look like hobgoblins."

A shrill feminine cry sounded from the marketplace. Thomas chuckled. "I'd wager there is the result of your fanciful stories. No doubt some poor child is now having his ear pulled for lifting a noblewoman's skirt."

"I seem to recall our lord father pulling your ear more than once for lifting a woman's skirt," Juliana teased.

Thomas tried to look stern and failed. "Talk like that will ruin your reputation, my lady."

"Do you think it would keep Lord Eadward away longer?" Juliana asked, her smile faltering.

"Still not pleased with Hugh's decision?"

"How could I be?" Juliana sighed, doing her best not to look depressed even if she was to be married soon. Thomas was home, Hugh was in residence and William was due the next morning. Now was not the time for self-pity. "The man lives not far from here. If I must marry, why should it be to a neighbor? I know what his lands look like, for they're like ours."

Thomas chuckled, nodding to several nobles who passed. Neither of Thomas nor Juliana wished to interrupt their private conversation, so they continued on through the gatehouse. Passing under the dark entryway, he said, "You're a curious one. Most ladies would complain Lord Eadward was nearly thirty years their senior. You complain he doesn't live far enough away to be considered an adventure."

A low wall separated the outside world from the outer bailey. A taller wall, made of stone and timber, guarded the main part of the keep. They walked under the second gate to the main courtyard. The castle itself sat atop an enditched mound of earth and rock. It towered a good fifty feet above the bailey. In front of the castle was the courtyard. The only way in and out of the yard was through the front gatehouse. Contained within the inner courtyard was the exercise yard for the knights, a small chapel, the stables, a barn, a few workshops, and a small brewery.

When they were before the castle, Juliana said, "Lord Eadward is kind and his age doesn't bother me. Hugh says the marriage will be good for the family and I'm willing to do my part."

Thomas nodded.

"Even so, it could be worse." Juliana made a face. She'd been feeling a strange sort of melancholy lately. Marriage was always said to be the start of a young maid's life, but to her it felt like the end of it. She loved Bellemare and she loved her brothers. If she had to stay in one place, she'd rather it was with her family. She hid her thoughts from Thomas. "I could be betrothed to his son, Sir Humphrey the Foul."

"I forgot we called Nicholas that," Thomas said, chuckling. He glanced up over the high castle, prompting Juliana to do the same. The stone was painted white with lime, causing the castle to gleam in the sunlight. She loved her home, but she longed to see more of the world. Thomas sighed. "I've missed being home."

"How else were we to speak ill of Sir Nicholas when he was always underfoot?" Juliana smiled. "The poor man still thinks I had invisible companions as a child."

"I know you have invisible companions," Thomas teased. "I'm surprised Hugh has yet to lock you away in a tower."

"You are hopeless when it comes to gallantry, brother." Juliana punched him lightly in the arm even as she laughed. "Nicholas used to tell me I ought to be careful, lest the devil hear me and take me away with him."

"Methinks that would have encouraged you." Thomas let her walk before him up the circular stairwell to the great hall.

"It did," she admitted, trailing her hand over the stone. She stopped, turning to look down in the dim light. Juliana couldn't read Thomas' features. "Nicholas won't be here for the wedding. He, ah, doesn't approve of it."

"Nonsense," Thomas said, but his tone was unconvincing. "You and he are friends, Juliana. How could he object? Oft, as boys, methought there might be more between you. I know our father hoped as much."

"Hm, if you say so. Though, there is nothing between Nicholas and me. I feel friendship for him, as I do all my brothers. He's never declared that he feels differently." Juliana sighed softly, continuing the climb up to the great hall.

"And if he did?"

"Nicholas is…" Juliana hesitated. Nicholas was what? "Nicholas."

"Ah." Thomas nodded knowingly. Juliana wasn't sure exactly what he thought to know.

Servants put empty goblets out on the tables, readying it for the eve meal. Along one wall was a platform, set up from rest of the hall. There, the family dined, along with honored guests. Blue tapestries hung on the wall, along with the Bellemare crest—a black stallion statant on a field of green. Below the high table were the permanent dining tables and benches set up for the servants, soldiers and freemen of the keep. The fact that the tables were permanent fixtures in the manor, and not the usual portable kind, showed the large extent of the Bellemare wealth. A large stone fireplace sat along the wall opposite the head table. A fire burned brightly, giving the hall light when the sun did not shine through the iron grated windows or when the oak shutters were closed. There were also many candles, made from animal fat and beeswax, placed along spikes in the stone walls.

Juliana wanted to say more, but Thomas was greeted by servants and knights excited to see him home. She kissed her brother's cheek and promised to find him later, after he met with Hugh. Standing in the doorway

15

to the stairwell, she watched him for a moment, proud of the man he was. She loved all her brothers for they were each great men—honorable, brave, handsome, loyal. Sighing wistfully, happy Thomas had finally come home, she walked out of the hall to leave the way they'd come.

Thomas watched his sister walk away from him before cheerfully returning the good wishes he received from the servants. Juliana was pale, thin. Her blue linen gown hung loosely on her frame, showing the cream chemise underneath at the forearms and neck. The sleeves of the overtunic trailed down to the floor from her elbows. She was a beautiful woman, made more so by the kindness in her. Even her naivety added to her innocent charm.

Juliana had grown up in the protection of Bellemare, spoiled by parents who loved her before their deaths and guarded by brothers who adored her. Thomas knew the idea of marriage was hard on her in many ways. His sister had always been a dreamer. He loved that about her, all the brothers did. But the look in her eyes this day was different. She was sad, bothered, almost haunted.

Juliana just celebrated her twentieth year, well past the time young women married. Although the brothers would gladly keep her well into old age, it wasn't fair to her. She deserved a family of her own, children of her own. At least with Eadward, she'd be close to Bellemare, should she ever need them.

In the world they lived in, Lord Eadward of Tyrshire was a good match. He was the younger brother of a rich Marquis, a Marquis who had no other heirs as of yet. He had many knights under his command and political alliances. His land was prosperous and adjoined their own. But, in the world Juliana lived in, the marriage was more like an imprisonment.

Thomas knew Lord Eadward to be a kind, generous man. He'd make her a good husband. His son, Sir Nicholas, had grown up with them. Hugh would have given Juliana to Nicholas, as they were of like ages, if she'd ever shown the smallest inclination toward him. Juliana didn't and Nicholas never once asked for her hand. Given that, Lord Eadward was the better choice.

Hugh struggled with his decision for nearly a year, though the brothers never told Juliana about it. The Earl only signed the betrothal agreement after he, Thomas and William were of a like mind. In the end, it was decided it was better to marry her off to a man of their choosing before she caught the king's notice and he married her off to a man of his.

"Sir Thomas, it's good to have you home," a pretty servant said. She curtsied before handing him a goblet of mead.

"Aye, Tressa, it's good to be back at our beloved Bellemare." Thomas smiled, his gaze alighting on the woman. He knew her well, so well that he could easily picture the speckled birthmark on her inner thigh. When her eyes met his, he glanced toward the ceiling in invitation.

The woman bit the corner of her lip and gave a quick nod. Thomas' grin widened with anticipation. As she scurried off, he thought, Mm, it's good to be home indeed.

Juliana glanced around the side courtyard from the kitchen's entryway. She heard the sound of servants busily at work behind her, preparing a great feast. With all the noble families at market, the hall would be filled during the evening meal. The smell of baking bread and roasted chicken permeated the air. A small herb garden was nearby. Being spring, the plants were young, but soon their fragrance would fill the air to war with the smell of the kitchen.

Juliana looked around. The side yard was empty, as she knew it would be. The area was private, accessible from the main courtyard, but not obviously so. She took a deep breath and then another. It did little to calm her. Tomorrow she'd be married. She wasn't as nervous as she should have been, but she wasn't excited either. If anything, she was sad. Her eyes tried to fill with tears, but she wouldn't let them. She knew the world she told the children of didn't exist, but it didn't stop her from longing for more, from daydreaming. Some nights the yearning inside her was almost unbearable. On those nights she would dream. The images were blurry, but the feelings of desire she awoke with were real—desires of the flesh, desires of the heart, desires of her very soul.

She longed for a man of that other world to come for her. Sure, it was a fanciful dream—one told many times by young maidens wanting to escape. Still, as she lay awake at night, she could almost feel him watching her. Juliana had always had a vivid imagination.

A chill washed over her, causing her to tremble. The air felt cooler, but she could attribute that to the evening being close upon them. Eadward was coming for her, could possibly even be there that night. Tomorrow they'd be wed. He was a good man and would make an adequate husband. He'd been a friend of her father and was now one to her brothers. The wedding night would be a little awkward, but such was the burden of being a woman.

Nicholas wasn't happy about the match and she suspected he didn't want her as his lady mother. She couldn't blame him. Nicholas would never feel like her son. Though they teased each other often as children, he was her friend and his opinion mattered. Regardless of how they felt, there was nothing to be done about it, for the marriage wasn't her decision to make.

"Where are you, Sir Knight? Why haven't you come to rescue me? I'd trade my soul to you for an adventure," she whispered to herself, closing her eyes. She reached out with her feelings, willing him to come to her. "Just one good adventure. Take me away with you to foreign lands. Show me the castles and palaces of enemy kings. Dance with me under stars by the light of a dragon's breath. Please, rescue me, Sir Knight."

"I wouldn't demand your soul, my lady, just your undying loyalty for an eternity."

The tone was low, gravelly. A blush heated Juliana's features as she realized she'd been overheard. What would Hugh say if he found out she'd been talking to herself? Again. She suppressed a loud groan as she quickly turned to see who spoke.

Dark eyes stared at her from a handsome face. His skin was tanned, his features hard. Leather bound back the locks of his unfashionably long blond hair, winding down the length from his temples to just above his waist. She swallowed, suddenly very nervous. Her heart beat faster, quickening like it did in her dreams.

He had to be a knight, for he looked strong and broad of shoulders. Juliana knew she stared, but she couldn't seem to gather her wits. She took a deep breath, forcing her mouth to close. He was most likely a foreigner, though it was hard to distinguish from his tone where he was from.

His clothing was nothing like she'd ever seen. The black breeches pulled tight to his legs and hips, showing every indention of muscle. He wore black leather boots that gleamed in the late afternoon light. They were high over his calves, lacing along the side so they fit snug. His black undertunic was of a lightweight material and tucked into the top of the breeches. Unlike the knee length overtunics of Bellemare knights, his was sleeveless and hung open in the front, falling to the ground like a cape. The black material was embroidered with silver, the front held together by two silver chains that draped along his chest. The upturned collar framed his face. As she stared, his head tilted to the side and his mouth curled in amusement. Her heart skipped erratically, thumping hard in her chest, reminding her to speak.

"Forgive me," Juliana managed, unsure how much time had gone by. "Did you speak?"

He took a step toward her. Juliana couldn't move. She couldn't see anything but the man. It was as if the world faded away, taking all her cares with it.

"I was merely taking you up on your offer, Juliana. You offered your soul, but I'll only demand your eternal loyalty and obedience. The soul you can keep, I have no use for it."

"Do I know you?" she asked, wondering how he knew her name. "Have we been introduced?"

"Tonight," he said. "I'll come for you tonight."

"For my wedding?" she asked. "It isn't until tomorrow."

"You're to be married?" His face turned instantly from amusement to darkness. His eyes narrowed in obvious displeasure.

"Aye, to Lord Eadward of Tyrshire."

"Not anymore," he said, stepping closer. "You will wed no one, Juliana. I will see to that."

The words were low but unmistakable. Juliana wanted them to be true. Deep inside, she didn't wish to marry Eadward. "I'm afraid, Sir, you have no say in the matter. The bans have been posted. It's done."

The man laughed softly. He moved closer to her still. His low voice was like a whisper on the wind. "The bans may have been posted, but the vows have yet to be said. It is hardly done. It will never be done."

Juliana shivered, unable to back away. Her gaze dipped to his mouth. They seemed so close. She'd been kissed once, by a knight, but he'd never made her heart beat so fast or her mouth go dry. Afterward, she'd been ashamed of kissing him because she knew her duty to her family name. Luckily, Hugh never found out, though she'd agonized for weeks. The man edged closer. Time stood still as he held her transfixed. Logic told her to move away. Her body wouldn't listen. It wanted this moment, wanted the danger of it, the unknown.

Licking her lips, Juliana let her lids fall heavy over her eyes until she was staring at him dreamily through the narrowed slits. One kiss wouldn't hurt. She wasn't married yet.

Juliana waited for the man's touch. She felt the heat of his body next to her. The scent of the man overwhelmed her, blocking out the fresh air, the food cooking in the kitchen. He smelled just as a man should—clean, strong, virile. Without thought, she parted her lips, offering them up to him.

No harm ever came of a simple kiss, she assured herself. *Just a kiss, a friendly, innocent kiss.*

Juliana watched him come for her, his lips moving closer. An eternity passed, eaten away by mere seconds. Dizzy with anticipation, she waited for his touch, his taste. She wanted to experience just once what it would be like to feel overwhelming attraction. Lord Eadward would be kind, but they would not have passion. He would never make her heart beat fast or her breath deepen.

"Tonight," she heard him whisper. Juliana felt the hiss of his breath against her lips with that one word. Her eyes closed completely. The wind stirred, blowing her hair. She lifted her hand, reaching for his chest, wanting to feel him, needing to know that he was real. Her hand fell through the air. She gasped in surprise. Opening her eyes, she saw that he was gone.

"Sir?" she said, breathless. Her lips stung with the rejection. Loneliness coupled with desperation overwhelmed her.

Juliana looked around the small yard, before running to the narrow entryway that led to the main courtyard. It was filled with guests, but no dark stranger. Blood rushed in her ears, drowning out sound. Her lips stung. Her heart pounded so hard that she felt numb and elated at the same time. Moisture welled within her eyes. She couldn't explain it, but she didn't want the man to go. With that in mind, she turned back to the side courtyard and ran to the kitchen. The servants stopped to stare at her.

"Tonight? Who's coming tonight, my lady?" Margaret asked, stepping toward her. Juliana looked at the cook. The woman's wiry grey hair sprouted out of her head in disarray, as she took up her stained apron and wiped her hands. "My lady, is all well? You're as pale as the linen. What about tonight?"

Juliana stared at the cook, unable to remember speaking the word "tonight" aloud. "Did someone come through here? A nobleman, strangely dressed?"

The servants giggled.

"My lady!" Margaret scolded playfully, shaking her head. "You come in here looking like death only to tease us. For shame! Now, off with you. I hear Sir Thomas is in residence. Go tell your stories to him. We have a castle to feed."

"But..." Juliana said, only to nod in agreement. The man wasn't a figment of her imagination, was he? She couldn't have dreamt up someone so real. She walked toward the great hall to find Thomas. Perhaps the wedding was getting to her after all, for now she was seeing things.

"Hugh, I don't want to be married." Juliana's voice was a mere whisper, as she looked at her oldest brother's back, waiting for him to turn to her. He was the tallest of all the siblings, with a noble bearing that had been bred into him since birth. She didn't know where the words came from, or how they managed to escape her lips, but she didn't want to take them back.

"Juliana, we were just talking about you," Hugh said when he turned. He didn't smile, he never really smiled, though his voice and eyes were kind as he looked at her.

Juliana hid her frown. Hugh hadn't heard her. It was probably for the best. She glanced over to see Thomas studying her intently. Thomas had heard what she said, but luckily out of the group of men standing there he'd been the only one. She gave a slight shake of her head, keeping him quiet. Then, looking at Hugh, she said coyly, "I should hope everything you said of me was very wicked. There's no fun to be had in the truth."

Hugh laughed, causing the group of men to join in. She recognized many of the nobles, even knew some of them by name. It was a good thing none of them had heard her disheartened comment. Her upcoming nuptials really must be affecting her judgment. First she saw people who weren't there and then she talked without thought or care.

"I wouldn't be so sure, my lady," Sir Geoffrey said. He was one of Hugh's loyal knights.

"Why do you say that?" Juliana asked, looking around at the men's smiling faces.

"Some of the children," Hugh explained. "Have been..."

"Reprimanded," Thomas supplied.

"...ah, aye, reprimanded," Hugh paused, clearing his throat, "for lifting noblewomen's skirts in the market today. They said you told them to look for Nixies."

Juliana gave a guilty glance around the small group. She knew from past experience that Hugh was amused by it more than anything. "What did you do to them?"

"I imprisoned them, naturally. The ladies demanded they be punished," Hugh said. Juliana blinked in surprise, worried. Leaning down to her, he whispered, "They feast in the dungeons as we speak, away from the real prisoners."

Juliana smiled. She should have known Hugh would never be so cruel. The children would think it a great game to be kept "prisoner" for the evening. Juliana nodded. "A suitable punishment for such a heinous offense. To imagine I would tell them to do such a thing. Honestly, I don't know where they come up with such fanciful ideas."

Juliana tried to look innocent. The others merely laughed. They all knew the truth. Juliana's affection for children and for stories was widely known throughout the countryside.

"Speaking of the children, I'm afraid I might have been telling them too many tales. I promised to ask, though, even at the risk of sounding absurd." Juliana paused, wondering if she was indeed insane. "Have any seen a stranger amongst us today? He sounds as if he'd be easily recognized. Long blond hair to his waist and all black clothing. A foreigner to be sure." Juliana bit the inside of her lip, trying to keep her expression calm as she awaited their answer. Such a man as the one in the garden would be hard to miss. The men looked at each other, shaking their heads.

"Nay, my lady," Sir Ivon, a towheaded knight said.

"I haven't heard of such a man," added Sir Pieter, an English Baron.

"Sounds as if we have an elf walking about the castle," Hugh laughed.

It was just as she suspected. She'd imagined the dark stranger. A hollow formed in her chest. She wanted so badly for him to be real. Thomas gave her a curious look, but she ignored him. Forcing an easy chuckle, she said, "Methought as much. The children must be trying to tease me for they swore he was out walking the courtyard."

The men laughed. Juliana bowed her head, curtseying, as she said, "If you would excuse me, my lords. Sirs."

They bowed low to her. She turned to go. Thomas took up her arm. When they were out of earshot, he said, "Juliana, there's still time to—"

"Nay, Thomas, nay." She smiled for him, but it took all her willpower to keep the look intact. "I'm just being foolish. Women get this way the day before they are to marry. Lord Eadward is coming tonight...and...well...I..."

"We want you to be happy. You know that, don't you, Juliana?" Thomas insisted.

"Is all well?" They turned to look at Hugh.

"Aye, all's well. I wish you two would stop worrying like old washerwomen." Juliana leaned over and kissed Thomas' cheek and then Hugh's. "I ate in the kitchen. Make my excuses. I'm going to go lie down. Send someone to me if I must greet Lord Eadward."

"Good eve," Hugh said, touching her cheek softly. Juliana closed her eyes briefly and turned into his hand.

"Sleep well, sister," Thomas added.

Juliana curtseyed, stopping to impishly wink at them before moving toward the stairs. She knew she should stay and entertain the guests, but she just couldn't do it. She was tired and wanted to be alone. As soon as she was hidden from the great hall's view, she let the smile fall from her features. Her head drooped forward and she held onto the wall as she wearily climbed the stairs. Tonight was going to be a very long night.

"She's not pleased with this," Thomas said to his older brother. "Methinks we should reconsider."

"I heard her as well. She's just nervous, Thomas. Besides, I have already given my word on the matter and she has given hers. The bans have been posted. Lord Eadward is a good man who will treat her well." Hugh's expression didn't change as he looked at the place where their sister had disappeared.

"We keep saying that," Thomas said. "I have yet to know who we're trying to convince—Juliana or ourselves. Mayhap, we should go talk to her."

"Come, brother, we have guests to tend to." Hugh took Thomas by the shoulder and pulled him toward the head table where the servants served pitchers of wine. "Juliana will be fine. She's strong. Always has been. And she'll do her duty."

"It's not her strength I worry about," Thomas answered, giving one last glance at the stairwell before letting Hugh lead him back toward the high table. "It's her spirit."

Chapter Two

"Ju-li-an-a."

Juliana stopped on her way up the stairwell, frowning slightly in confusion. Laughter rang softly from the hall below. She glanced behind her, the way barely lit by the firelight from the great hall. No one was in the stairwell with her. She shook her head, continuing up. Hopefully a full night's sleep would set her head straight.

Abovestairs there were enough bedchambers for all four siblings and a few guests. Juliana's was to the left, next to small rooms set up for sewing with weaving looms and cutting tables. Her chambers were separated from her brothers'. Hugh thought to give her privacy, or so he claimed. Juliana knew it was to keep her from being offended when they brought maids up to their beds for the night. Thinking of it, she smiled. She let her brothers pretend they got away with their affairs without her knowledge, but there was little that happened at Bellemare she didn't know about.

"Juliana."

Juliana stopped. That time the whisper was louder and came from above. "Aye?"

Above her the halls were dim. The sun had set and now moonlight shone through the narrow window slits above. Since she wasn't expected to retire so early in the eve, the servants had yet to light the torches. She took a hesitant step up, nearing the top.

"Is someone there?" she called.

"Juliana," the voice whispered again, raspy and low. A figure moved from the shadows, running across the top of the stairs. She jumped in surprise, nearly falling down the stairwell. Righting herself, she leaned to the side, trying to get a peek. The figure had been small, like a child.

"This isn't funny," Juliana said, relaxing some. The children had played pranks on her before. "Come out, please. You shouldn't be here. These are my private chambers."

"Juliana." This whisper was different, raspier than the first, the tone higher. No doubt it was a girl. At least one torch was usually left so none had to wander around in the dark, but the children must have put it out.

"Lord Bellemare will not be pleased!" Juliana smiled, despite the scolding tone of her words. Obviously, some of them had escaped imprisonment. They had to be waiting in ambush. Not wanting to disappoint their game, she edged into the passageway. It only seemed to get darker, but she'd walked the halls to her bedchamber many times and knew every hidden nook. From what she could see, the hall was empty and there would only be a few inlets to hide in. Her voice ringing softly, she said, "He's likely to imprison you with the others if he catches you."

"Juliana," came another whisper, this one from behind.

Juliana turned, ready to grab a child into her arms. The moonlight silhouetted a hairy figure. It was too short to be a child, too human in form to be an animal. Its foot lifted to step and she thought to see a talon in place of a foot. She screamed, jumping back. Mocking laughter sounded all around her, coming from at least a dozen voices. She looked up. A dark, wrinkled face grinned at her, hanging on the stone above. White hair sprouted from his head. His nose hung low over his thick, wide lips. When he smiled, he had sharp, pointed teeth.

"Juliana," the creature above her rasped, following the terrifying sound with a hard, uneven laugh.

"Ahh-hha," Juliana cried, stumbling back from them. She glanced from the ceiling to the top of the stairwell in stunned horror.

"Juliana," the higher pitched voice said behind her.

She spun around, screaming. Her heart pounded a violent rhythm. A being with long arms stood in her way. Instantly, the hall filled with frightening creatures. They grew from the shadows, crowding her in. Seeing that her bedchamber door was the closest, she ran for it. Something touched her leg as she hastened by. She yelped, terrified, as she pushed through the door. Slamming it shut, she bolted the lock.

There was complete silence, except for her gasping breath. Juliana leaned her back against the thick oak. From what she could see, her room was empty. The fireplace burned brightly, illuminating her narrow bed and trunk. A red coverlet with gold embroidery lay over the mattress, still smooth from that morning. Her white wedding gown was folded neatly on the end of the bed. She looked at the ceiling. The rafters were empty.

The silence continued and she let loose a small laugh of relief. She was imagining things. She was safe. It was nothing, just the shadows of the dark hall. It was her vivid imagination tricking her into believing that...

Suddenly, the cold laughter started anew. Juliana screamed. The creatures pounded on the door, vibrating the hard oak against her back, as they called out her name. "Juliana! Juliana!"

"Stop!" Juliana cried out, jumping away from the door. "Leave me alone. What do you want?"

"Methought I answered that question already," a voice behind her said. "How easily you forget. And I had hoped to be more memorable to you."

Juliana twirled around, her gaze moving to the bed. The stranger lay atop the coverlet, the black of his clothes contrasting with the dark red material of her coverlet. He lounged on his side, lazily drawing a long, manicured fingernail over the embroidered gold pattern. His silver and black overtunic was gone, and she couldn't help but think how devilishly handsome he looked, lounging half-dressed on her bed. His hair spilled over his shoulders like silk strands, framing his dark, handsome features.

The pounding continued on the door, as did the sinister laughter. Juliana ignored it, becoming transfixed. He wasn't like the men she knew. There was an energy, a vibrancy that poured off of him. He was primal and strong, alluring and frightening at the same time. She watched his finger stoke the coverlet, the caress so light and tender it made her shiver.

The moment he looked up, his dark eyes meeting hers, the pounding on the door stopped to be replaced by the sound of crackling wood in the fireplace. More of his blond hair spilled over his shoulders, soft and inviting. He stopped moving, holding as still as a statue. She stepped back. Her breathing heavy, she managed to ask, "How did you get in here? You can't be in here. You control the demons, don't you?"

The man pushed up from his side, smiling. He draped an arm over his bent knee, his wickedly dark eyes watching her. She took another quick step back. His expression lightened, looking almost amused by her reaction. "Nay, you're thinking of King Lucien. He controls the demons. I'm Merrick."

"What do you want, Merrick?" Juliana couldn't take her eyes off him. Her heart beat fast. It seemed so intimate, being alone with him in her bedchamber. The knights were far below and, if they hadn't heard her screams already, they'd not hear them now. She swallowed, wondering if she should brave the hall.

Merrick chuckled. "I wouldn't try it. They haven't gone away."

Juliana stiffened, raising her chin. "What do you want with me?"

"To take you up on your offer," he said, his lips curling a little more. It was a seductive look, even as it was dangerous. He swung his legs over the side of her narrow bed. His polished boots landed neatly on the floor. Pushing up from the bed, he didn't take his eyes off of her.

Juliana much preferred him lying down. Standing, he appeared to dominate the very room, including her. The orange of the firelight reflected in his dark eyes, making them glow. Merrick came for her, stalking her slowly as he crossed the distance. She tried to pull away, but found she couldn't move. So help her, she wanted him to touch her. "What offer?"

"Mm, so easily you forget. I might start to take offense, Juliana." Merrick lifted his hand, grazing her cheek. His touch was warm, gentle, as it glided down her throat. He stopped at her pulse. It quickened beneath his fingers until she was sure her heart would leap from her chest. Pulling his hand away, he said, "No matter."

He turned his back on her, moving with infinite grace and refinement to the small table along the wall. His brief touch left her weak, but the absence of it left her powerless. Lifting the pitcher of clean water left for her by the servants, Merrick poured the liquid into a bowl.

"Tell me, my lady," he said thoughtfully. "What do you hold most dear?"

Juliana didn't dare answer.

"This castle?" He picked up the bowl, swirling the water lightly as he watched it. Meditatively, he continued, "Your reputation? Your family? Your brothers?"

"Why do you want to know?" Juliana demanded, doing her best to sound unafraid. It was a weak attempt and he merely arched a brow in question as his eyes met hers.

Merrick grinned, a devilishly wicked look. "Thomas?"

"What are you doing?" Juliana tried not to breathe too loudly. She swallowed back her fear, stiffening her resolve. The man excited her, even as he frightened her.

"I know," Merrick said. He lifted the bowl in one hand, letting it rest on the tips of his fingers, before moving to the narrow slit in the wall. Moonlight fell over the bowl. He tapped his finger on the surface of the water. Then, gazing into the bowl, he said, "How about the children you tell your stories to? So young. So innocent."

A tear slipped down her cheek. Her lips trembled and she swallowed nervously. He lifted the bowl toward her in one graceful movement. A soft glow shone from within. Juliana stepped forward, slowly moving to look into the bowl. An image of the children undulated gently on the water's surface. They were in the Bellemare prisons, laughing and eating their feast. She couldn't hear them, but she could see them just fine. She lightly touched the edges of the bowl, unsure as to whether or not she wanted to take it from him.

Merrick waved his hand languidly over the water's surface. After his fingers passed, the children were gone and she stared at an empty prison cell filled with half-eaten trenchers of food.

She gasped, looking up at him. "What happened? Where are they?"

"You wished for an adventure," he said softly. He let go of the bowl. It slipped through her fingers and crashed onto the floor. The bowl cracked in two and water spilled over the dark stone. The image disappeared completely, as he repeated again, "You asked for an adventure. I shall give you an adventure, Juliana. And, in return, you will belong to me."

"Nay, I don't want it. I was just…daydreaming. I won't do it." She glanced down at the puddle. "I don't agree. Take your bargain elsewhere, devil."

"Then you'll never see the children again," Merrick stated. "Your task is a simple one, my lady. You shall go to my realm, the realm of all that is magic and immortal. You know it as the Otherworld. There, you will journey to the Kingdom of Valdis."

"Please, I'm begging you, Merrick. I'm getting married tomorrow. I can't go on an adventure. I'm to be a wife. Please, return the children. I'm begging you. Don't hurt them."

"Nay, Juliana, I told you I wouldn't allow your marriage. There will be no wedding, regardless of what you decide. Don't anger me in this." Merrick's voice lowered in warning. His dark eyes pierced into her. All pretense of smiling was gone. He took a menacing step, forcing her to stumble back.

"What do I do in Valdis? How do I get there?"

"I will show you the door to the Otherworld. It is up to you to find your way from there," he said. "Your task is a simple one. You must find the King of the Unblessed and ask him a simple question."

"What question is that?"

"If you ask him, he'll give you anything you desire, so long as it doesn't interfere with our bargain." Merrick studied her for a long moment.

"Please," she begged, "what question?"

"That is for you to determine." Merrick touched her cheek. She jerked her face away from him, causing a soft laugh of amusement to escape him. He pulled his hand away, a strange look upon his face. "I warn you, it won't be easy. You could be killed."

"Please reconsider—"

"Feel fortunate I'm not King Lucien, or I would have taken your soul for much less adventure than I am giving to you now." His tone was hard, almost deadly. "You wanted an adventure, begged for one. Well, you should have taken more care in what you wished for, my lady. Not all adventures are happy ones. Lucien would have made you prisoner in the bowels of a ship, sold as a slave at a distant land. I merely ask you to journey to Valdis and ask a simple question."

Juliana didn't move. Her mind raced with thoughts, none of them rational.

"I can feel the excitement in you even now, as you damn yourself for it. I feel your fear, Juliana." A low, pleasurable growl sounded in the back of his throat as he pressed his cheek to hers. "This excites you, doesn't it, my lady? Your heart is beating so fast and your breath catches each time I touch you."

Julian turned her face away. "Where do I find this King of the Unblessed?"

"He lives in the Black Palace." Merrick started to turn, only to stop. Tapping the side of his mouth, he said, "Oh, I almost forgot. Every great adventure has to have perilous odds. A time frame, methinks. You have one week to do what I ask, or both your life and those of the children will be mine to do with as I will."

"You're a beast!" She balled her hands into fists.

"I've been called much worse." He laughed, though his face remained blank and his eyes looked dead of all emotion.

"How do I know I can trust you?"

"You don't." Merrick touched her cheek, rubbing his palm over her skin. His hand was warm, making her shiver. Juliana closed her eyes. Why did he have to keep touching her? He stood so close she could feel his warmth. "It's up to you. Really, what choice do you have, my lady?"

"When does this madness start?" Lifting her chin, she again pulled away from his touch and refused to meet his eyes. She couldn't. He was too close. His finger grazed the side of her mouth, pausing along the seam. The feelings inside her were insanity and she wouldn't succumb to them. She wanted to kiss him. She wanted to throw him down on the bed. What she'd do to him once she had him down, she wasn't exactly sure.

"Now." He let her go.

"And how do I get to your world?"

"Your journey starts as all journeys do, by walking out the front gate of your castle." His body glimmered, fading until he was transparent. Juliana stared, unable to look away. "Tell no one from your world of this, Juliana. I will not be pleased if you do."

Merrick disappeared. She shook her head, finally letting the tears of worry fall from her eyes unchecked. How could she have wished for him to come back? To be real? Whatever he was, it was surely a demon, a beast, a fiend. For only a true devil would threaten the lives of innocent children.

She looked at the door, trying to get her wits about her. She needed to be careful, needed to think. Juliana sighed. She had to do it. How could she not? But, then again, how did she know he told the truth? The dungeons. She'd go to the dungeons and see for herself.

Her blue linen gown and cream chemise weren't ideal for travel, but she didn't want to waste time changing her clothes. She did slip out of her shoes, opting for sturdy leather boots. Grabbing a thick cape from her trunk, she slipped it over her shoulders. It was made from brown wool and would serve her well for travel.

Going to her bed, she pulled a jeweled dagger from beneath the mattress and slipped it into her boot for safekeeping. It wasn't much, but having three brothers she knew how to use it. They'd given it to her on her fourteenth birthday.

"I can't believe I'm even considering this," she whispered, looking around her chamber one last time. "Then, again, what choice do I have?"

***

"Lord Bellemare!"

Hugh, who was discussing the fine points of jousting with Sir Pieter, stopped talking in mid-sentence at the interruption. Glancing down from the high table, he frowned to see the look on his guard's face. Euric was supposed to be watching the main gate, a very important duty especially since the gates were left open all night for the castle visitors.

Hugh glanced around at his guests. Bellemare's hall overflowed with visiting nobles and their families. Minstrels played lively tunes as a jester danced around the crowd, tripping over his feet. Outside near the marketplace, the servants and many of the knights enjoyed their meals by bonfire. At Euric's call, the crowd fell quiet. All eyes were on the Earl. Hugh didn't mind. He was used to the attention.

"What is it, Euric?" he asked, not standing from his chair.

"My lord." Euric bowed. "Sir Nicholas arrives."

"Ah, he must be with his father," Hugh said, nodding. He waved his hand, dismissing the guard. "Well, man, let him cross."

"I have, my lord," Euric said, his eyes widening as he tried to impart some unknown meaning to the Earl. "He wishes to speak with you. It's most urgent."

Glancing at Thomas, Hugh motioned for his brother to follow. They stepped down from the platform and followed Euric to the stairwell. When they were away from the great hall, Hugh asked, "Is Lord Eadward with him?"

"Nay, my lord," Euric said. "Sir Nicholas is alone."

Hugh shared a look with Thomas. He knew his brother well enough to interpret his blank expression for concern. All three men were silent as they climbed down the dark stairwell to the courtyard. A warm breeze filtered in, the temperature pleasant.

"Sir Nicholas, welco—" Hugh began, as he walked outside. Nicholas' look cut him off. The courtyard was empty, but they could hear laughter from outside the bailey walls. The walls were illuminated by the outside bonfires, casting the darker yard with a soft orange light. The night sky was clear, littered beautifully with stars that blanketed the heavens for miles.

Nicholas' green eyes were swollen red, though they looked more angry than sad. His short brown hair was tousled about his head, attesting to a fast ride. Hugh assumed he must have come straight from his father's castle to get there. His father's head knight, Vincent d'Avre, was with him. He looked just as upset.

"What is it? What has happened?" Hugh demanded.

"I have come...to..." Nicholas said, his voice hoarse. He shook his head, unable to say more. He turned his back on them, lowering his head into his hands.

"Master d'Arve?" Thomas prompted.

"Lord Eadward was attacked," Vincent answered. The man looked at Hugh. "He's dead, my lord."

"Attacked? By whom?" Hugh demanded, scowling in outrage. "Who here would dare attack him on my land? Coming to my home?"

"He was attacked in his sleep last night, my lord," Vincent said. Nicholas' shoulders stiffened. Faint shouts followed by more laughter rolled over the night sky from the marketplace. "At his home."

"Who?" Thomas said, anger thick in his voice.

"We don't know," Vincent said.

"He was murdered." Nicholas turned back around. He was stiff with control as he eyed the two brothers. Hugh's gut tightened with anger and grief. He'd known Lord Eadward for years, and Nicholas was his friend since boyhood. He knew Nicholas for a good, honest man, whose bravery on the field of battle was well known. "Massacred in his bedchamber, gutted like a pig, torn apart until only his face was recognizable. We couldn't even carry the body from his chamber. We had to wrap it in a blanket. I have never seen anything so…"

Nicholas choked on his words, but his look said more than his voice ever could. Whatever it was he'd seen, it had to be horrific to make a knight tremble in such a way. And to see it done to his own father? Hugh couldn't imagine.

"Nicholas, we will punish the man responsible," Hugh swore. "Are there no suspects? No witnesses?"

"None," Vincent answered when Nicholas couldn't.

"My father's sword was still sheathed. He didn't try to fight back." Nicholas took a deep breath and Hugh knew he fought to stay calm.

"Or didn't have time to," Thomas said softly to Hugh.

"Was anyone unusual seen about the castle?" Hugh asked.

"Nay, my lord," Vincent said. "The gates were down all night. We had no visitors into the keep. It's as if…"

"As if it were someone he knew," Nicholas finished, his tone cold. "Someone he trusted."

"You said his bed. A woman?" Thomas asked.

"My sire took no lovers at Tyrshire these many years past," Nicholas answered.

"That doesn't make sense," Hugh said, scratching the back of his head. "Lord Eadward has no enemies, none that would profit from his death. He hasn't even been active in the king's court for nearly ten years. Aside from the wedding to…"

Hugh tensed, glancing back at the castle.

"Juliana," Thomas whispered. The men exchanged looks before running up the stairwell to the great hall. They crossed through the room, drawing the looks of those gathered. Hugh motioned his knights to stay seated.

Jogging up a second stairwell that led to the noble bedchambers, Hugh called, "Juliana!"

"Juliana," Thomas repeated, sounding just as concerned.

They rushed through the darkened hallway to her bedchamber door. Hugh held his breath, stopping to pound on the thick wood. The door creaked open with the force of his blows. A fire burned brightly in the fireplace. The four men made quick work of checking her chambers. Her bed was made, her wedding gown untouched. There was a pair of her shoes and a broken bowl on the otherwise clean floor. She wasn't there.

Thomas reached beneath her mattress. "Her dagger's gone."

"Juliana wouldn't have..." Nicholas instantly defended, shaking his head. Hugh studied Nicholas, watching how the man's eyes turned away as he said Juliana's name. His face was pale, drawn. "Nay, you mustn't think she would...my lord father..."

"We don't," Hugh assured the man. "She was here all day with us."

Nicholas nodded once.

Hugh's gut was tight with fear, but he forced the emotion down, locking it away. Frowning, he said, "She would only take the dagger if she suspected danger. Vincent, go to the front gates, tell them that Lady Juliana is missing. Don't let any carts pass until she's found. Tell them to send knights into the marketplace."

Vincent glanced at Nicholas, who nodded that he should obey. Vincent ran from the room.

Nicholas looked lost. "She's probably about."

The brothers ignored his words, as they went to check the remaining chambers. Their bedchambers, the sewing chamber, all of them were empty.

"I'll go to the hall," Thomas said. "If she passed there, she would have been seen."

"I'm coming with you." Hugh followed him down the stairs. "We need to send out search parties. No one will rest until she is found."

❦❦❦❦❦

Giles poked his head up from inside the barrel of ale, covering his mouth as he hiccupped. Liquor dripped off his small cap, running over his sticky face, but he didn't care as his kicked in the ale to keep his small body afloat. He knew the lady that passed through his dusty pantry wouldn't see or hear him. None of Bellemare's humans could see him. He was a brownie, Bellemare's household brownie to be exact. It was a sweet life for he'd been blessed with keeping stock of the ale. Everything he needed was right here in this room—food, drink, bolts of cloth to make clothes for himself. Looking down at his ragged suit of green and blue that he'd worn for the last hundred years, he hiccupped again. Aye, maybe someday he'd make new clothes.

The two small holes that made up his nostrils expanded and contracted on his flat face with each rapid breath. Only a foot tall, he had to climb on top of the barrel's edge, hefting himself up with his long, nimble fingers to see Lady Juliana better. All the creatures of Bellemare liked Lady Juliana. She was kind and they loved to sit around listening as she told stories from their world. She didn't always get the tales right, but it was a piece of home.

Whenever she gathered the mortal children, the immortals would come too, sitting around in the blades of grass to watch her. They'd been there earlier that day as she spoke of Nixies. Giles rubbed his backside. A mortal boy had nearly trampled him to get to the marketplace.

"What is she up to?" Giles wondered, squinting to watch her. He smacked his lips, frowning. She looked worried. Perhaps he should follow her, just to make sure she was all right. Hiccupping, he looked down at the barrel. "Ah, but first, *hiccup*, a drink!"

He fell back into the ale, a drunken grin on his face.

Juliana hugged her wool cloak tightly around her shoulders, as she made her way through the castle undetected. She passed under the great room floor, crossing through the pantry so as not to be seen. A few servants were about, but most were too busy serving the guests to pay her much mind. She knew every inch of the castle, had played in it since girlhood, and it was easy to slip through unnoticed.

Luckily, the children weren't being kept in the gatehouse prisons, but in the lower dungeons of the main castle. Pressing her hand against the cool stone wall, she hurried down the stairwell. Seeing the dungeon, she froze. It was as Merrick said. The children were gone.

She shivered, wondering if Hugh had let them go. Seeing the half-eaten trenchers of food, she frowned. The door was still locked as well. Going to the bars, she looked in. No, the children hadn't been let out. They were just gone.

"You didn't believe me?"

Juliana gasped, jumping in surprise. She turned to look at Merrick. He lounged against the wall, watching her expectantly, his arms crossed over his chest.

"I'm hurt."

"Stop this." She took a step toward him, casting her eyes down. "Tell me what you want from me. I'll give you...anything. Just stop this."

At that he merely smiled. His gaze dipped over her body and she shivered to imagine just what his "anything" would be. So help her, she'd succumb to his demands almost willingly. Fortunately for her sanity and virtue, he didn't make them. He lifted his hand, brushing his fingers over her neck. Juliana shivered at the light caress. His nearness did something to her, despite the hate for him which grew with each passing second.

"You waste precious time, my lady," he said. "The King of the Unblessed awaits."

"I'll find your King Lucien and I will get those children back." Juliana lifted her chin and walked past him, head held high. She hurried up the stairs, leaving him to watch after her.

When Juliana looked away, Merrick waved his hand, lowering the glamour over the children. They appeared once more, though he blocked the sound of their laughter from her ears. The children couldn't see or hear him and he preferred to keep it that way. What did he want with a bunch of human children? So long as she believed he had them, she would go on his adventure.

He moved to follow her up the stairwell. So, she thought he meant for her to seek out King Lucien? Merrick easily saw how she came to that conclusion. He said Lucien controlled the demons. Being human, she naturally assumed his unblessed goblins were demons.

This would be easier than he'd first imagined. The whole of a week could go by before she even realized she sought the wrong man. Merrick laughed. She'd be bound to him for an eternity and it would be of her own doing. She asked him to come and give her an adventure. She offered her soul for it. In the laws of magic, her soul was worth far more than obedience and the amendment he made would keep the bargain between them. Regardless of what happened, she would be his until he let her go. King Merrick knew he would never let her go.

A cold wind whipped down the stairwell, too cold for the spring evening of the mortal world. Juliana was stopped at the top of the stairs, staring out at the courtyard. The land was covered with snow where there had so recently been grass. The courtyard was empty, the snow so fresh that tracks had yet to be made in it. She glanced at him as he moved to stand beside her. Her eyes were hard and her cheeks flushed red with both anger and cold. He grinned, enjoying their silent battle of wills.

Merrick was glad she didn't smile at him, didn't offer her lips. He'd been tempted to kiss her in the side courtyard, tempted to take her mouth and her body for his own right there in the garden—had he been more than a glamour to her, he might have. He was unable to visit her realm in person, at least not wholly. It was too hard to keep a solid form for too long, but he could appear real enough to her. However, if he just wanted pleasures of the flesh, he could easily find them. He wanted more from Juliana. He wanted to see her soul shining out of her eyes. He wanted to hear her heart race in fear, longing, anger. Most of all, he wanted to control her completely, wanted her pledged to him, not magically, but by her own will. Know it or not, Lady Juliana would be his slave…for an eternity.

That was, if he didn't kill her first.

Juliana sighed, surprised to see that Merrick followed her as she trudged through the snow to the gatehouse. He didn't say a word. Snow fell in light flakes over the land, but he didn't seem bothered by the cold. There was no sign of the guards, of the visiting nobles and their servants, no songs from the minstrels, no glow of a campfire along the wall.

"Where is everyone?" she asked, going to the front gate. Merrick merely smiled. The surrounding landscape looked the same, only it was snow-covered and barren. A large, black-colored bird squawked overhead. Juliana pulled her cloak closer to her body. She didn't know if she trembled from the cold or from fear. Understanding it was pointless to again beg him to end his madness, she asked, "Which way to the Otherworld?"

"You're already here," Merrick said. He lifted his hand, gesturing to the far off forest. "Your adventure begins, my lady."

Juliana shivered, pulling her cloak tight. He disappeared, fading into nothingness. She walked toward the nearby trees. The landscape looked the same as her home. As she marched through the snow, she put her head down, blocking the cold wind. The moon was bright and the silver light guided her, glistening on the snow like diamonds. She hadn't slept, but her heart beat so fast in uncertainty that the fear kept her moving, kept her immune to the weather. After several paces, she glanced up, turning to look back at her home. She gasped. The castle was gone. All that lay before her was the long stretch of snowy fields.

"Don't you dare cry," she told herself sharply. "You will not be weak. You will find this Lucien, King of the Unblessed Demons. You will find him and ask him to free the children."

Fear and anger could only keep Juliana moving for so long before the cold forced her to seek shelter in the forest. Icicles hung from the tall trees, like shards of broken glass, so eerily smooth. They reflected the moonlight, illuminating the pathway before her. The trees blocked the wind, but her breath still came out in white puffs and she couldn't feel her nose. Seeing a small outcropping of rocks, she crawled beneath it, away from the snow, and huddled in a ball.

"I really, really hate you, Merrick," she whispered, closing her eyes to sleep. "I will make you pay for this."

Merrick frowned, glancing up from the garden basin. He waved his hand, making Juliana's image disappear before threading his fingers behind his back. He was used to people hating him. Why should her hatred be any different? It was too bad the wizards decided to pick this night to make snow, but what could he do about it?

Turning on his heels, he strode from the black garden. The stone maze parted to let him pass, soundlessly changing. His black overtunic fluttered behind him. The red flowers bloomed and died, rippling like a wave over stone as he walked by.

The Black Palace was vast, reaching up into the dark night sky. It loomed before him like a mortal's gothic cathedral, only the spires arched and twisted in a way that would never be possible in the mortal world. They were decorated with hooked stone spurs.

The pointed lancet windows gave off a soft orange glow from within. The torches always burned, never needing to be replaced. Above his private entryway to the gardens was a small round window, the stone was carved with great detail, depicting the silhouetted head of a dragon. The round window was a smaller version of the one in front of his palace.

Inside, the black stone swallowed the light into its inky depths. The orange glow of torches mixed with moonlight streaming through the long windows. The narrow halls were plain, except for the decorative arches overhead.

The castle was alive with magic and it was all connected to him. Merrick didn't build the castle. It simply was, because he was. Merrick could walk along the hall from his garden and get to any place in the castle just by reaching the single door at the end. All the doors in the palace were like that. They led to wherever he wished—the hall, his bedchamber, the dungeons. For everyone else, the doors were simply doors.

The moment he stepped foot into the great hall it would change to his mood. Most of the time, the décor was black, gothic, dark. It was the same with his clothing. With the mere suggestion of his mind, his tunic would change to suit him. Sometimes, very rarely, he'd dress himself, as he did in the old days, pulling his pants on, lacing his own boots.

Merrick opened the door at the end of the passageway and walked into the great hall. The room stayed black, all but the dark blue tapestries behind his throne. They fluttered, changing to crimson red with gold embroidery. The pattern looked suspiciously like Juliana's coverlet. Seeing a goblin huddled in the corner, his face scrunched up in mischief, Merrick ordered, "Iago, fetch me a wizard. Any wizard."

"Aye, my king," Iago answered, his voice rasping. He didn't move right away and Merrick turned to look where the goblin stared. Iago snickered behind his hand. A fireplace surged, lighting the goblin Borc on fire. Borc yelped, jumping around in circles before finally dousing his head in a bucket. The bucket steamed. The goblins laughed, a jeering sound that filled the hall.

The goblins were small, withered looking creatures. Some danced in the corner. Some fell over themselves in laughter. Others plotted mischief, drawing maps on parchment with crude quills as they fought amongst themselves. Low tables were set up in the back, just the right size for short goblin legs. They were filled with food, disgusting things Merrick couldn't stomach—live bugs swimming in a slimy sauce, rotted vegetables, eels and snakes.

Volos, a troll, made a strange contrast to the shorter creatures, often drawing his eye because of how he stood out. Usually trolls stayed out of the palace, preferring to live a solitary existence in caves. Volos stayed in the palace with the goblins. Trolls by nature were much larger versions of goblins, but Volos was particularly ugly and unintelligent. Long ago, he'd been taken in and raised by the oldest goblin, Bevil, who he now sat in the corner listening to.

Merrick shook his head as he crossed to his throne, choosing to ignore his goblin subjects. He was tired of their antics. All they ever thought about was mischief. Sitting on his cushioned throne, he lounged back, resting his chin on his fist. His gaze roamed over the ribbed vaults of the ceilings held up by giant Corinthian columns, to the five giant fireplaces that always burned along the walls. Borc was again by the fire, though not as close to it as before.

The king found pleasure in none of it. Reaching over to the empty arm of his throne, a silver chalice of wine appeared just as Merrick wrapped his fingers over nothingness. He drank deeply. Throwing a leg over the side of his throne, he rested the chalice on his knee.

"Music," he said, softly. A few goblins glanced at him, but did not answer. They kept their distance as music showered over the hall, coming as if from the stone. Their voices lowered to a soft hum. The song was forlorn, sad in its melody. Merrick closed his eyes and listened. Why should he care if she hated him?

Chapter Three

A loud boom echoed over the forest followed by the sound of birds taking to flight. Juliana jolted awake, blinking rapidly as she scrambled to her feet. It took a moment to get her bearings, as sleep still clouded her mind. She'd been dreaming of Merrick. Sad music was all around them like a cloud and he was offering her his hand. She wouldn't take it because there was blood on it, but part of her desperately wanted to. Behind him a black stone angel stretched out her arms. Death and blood? Is that what Merrick had to offer her?

When Merrick was near, she felt as if she couldn't breathe. Every nerve in her body reached for him, making her anxious and excited at the same time. But there was a darkness in his eyes which frightened her and she knew it was best to stay away. Surely anything she felt was just a trick. She'd always wanted to believe in magic and now here it was, in front of her. She hated the pleasure she felt in the adventure and tried to bury it deep inside herself. It was wrong to take joy when Merrick kept the children prisoner. She might want an adventure, but not at their expense.

Another boom sounded, crackling over the forest. Juliana cried out. Her heart leapt in surprise as she looked around. The snow was gone and it was spring, the air warm. It shouldn't have been possible. When she went to sleep it was the dead of winter, but now water dripped off the trees where icicles had been. The ground was damp, making the floor of the forest soggy. Her boots squished in the mud as she walked over it.

Juliana slipped the wool cloak off her shoulders, folding it over her arms. This time when a boom sounded, she didn't jump. Drawn to see what made the horribly loud noise, she walked down the forest path, stopping to pull the dagger from her boot.

"That's not right!" a voice screamed in irritation. "Here, give it to me!"

"The muse told me how to do it, not you!" another voice answered.

"If you're so smart, then how come the wizards made the winter only last one night?" the first voice yelled. "They've never done that before, have they?"

"That's easy. We must have slept longer than one night!"

Juliana slowed, as the sounds of a struggle ensued.

"Let me!"

"It's mine! I made it."

"You did not!"

"Did so!"

"Did not!"

Juliana pulled back a tree branch, looking out into a small clearing in the trees. Sunlight glowed over the pretty clearing covered with tiny blue flowers. The ground was blanketed with them and the air was sweet with their perfume, combined with the robust scent of earth.

Juliana frowned in confusion. She didn't see anyone in the clearing. The voices kept arguing back and forth.

"Did not!"

"Did so!"

"Is someone there?" Juliana asked, her voice soft.

"Is someone there?" the first voice repeated. "Of course someone's there. Who would you be talking to if no one was there to answer?"

"Maybe she's talking to herself," the second voice argued.

"Why would she ask herself if she was there?" the first demanded.

Juliana heard the words, but didn't see anyone to speak them. "I can't see you."

"Of course you can't see us, you're not looking at us, are you?" the first voice continued, huffing. "Halton, give that back to me!"

"You stop it, Gorman, lest I turn you into a piskie!" Halton yelled.

"A piskie? Me?" Gorman sputtered in outrage. "I look nothing like a piskie!"

"Not yet, but that's because I haven't changed you!"

Juliana frowned. Slowly, she leaned forward. She lowered her dagger, hiding it behind her leg. Two tiny creatures were on the ground, their voices nearly ten times as big as they were. Aside from their stature and a slight point to their ears, they looked like two small human males in bright green tunics. There was something oddly familiar about them, but she shrugged the notion off.

Halton pointed a small stick at Gorman. "I'm warning you. Stay back!"

"Excuse me," Juliana said. They both looked up at her, their wide blue eyes rounding. A slight breeze tousled their already messy brown hair.

"There," Gorman said, motioning up. "You can see us now."

"Now, quit staring, if you don't mind. It's not polite." Halton pointed the stick up at her. A small stream of light came from the tip, whizzing past her face. Juliana gasped, jumping back. The light hit the tree limbs above them with a loud boom. A limb snapped off, crashing to the forest floor. Juliana scrambled to get out of the way, falling against the trunk of a tree.

"Watch it!" Gorman screamed, hopping on top of the fallen limb. He looked at the charred end, still smoking and then up at the tree it came from. He nodded thoughtfully.

"Watch it do what?" Halton asked, joining him up on the branch. Juliana stood, brushing off her skirts.

"Give me that. You almost hit the little giant." Gorman pulled the stick from him. Then, to Juliana, he said, "He didn't mean to frighten you. Don't look so scared. We mean you no harm, little giant."

"I'm not a little giant," Juliana said. She eyed the stick, curious. She'd never seen anything like it. "What is that thing?"

Halton laughed. As if she couldn't hear him, he mumbled to his friend, "Well she's not a big giant now is she? Poor little thing, she's sensitive about her height."

Juliana grimaced. She was being called little by creatures no taller than her knees—and that was if she stacked them one on top of the other.

"It's a wand," Gorman said. "Haven't you ever seen a wand?"

"Nay." Juliana shook her head.

"You're not a very bright giant, are you?" Halton snorted. Speaking very slowly, he said, "Little stick make big boom. Magic. That's a wand."

Gorman hit his friend over the back of his head. "That's not all a wand does!"

"Well, she doesn't need to know that. Ah, just look at the poor, simple creature. She's already confused. Well, giants never were the brightest creatures. You know what they say. The bigger the body, the more dull-witted they be."

"Who says that?" Gorman asked.

"You know, they." Halton shrugged.

"Right, they." Gorman gestured in understanding. "But wouldn't that make her smart for a giant, being as she's so little?"

"Well..." Halton tilted his head, seemingly perplexed as he contemplated the question. "Ah, but she's still a giant and so can't be too smart."

"Ah, right," Gorman agreed.

"Right," Halton said, nodding emphatically as if they'd just come to a major decision.

"I know," Gorman said, smiling at Juliana. "Let's keep her. I always wanted a pet giant."

"You have?" Halton asked.

"I'm not simple," Juliana said in irritation, interrupting their discussion.

"Oh, nay, of course you're not!" Gorman said, a little too eagerly in his agreement. Then to Halton, he said, "Just think of the berries we could reach with her helping us out!"

"What are you exactly?" Juliana asked. At the thought of food, her stomach growled. She shouldn't have skipped supper the eve before. She leaned over to get a better look at them. "Faeries?"

"Faeries?" Halton frowned. "Do you see us flying around with wings on?"

"She might not know what wings are," Gorman whispered, though Juliana could hear him just fine. It was obvious they didn't know how loud they were.

"Ah, smart thinking." Halton flapped his arms like a bird, bending his legs as he moved in a circle. He wiggled his backside and yelled up at her, "Do you see wings on us?"

"Never mind." Juliana slipped her dagger back into her boot and stood up. Glancing around, all she saw was trees. It was doubtful she was going to get any help from these two. However, who else was she going to ask? "Tell me, do you happen to know in which direction and how far it is to King Lucien's palace?"

Both creatures paled. They stared at her, jaws dropped.

"She says she's not simple," Halton tried to whisper through the side of his mouth, "but she seeks out King Lucien of the Damned."

"I know what he's king of," Gorman grumbled.

"I'm just saying," Halton defended.

"Quiet, Halton, I'll handle this." Gorman held up his hand for silence. He puffed out his chest with importance, before calling to her, "What's a simple creature like you want with King Lucien?"

"I have to speak with him." Juliana again glanced around the forest. The noise of their wand must have scared even the birds away. All was quiet. "I have to ask him something."

"I knew it, she's going to sell her soul," Halton said, turning to Gorman. Motioning vigorously toward Juliana, he said, "I told you she was sensitive about being little."

"Nay, I told you she was sensitive about being…ah, now quiet! Shh, I'll handle this." Gorman gestured to his friend for silence. "Do you know what happens when you sell your soul, giant?"

"I'm not a giant," Juliana answered.

"First she's not little, now she's not a giant." Halton laughed. "Can't seem to make up her mind, can she?"

"And I'm not going to sell my soul," Juliana said before they could start another tangent. "I just need to find the king. I can't tell you why."

As if he didn't hear her, Gorman continued, "He sucks it right out of you, he does. He doesn't wait for you to die a natural death like some think. He sucks it right out of you as soon as you make the bargain. Have you ever seen a creature with no soul? Their eyes are dead. Their faces pale. Their bodies carry the demons and they don't—"

"Hey! When did you ever see a creature without a soul?" Halton demanded.

"Uh, you weren't with me." Gorman scratched his head, looking away.

"I'm always with you," Halton argued, giving him a small push.

"Well, you weren't this time." Gorman pointed the wand to emphasize his words. "It was a Wednesday."

The wand shot a spark of white into the forest. It hit a nearby tree, ricocheted off the trunk, bounced in the other direction, hit another tree and bounced again. The two little men covered their heads, ducking as it whizzed by. Another loud boom sounded moments before a tree was set on fire.

"Give me that! I told you, it's mine. The muse told me to make it. She said I'd need it for a great task." Halton reached for the wand. He stuck it under his tunic, lacing it to his belt.

"You don't know any muses," Gorman said.

"Do so! She came to me in a dream."

"Did not!"

"Did so!"

"Did not!"

Juliana sighed as they again argued. Shaking her head, she walked back toward the forest path. She'd just have to ask someone else. That was if they hadn't scared everyone off with their loud noises.

"Ah, now look what you did. You frightened the simple thing away," Gorman said. "Come on! Let's go find her. It's obvious we were meant to help the little thing out."

Juliana intended to keep walking, never thinking they'd be able to catch up to her on their short legs. She was wrong. The two men leapt from the woods, flying through the air. Juliana swatted at them in surprise, barely missing them. They landed in her hair, swinging on it like vines to settle on her shoulders—one small man on each side. She stopped walking.

"Get off me," Juliana said.

"Ho, easy there, easy now." Halton patted the side of her head. She jerked away from him and knocked Gorman off her shoulder. He fell on the ground with a loud thump.

"Oh, sorry!" Juliana leaned over to look at him. "I didn't mean to. Are you hurt?"

"Well of course I'm hurt!" Gorman stood. His clothes were muddy from the wet path. "Ah, just look at what you've… Come on, then, pick me up. There's a stream just up ahead."

Juliana scrunched up her face. She went to grab him, stopped, and then held her hand flat, palm up. He nodded his thanks and stepped on.

"Easy, not too fast," Halton said. It felt like he was screaming in her ear. Juliana flinched. "That's it. What's your name anyway, giant?"

"Lady Juliana."

"A lady, you say? I didn't know giants had ladies," Gorman said. He sat down on her hand and motioned into the forest for her to walk. The mud on his pants adhered to her palm. He leaned toward Gorman and whispered loudly, "They don't, do they?"

"Ah, let's leave the simple creature be. We can call her a lady if she wants us to," Halton said. "As little as she is, it's possible she married an elf."

"I can hear you," Juliana answered. Even if they were annoying, she was glad for the company. "And I really am a lady and not a giant and I am not..."

She'd been about to say she wasn't married. Her gut knotted and her relief in having her nuptials delayed mortified her. What kind of person was she to want to run away from duty? Had she no honor? Well, to be fair, it wasn't like the choice was hers. Merrick had forced her hand. She swallowed, not liking herself very much at the moment. Last night in the snow, she'd worried about what her brothers would think to find her missing, but she'd not once thought of Eadward.

"Oh, there, there," Gorman said, interrupting her thoughts. Juliana felt Halton patting her earlobe, as if trying to tickle her. "Don't be so hard on yourself. We think you're an excellent giant, my lady."

"Forget it," Juliana mumbled. "Which way did you say led to the stream?"

Thomas rubbed the bridge of his nose. His eyes had been open for so long, they ached when he moved them so he instead stared off into space, looking at nothing but thinking of everything. He wasn't worried about his own discomfort. Hugh looked as tired as he, as did Nicholas and Sir Vincent. None of them said a word as they sat in Bellemare's great hall drinking the wine servants set before them. They didn't touch the food. None of them had an appetite for it.

They'd searched all night, but there was no sign of Juliana. She'd just disappeared without a hint of what might have happened to her. It was almost as strange as Lord Eadward's murder. The whole affair screamed of conspiracy, only they couldn't think of who might conspire against the houses of Bellemare and Tyrshire.

"Perchance, we underestimated Lord Roeland? He wasn't pleased when you turned down his offer," Thomas said, looking at Hugh.

"Nay, he'd not go so far as this," Hugh answered, shaking his head. "He was disappointed that Juliana didn't want him for husband, but he wasn't vindictive on the matter."

Nicholas frowned. "How many suitors does your sister have?"

Thomas shared a look with Hugh and grimly chuckled. They'd been weeding through a list of them all morning. "She's had what? Fifteen proposals this last year alone?"

"More like eighteen. Every eligible noble sees her and the Bellemare name she is attached to and within a fortnight they ask for her hand." Hugh sighed in thought. "And there are more still, if you count the knights of lesser breeding.

"More?" Nicholas asked, quietly. He looked into his cup. "Then why did you agree to my father's suit? Surely, a young husband with prospects of his own? A man with promise and…"

Nicholas frowned and said no more. Hugh sighed, raising his goblet to a servant. The woman came to the head table with her pitcher and filled it. She didn't even try to smile at the Earl's distracted attention. When she left, standing politely at the other end of the room to let them talk in private, Hugh said, "We approached Lord Eadward, not the other way around. He was a good man, a trusted friend."

Nicholas took several deep breaths, before abruptly standing. He started to nod, but couldn't finish the weak gesture and instead strode from the great hall. Vincent moved to go with him.

"Brothers, I came as soon as I heard."

Thomas turned at the solemn greeting, automatically knowing to whom the voice belonged. Their youngest brother, William, hurried into the hall. The brown robes he wore when studying at the monastery hung over his thin frame. His hair was too long for fashion, hanging shaggily over his ears and forehead. His brown eyes glanced over his older siblings in question. If not for his slight stature and younger age, he'd look like Hugh's identical twin.

"Has he said what he wants?" William asked.

Thomas sighed. Hugh didn't move.

"Well?" William prompted.

"There's been no word of ransom," Hugh said after a long pause, his words as stiff as his body.

"What mischief is this?" William whispered. He began to pace, mumbling to himself. It was a sight they had seen often as boys.

"William," Hugh stated, his voice stern. "There's no time for this. We must concentrate and come up with a plan."

"What?" William blinked. He scratched behind his ear, humming thoughtfully. "So, no ransom? Did he say what he wanted with our sister?"

"William," Thomas said, able to tolerate his oddness better than Hugh. "Do you know something? What have you heard?"

"Well, the king, he took her," William said. He studied them carefully before shaking his head in distraction.

"King Henry kidnapped our sister?" Thomas repeated carefully. The very idea was ridiculous.

"Nay, nay, that's right. They don't know, do they?" William turned to look his brothers in the eye, adding, "You don't know, do you? I forget sometimes. To me it's as common as the sun shining and you don't know."

"He's gone mad," Hugh said under his breath. Thomas saw the concern in him. He felt it too. William had been away the good part of five years, studying with the monks at a nearby monastery. Every time they met with the youngest brother, he'd become stranger and stranger. Both Hugh and Thomas were sure William would someday take his orders, and for that reason they left him where he was, though the youngest had never given any real indication one way or another. "I feared this would someday happen. William, what has gone on with you?"

"Are you seated?" William said, glancing back and forth quickly between them.

Thomas frowned. They were both seated. He was tired and had an ache in the back of his skull that radiated down his spine.

"William, concentrate!" Hugh said.

"Right, right." William nodded, looking around. "Let's see. The castle? Aye, you're right, start with the castle."

"William?" Hugh said, standing. "Who are you talking to?"

"Nay, nay, sit." William waved Hugh down. "You're too big to pick up off the floor. Let's see, ah, aye, a simple trick should do it."

William reached into his robe and pulled out a wand. Licking his lips, he cleared his throat. "Something small, I think. Ah, wine."

William flicked his wrist, mumbled something they couldn't understand under his breath and then grinned. Thomas frowned. He glanced over his shoulder. Nothing was changed.

Hugh scowled. "What?"

"I filled your wine," William said, pointing at Hugh's goblet. "There, see."

Thomas and Hugh both leaned over and looked into the goblet. It was full.

"The servant was just here," Hugh said. He stood, prompting Thomas to do the same. They walked around the table, coming down off the platform. "I will get you a physician and a priest. The best care, but I want you to come live here at Bellemare. I promise, William, you will be looked after."

"Ah, nay, wait. I'm not mad. I can prove it." William looked quickly around the hall. Seeing the servant girl standing in attendance with her pitcher, he pointed at her and blurted, *"Digitalis purpurea!"*

She gasped, her eyes widening as she stayed frozen to her spot. Thomas and Hugh studied her from across the long hall. She looked unchanged.

"Wil—" Thomas began.

"Nay, shh, just wait." William waved his hand for silence, staring at the servant. He moved toward her. Thomas and Hugh shared a look and then moved to follow. "I'm still young and it takes awhile."

The woman glanced from one brother to the next, shaking uncontrollably at their rapt attention. The pitcher of wine dropped from her finger, crashing on the floor. Suddenly, brown and red scabs formed on her hands, growing on her skin. She screamed, a high pitched sound of terror. Her body jerked. She couldn't move. The scabs traveled over her arm, up her throat, covering her mouth until her voice stopped.

William grinned. "There, see."

"What devil's madness…?" Thomas' jaw dropped in awe.

"Cease at once!" Hugh ordered. "William!"

"Cease? Oh, right, cease." William pointed at the servant and said, *"Aeruprup Silatigid."*

Almost instantly her skin cleared. The sounds of her screams echoed in the hall as she ran away, terrified. Thomas couldn't move as he stared at his younger brother.

William frowned after her. "Wonder what's the matter with her? It was just a simple spell."

"What kind of monk are you?" Thomas asked in awe. He'd never seen anything like it in his life. He shook his head.

"Monk? I'm not a monk," William said, chuckling. "I'm a wizard, well, an apprentice anyway. A monk? That's what you thought I've been doing all these years?"

"You were at a monastery," Thomas reasoned.

"We're all tired. We're seeing things that cannot be," Hugh said. "We should try to sleep for an hour before we renew our search. I've already sent men to the west boundaries. There's not much else we can—"

"Do you truly know about none of this?" William looked surprised. "I mean, I know you don't know Rees, but have you never suspected the truth?"

"About what?" Thomas took a deep breath. He knew what he'd seen with his eyes. He just didn't know what to make of it. "Who?"

"Well, about magic?" William asked.

"Magic?" Hugh repeated. His voice rose, as he swore, "I will not have this family making deals with the devil."

"But, Juliana, she knows?" William looked from one man to the other, confused. Thomas shook his head. His gut tightened, thinking of his sister. "Her stories...I...I just assumed she knew. We never talked of it, but... Well, then, how did she know to draw his notice? I just assumed she'd asked him to come to end the wedding and got more than she bargained for."

"So help me William, you had better collect yourself," Hugh warned. He pointed a finger at him. "My patience is thin as it is. I will not have you speaking of our sister making pacts with the devil."

"Nay, hardly the devil. Have you never wondered how it is our family is so blessed?" William asked. "Our horses breed the best stocks, our weather is always the fairest, our lands are fertile, our armies strong, our—"

"We get the point," Thomas interrupted.

"It's because we work hard," Hugh asserted.

"It's because we have help. We're blessed," William added.

"By God, aye." Hugh nodded.

"Him, too." William paced the floor as he talked, waving his hands. "But we're also blessed by the King Ean of Tegwen, ruler of the Blessed Kingdom. It goes back to our great-great—well, an ancestor of some sort who saved the old King's daughter and married her. She became mortal and died. The king was sad, he died, and now Ean, his grandson rules Tegwen. Oh, why didn't I think of it before! That has to be what this is about."

Thomas shivered. William was serious. Their brother had never been one to lie. He might be eccentric, but he was always honest.

"Our ancestor was the daughter of a king?" Hugh prompted. 'Nay, such things would be in our records.'

"Aye, though I believe she was married to a brother of our direct bloodline. As far as I know, they had no children of their own but claimed their nieces and nephews," William answered, before mumbling, "That's why Merrick... He seeks to... Aye, aye. Oh, nay, nay. That cannot be good."

"What?" Hugh demanded. "William, explain yourself!"

"Methinks the King of the Unblessed takes Juliana for revenge against his brother. You see, King Ean took Merrick's throne and cursed him. Or so some of the legends say." William paled dramatically. "If this is about revenge, then you have to go after her. She's in grave danger."

"Wait, how do you know all this? How do you even know this Merrick has her?" Hugh asked.

"Merrick is King of Valdis, Ruler of the Unblessed," William said. "He is...was Ean's brother. He was supposed to be King of Tegwen, but something happened. None of us are sure what."

"Aye, good and evil, blessed and unblessed," Thomas answered, trying to make sense of it.

"Nay, evil would be King Lucien of the Damned. When you go to the Otherworld, stay away from him. He's pure evil. King Merrick is more of a necessary evil. He'll not save you, but he'll most likely not kill you either without cause. But let me tell you, there are worse things to be had at his hand than death. Now, King Ean is basically good but, as with all things, good is subjective to the beholder. Watch for him as well. There isn't much to be said of him in the scrolls. Oh, and it'd be best not to draw the notice of the lesser kings or the faery queen. They don't have as much power, but they can be a tad meddlesome at times. Other than that, you should be well. At least, I can't think of anything at the moment."

"And you think this Merrick has our sister?" Thomas shook his head. This was too much.

"Thomas, you're listening to this?" Hugh asked.

"How can I not?" Thomas believed what William said. Somehow, he just felt it was true. "I mean, think of it. Haven't you always known but never wanted to question? In tournament, haven't there been times when the lance should have struck you from your horse and hasn't?"

"Aye," Hugh whispered, nodding slowly. "Oft."

"And haven't you felt it?" William asked eagerly.

"I know Juliana has," Hugh admitted, though his words were reluctant. Thomas studied William. "How is it you know all this and accept it? Why you?"

"When I was younger, after one of Juliana's stories, I trapped a...ah..." William's words trailed off.

"A what?" Thomas insisted, impatient. If their sister was kidnapped by an evil king, they needed to go get her. They didn't have time for childhood stories.

"I caught a nymph in the woods. Her name was Meliades. She was beautiful and naked and had great breasts." William grinned. A besotted look clouded his eyes. Thomas cleared his throat to draw his attention back to the matter at hand. "In exchange for her freedom, she introduced me to Father Gerald and he's apprenticed me ever since. It was he who got the message that Juliana was taken by Merrick to the Otherworld. Though, I'm not sure who told him."

"William, I do want to believe you, but it's—" Hugh began.

"Then believe me," came a strange voice.

Thomas' gaze darted to a little creature that appeared by William's foot. His short brown hair was unkempt and he wore a bright green tunic that fell to his thighs. His wide blue eyes looked up at them, almost too big for his face.

"What is that?" Thomas asked William, pointing at the small creature and not sure if lack of sleep was getting to him.

"The name's Rees," the creature said, bowing gallantly. "I'm a spright. More importantly, I'm Bellemare's spright. I help breed the horses. Now, Heinic, the garden gnome, he's who you thank for that little piece of heaven out by the kitchens. Giles is your household brownie, though he be scarce most days. Quite taken to drink, that one is. That's why your pantry is collecting dust. There are more of us. Your brother's right when he says you're a blessed lot. King Alwyn, rest him, ordered us here to your keep many, many years ago and here we've been, watching after you. Right proud we are of you, too. We especially like sitting with the children to listen to Lady Juliana tell stories. You're a noble, honorable lot of—"

"And you believe this Merrick killed my father." They turned, seeing Nicholas in the entryway to the stairwell. Thomas wondered how much he'd overheard. Nicholas' gaze roamed over the small man, but he didn't acknowledge him otherwise. His face turned red and his breathing deepened. Looking to the three brothers, he said, "I'm going with or without you. I will find this Merrick and avenge my father. I will not let him have Lady Juliana."

"Merrick killed Lord Eadward?" William asked in surprise. "When?"

"Last night. Around the same time Juliana was taken." Hugh eyed the spright warily. Rees grinned up at him and winked. Hugh drew back ever so slightly.

"He was slaughtered like an animal in his bed whilst he slept," Nicholas spat. "And all so this coward, Merrick, could come steal his bride."

"Slaughtered?" William frowned, shaking his head. His confusion only deepened on his face. He looked at Rees. "That makes no sense."

Rees only shrugged. He still stared dreamy-eyed at Hugh. Hugh shifted uncomfortably on his feet. Rees leaned forward and said, "My lord, I've been meaning to talk to you about your sword arm."

Hugh shook himself, ignoring the creature as he said to William, "So you think this Merrick couldn't do it?"

"Could? Aye, he could. He has the magic to go where he will. It's hard to explain. In his world, he's more limited, though still very powerful. Here, in our world, he's freer, especially since we only use small protection magic—a strand of garlic in a threshold, holy water for demons, salt, poppy seeds—"

"Then he's the one," Nicholas said. "You yourself claimed he's a necessary evil. Well, then I say we rid the world of him."

"Another will only take his place," William said, his voice low. "There is no way to rid the world of what he is. There have been worse unblessed kings in his place and there will be so again."

"But I will rid the world of him," Nicholas swore, vehemently. His whole body shook. "You did not see my father's body. There is practically nothing left to bury."

"How do we get there?" Hugh asked, his voice practical.

"Getting there's easy. You get there the same way you get anywhere. You step out your castle gate prepared with the knowledge to go. It's getting home that is the hard part. You leave from one point to many, but you come back from many points to one."

"It doesn't matter," Hugh said. "Juliana's out there. She's our blood. We have to go."

"Rees, please inform King Ean of what has happened here. He might be able to talk some sense into his brother," William said. Rees bowed and disappeared. Then, to Thomas and Hugh, he said, "I wish you luck, my brothers. You'll need it,"

Hugh frowned. "You're coming with us. You know about this place."

"Ah, about that, I wish I could, but I can't." William shrugged, helpless. He motioned the men to follow him as he made his way abovestairs to the bedchambers. "I'm banned due to a rather embarrassing misunderstanding about a giant's daughter's virtue. With me on the journey, you'd be sure to attract some very large, very unwanted attention. I swear the baby's not mine, but Angus won't hear it. Until the matter's settled, I'm stuck in the mortal realm."

"They think...?" Thomas started to ask, frowning. William coupled with a giant? It was...impossible. Wasn't it?

"Oh, aye, that I did." William grinned, nodding. He paused in the stairwell, sighing dreamily. Hugh nudged his arm to get him walking. "Many, many times. But, you see, I was not the first to till that soil. Try telling that to the woman's father though. He was none too happy to hear it."

"What manner of creatures are you?" Juliana questioned the two men on her shoulder. They sat, lightly kicking their feet in an annoyingly steady rhythm against her skin.

"Us?" Halton asked.

"Of course she means us," Gorman answered. "Who else would she mean?"

She felt them jerk and knew they were fighting again. Gorman had already fallen off twice since they'd left the stream. It hadn't taken him long to clean off before they had her picking berries to break their fast. After which, Gorman and Halton hopped into the forest for a private conversation. She was amazed they had the presence of mind to do that much, since they said everything else they were thinking as if she couldn't hear. When they came back, they agreed to help her find King Lucien.

Juliana didn't get into details about why she needed to find him, but they didn't really ask either, convinced she was going to trade her soul to be a bigger giant. Merrick had said not to tell anyone from her world, but what would happen if she told someone from his? She didn't want to risk it if she didn't have to.

"We're sprights. Haven't you ever seen a spright afore—*Oh!*"

Juliana felt Gorman fall, obviously pushed by Halton, and moved to catch him. He landed between her arm and her breast.

"Hello!" Gorman said, pushing against her breast with his face. "What's this? Mm, I seem to be trapped."

"Agh!" Juliana pinched the back of Gorman's shirt and lifted him up. Holding him before her face, she said, "You stop that!"

Gorman grinned and shrugged sheepishly, even as his legs flailed in the air. Juliana shook her head and placed him back on her shoulder. When he was again seated, she heard him try to whisper, "Good thing she don't know about the view, eh?"

Juliana gasped. Halton and Gorman chuckled to themselves. She glanced down to her breasts. The cleavage was completely covered with her cream undertunic. She frowned, stopping to pull her cloak over her shoulders.

"Hey, watch it!" Halton yelled.

Juliana managed to get her cloak on without smothering her riders. "Why am I even bothering with you two?"

"Because we're helping you." Halton laughed.

Is that what they called it?

"How else are you going to get to the King Lucien's palace?" Gorman added.

"Right." Juliana sighed. They were right. She needed them and the company did keep her mind off other things—like her brothers who had to be sick with worry, and the children who were probably frightened to tears.

The forest stayed the same as she walked. Occasionally, Gorman would tell her to take a turn in the path. They were pleasant enough companions, even if they did speak too loudly at times. Morning faded to afternoon and afternoon to early evening. Gorman passed most of the day in banter and Halton passed it in song. His singing was worse than his loud voice.

"How close are we to Lucien's palace?" Juliana asked, cutting Halton off during a break in singing before he started another tune.

"Far," Halton said.

"Very far," Gorman said.

"Extremely far," Halton added.

"Exceedingly fa—" She felt Gorman shift on her shoulder.

"All right," Julian interrupted, stopping the argument before it started. Even combined they didn't weigh much at all, but her neck was starting to strain all the same. "I understand. We have a long ways to go."

The two sprights laughed. Halton burst into song. Juliana flinched, trying to close her ears to him. With him on her shoulder, it was near impossible. She walked faster. The sooner she got to King Lucien's palace the better.

Chapter Four

Golden Palace of the Blessed, Kingdom of Tegwen

King Ean smiled, though in truth he felt detached from the faeries being presented to him. They were pretty, but he had no real interest in their feminine wiles as they simpered and smiled before him. Their dainty bodies fluttered about, hovering above his great hall floor. Both were fair with soft white skin and rose-tinted complexions. Their hair looked as soft as corn silk, and still he had no desire to touch it, or them. Regardless, it was possible he'd take both of them to his bed that night. A man did have his appetites, after all.

The blonde fluttered forward, her white wings sparkling like stars against her dark blue dress. Her dark haired companion was of the opposite coloring. She had dark blue wings and a white gown. Next to each other, they were quite fetching.

"Lady Lily," Sigurd, his herald, announced. A small burst of light erupted over the blonde and within a blink she stood before him, curtseying at a height to complement his own. Her wings quivered, but she stayed grounded. The king nodded once. The darker faery was waved forward. Her wings were a translucent dark blue, fluttering wildly as she hovered overhead. She too burst to stand before him. They both wore sparkling dresses of fine silk, as did all faeries. The race did pride themselves on beauty. "And her sister, Lady Rhoslyn."

"My ladies," Ean acknowledged them with a tilt of his head. He didn't smile at them and their eyes fell slightly. It was well-known he did not seek a queen, but it didn't stop his people from presenting eligible maidens. "Welcome to the Blessed Court."

"My king," they said in unison, their voices rich and smooth as they curtseyed. Both poofed into their smaller forms and flew from the great hall. A streak of light trailed behind them, releasing their potent pheromones into the air. It signified that they indeed wanted him in their beds. Faeries were highly sexual creatures, getting their energies from pleasure. In that, they and the elfin king were much alike, for he too received power from pleasure. It was why elves and faeries made good lovers. As to mates though, they were almost always disastrous pairings.

Elves were respected for their wisdom and patience and Ean liked to think he was no different. He'd grown up in the palace, along with his brothers, Merrick, Ladon and Wolfe. Ladon and Wolfe were dead. Merrick, being the King of the Unblessed, was all but lost to him. Ean had no family left him.

The great hall of the Golden Palace was majestic in its great beauty. The walls rose high, like crystals, from the cream marble floor. Light from outside shone through the walls, walls that were thin enough for the light, but thick enough not to be seen through. A fireplace burned along the side, never needing to be lit. At night, the torches would automatically catch fire, lighting the halls of the palace.

The hall was always filled with faeries, elves, sprights and pixies. All blessed creatures fell under his rule. Sprights and pixies mainly kept to themselves. The elfin and faery men were strong, youthful. But, the elfin and faery women were something to be admired. They were beautiful— some dark and exotic with complexions to rival the pixies' smoothest chocolates, others as fair and smooth as cream with just a touch of fresh peaches. While at court they wore lovely gowns that glimmered when they moved, hugging and teasing the flesh in such a way as to drive the men wild with lust. Away from court they were as tough as the men, taking up arms when needed.

"My king."

At Gregor's summons, Ean glanced away from the lingering trails of faery pheromones. The man was his head knight and commander of the elfin guards. Being such, he wore the red tunic of the Tegwen guards. It hung down over his legs, parting in the front. He walked forward with dignity and grace, though Ean knew the man could be deadly with his sword should he be provoked.

"I must speak with you," Gregor said, pushing his light brown hair over his shoulder. It was long, as was all elves'.

"Speak," Ean allowed, weary. He'd been under a melancholy lately, one he could vaguely contribute to his lingering connection to Merrick. It happened sometimes and Ean knew it would soon pass, as it always did.

"Privately, my king," Gregor insisted. "It's about King Merrick."

At the words, the few lingering in the hall grew quiet. Gregor had long ago proven himself a good, loyal man, but one who did not care for Merrick. All eyes turned forward. The blessed were at odds with Valdis and that would never change.

Ean nodded, instantly standing from his golden throne. He stepped down the platform to the main floor. "Come Gregor, let us go to my private chambers."

Ean's long tunic glimmered with gold on white. As he walked, the material fluttered around him. A crown wrapped around his forehead, the gold dipping down in front before disappearing beneath the locks of his long blond hair. He knew well the image he presented, knew he was envied by men, desired by women. He was surrounded at all times by his subjects, and yet he felt always alone. He had thought of starting a war with Merrick to ease the boredom of his existence, but could not bring himself to take up arms against him. So long as Merrick did not seek to fight him, Ean would leave his brother alone.

The side halls were constructed of white stone. Colorful tapestries hung over them, depicting the history of the elfin race—many stories of the great kings who came before him. As of yet, Ean did not record the story of his rule, for there was much he didn't wish to say about it.

His chambers were abovestairs, taking up the entire top floor of the palace. A long window of magic stretched over an inlet in the wall, showing the vast beauty of the countryside. There were pillows and furs arranged on the floor. The king often lay there at night, contemplating the stars, instead of in his oversized bed that was along the opposite wall.

Coming to his solar, he waved the faery servants out. They flew away, leaving the two men to privacy. Ean took a seat next to a gaming table and motioned Gregor to join him.

"It's been reported that Merrick has brought the human, Lady Juliana of Bellemare to our realm," Gregor said, as he took a seat.

Ean frowned, confused. "Merrick has brought a mortal woman over? For what purpose? I should think he'd want little to do with mortals. They are...*mortals*."

"My king, not just a woman, your *ward*, Lady Juliana of Bellemare," Gregor insisted.

"Ward?" Ean sat forward. "Bellemare, Bellemare, aye, I remember it now. My grandfather offered his blessing to it. I've not seen it myself, or those who reside within. You say Merrick has taken a woman from this place. Why?"

"It's not known, my king, but surely it's to strike at you," Gregor said. "Being as he was..."

"Is my brother. Regardless of what he is, that will not change." Ean frowned, unwilling to admit that he'd lost Merrick. Even if at times he thought it himself, he would not say the words aloud and break the small thread that still joined them.

"Aye, my king."

"Enough with the formality, Gregor." Ean sighed. "I have known you since boyhood. Speak plainly."

"Merrick surely knows of Bellemare's blessing."

Ean frowned. He was king and he barely recalled Bellemare's blessing. Though it was possible, he doubted Merrick thought of Bellemare or the mortals protected by the Blessed Kingdom. "Why is Bellemare blessed again? Which family are they?"

"Saxons," Gregor supplied. "One married your Aunt Alyssin, who gave up her immortality to be with her husband in life and death. It was her wish that her husband's line be blessed. Your grandfather, King Alwyn, ordered they be helped until a time when they no longer deserved the blessing bestowed upon them. He dispatched those to see to it. Though they are still there, until now we've not heard anything for many years. Rees, the Bellemare spright has come to report Juliana's disappearance."

"And he's sure it's Merrick?"

"Aye, my king."

Ean took a deep breath. What would Merrick want with a mortal woman? Surely, if his brother wished to strike a blow at him, he'd choose something more substantial than his human wards. Perhaps Merrick discovered something about the human line he knew nothing about. If Alyssin married into it, did that make the Bellemare mortals part elfin? Was this Juliana their cousin? And, if she was, what did it mean?

"There's more." Gregor fingered a game piece, refusing to meet his king's probing gaze. "It's said he's killed the woman's betrothed, slaughtered him. Two of the brothers and the slain man's son come to rescue Lady Juliana and fight your brother. I fear they will come to harm. Mortals, no matter how many their numbers, are no match for the Unblessed King."

Ean stayed quiet. He'd like to think Merrick wouldn't slaughter an innocent, but the truth was he no longer knew his brother. The image of boyhood he held in his head was not the man his brother had become. Still, Ean was reluctant to sever his last ties to Merrick, even if it meant dealing with the melancholy the connection brought. Regardless of this, he had no way of knowing if Juliana's betrothed was innocent. Merrick could well have his reason for slaughtering the man.

"Should we send aid to them, my king?" Gregor asked. "They are ignorant of our world, having just with recent events discovered we exist, and they are still your wards."

"Nay, send someone to watch for now. Let us discover what this is about before we take action." Ean stood, moving from the solar to the large window. Magic kept the wind and dust from penetrating the room. He looked over the landscape, the view clear and perfect as if he were outside. A large dragon was silhouetted in the far off distance, spouting fire across the sky to leave a trail of smoke. The king threaded his hands behind his back. "I will go speak to my brother and try to discover why he's taken Lady Juliana. It may have nothing to do with us."

"My king, nay," Gregor said from the solar's doorway. "You mustn't. Send me instead."

"I'll go, but I'll meet him on neutral ground and only after I've consulted the sacred scrolls. If there is something to the Bellemare line, I will discover it first. Send a dispatch at once to King Merrick with my invitation. Methinks we should meet at our borders, Rivershire." Ean rubbed his bottom lip thoughtfully.

"I will deliver the dispatch personally," said Gregor.

Ean didn't turn back around, as he felt Gregor leaving to do as he bid. When he was alone, he sighed, lifting his hand to the magical barrier. He slid his fingers through to feel the wind on the other side. It stung him with cold, but he didn't mind it. In the distance, the dragon disappeared, dipping down into the trees. Softly, he whispered to himself, "What mischief are you about now, brother?"

<hr/>

"Run!" Halton ordered, gripping Juliana's hair. She sprinted faster, screaming as another blaze of fire lighted the sky behind her. The spright slid from her shoulder and she felt him bouncing on her back as he gripped her hair.

"I told you that cave was no place to spend the night, giant!" Gorman yelled. He too pulled her hair for support, letting loose a high-pitched wail each time the dragon's flame drew near. The cave had seemed like a good idea, though it wasn't her idea. It was Halton and Gorman's. "See what you did! You woke it!"

Juliana jumped over a log as she ran toward the forest from the clearing. Her only hope was that the beast was too large to follow them into the trees. She was tired from a day of walking and it only made her breath all the more labored. The dragon roared. Its purple wings spread wide as it stopped in midair to spout fire at them. Heat warmed her back, the sound of boisterous flames deafening. Orange lit the evening, showing her the way into the darker forest. She screamed again, holding her breath as she leapt into the protection of the trees.

The roars continued, but Juliana could no longer feel the heat behind her or the wind of the beast's flapping wings against her back. She glanced over her shoulder. The way was dark except for the distance spot of orange from the dragon. The beast stayed out of the woods. Her feet stumbled as she slowed. Juliana collapsed on her hands and knees, breathing hard as she fought to ease the stitch in her side. Halton and Gorman jumped off her.

"That wasn't too frightening," Gorman boasted.

"Aye, it was just a baby dragon, not that big at all. I'm not scared of him," Halton said, yelling loudly in the beast's direction. He shook his fist. "You hear that, dragon! You're not so scary!"

Juliana ignored the sprights. She didn't want to move from the ground. Swallowing, she pushed back onto her knees, sitting on her legs. Her cloak was gone, lost as they fled the horrible creature. Sweat beaded her body, sticking her hair and clothes to her skin. She was tired. It had only been one day and she was tired of her journey. How was she ever going to last a week?

"Why'd you run, my lady?" Halton asked.

"We could've protected you," Gorman bragged.

Juliana frowned, pushing awkwardly to her feet. The middle of a path was no place to make camp for the night. She didn't say a word as she staggered away from them. She missed her brothers, her home. She wished Hugh was with her, with his calming logic and expert sword arm. Or even Thomas, with his lighter wit. He too was good with the sword. In truth, she'd even welcome the less fierce William to her side just so she didn't feel so alone.

"Ha! We're not scared of a little dragon," Gorman continued.

She could hear the sprights following her. Juliana walked faster, despite the stitch in her side. Her feet tripped but she didn't stop. She needed to be away from them for a moment. She needed silence to think and all they did was talk. It was their bantering that had awakened the dragon in the first place.

"If you're not scared, then how come you were screaming like a piskie?" Halton taunted.

"Was not!"

"Was so!"

"Was not!"

Juliana began to jog, holding her waist. The air cooled by small degrees. The sun set in the distance and its magenta light peeked through the trees, combining with the silver moon overhead. She stopped jogging and looked down at the trail. Small flowers dotted along the side, intermingling with the weeds. Unable to hear Gorman and Halton, she glanced back. The chill grew, causing her to shiver. The flowers along the path pulled in on themselves, wilting as if an invisible wave washed over them.

"Gorman?" she whispered, trembling. She glanced around the darkening forest. All was quiet. "Halton? Where are you?"

"My lady appears to be a bit singed."

Juliana stiffened. Merrick? It couldn't be. Her body pulled toward him and her skin tingled, reaching for his nearness. She hated to admit she had longed for him, but her mind was stronger than her body. She would resist him.

I will not succumb, she swore. I will not succumb. I will not succumb. I will not suc... Lifting her jaw, she whispered, "Merrick?"

"Aye, Juliana." Merrick studied her from behind. She didn't turn to look at him, and he desperately wanted her to. He'd come to see her, to make sure she was unharmed, having watched the chase with the dragon from the garden basin. He silently beckoned her to him when she didn't come of her own free will, gently urging her with his power to come to him. She refused to move. "Did you miss me?"

"Nay."

"Pity." He whispered the word next to her ear and followed it with a flick of his tongue to her lobe. She jolted in surprise. Merrick blew warm breath along her neck, watching as chills worked over her flesh. A weak noise escaped her throat.

"End this, Merrick," she begged softly. "Let me go."

"I cannot." He closed his eyes. A strange pain welled in him at her plea, but he forced it aside.

"If not you, then who?"

Merrick took a deep breath. Her words rolled over him and he couldn't resist touching her, just as he couldn't help teasing her, mocking her. She had no idea the effect she had on him. He hesitated before moving his fingers to her shoulder, letting them glance down her arm in a light caress. He expected her to scream, to jerk away. She didn't move. "Merrick, please."

Please? Please what? The words were so light, a plea to him. He knew she wanted to be freed, but he couldn't let her go. The more she struggled, the more he wanted to tighten his grip on her. Merrick drew closer to her back, keeping his body a hairsbreadth away from hers. His blood stirred, as it always did when she was near. This time he didn't fight it. He let his arousal grow between his legs. It pressed along his tight breeches, straining to be free.

He smelled her perspiration, her fear, her longing for him that she tried so desperately to hide. Her fear fed his powers and his desire. He wanted to touch her, awaken her passions to him, but he wanted her to freely ask it of him first. Merrick didn't know why it should matter. If he wanted her, he could take her by force or by seduction. Either way, his body would be sated. With just a simple gesture he could whisk her away to his palace, to his bed, where he could bury himself repeatedly into her depths until he had his fill. No one would dare stop him.

Juliana swayed and he was surprised when she fell against him. His erection pressed against the small of her back. His chest supported her weight. He dropped his hand from her arm, not touching her further. It was torture, the ache she caused, but he was used to self-denial, to torment and pain. He told himself to leave her, to disappear. His body was reluctant to listen to the will of his mind, so he stood, waiting for her to speak.

"Why do you do this, Merrick?" Juliana had waited for him to speak to her, to give a hint of why he tormented her in such away. His body was close, too close for propriety, but she couldn't take the necessary step forward to free herself of him. He was warm, heating her so she no longer felt the cold. His strength supported her. Again, moments passed in silence. His chest rose and fell in even breaths. She shouldn't let him touch her like this, but she couldn't pull away.

"I am what I am, Juliana, I cannot do otherwise," he whispered at last.

"Everyone has a choice. Please, release us. Stop this game. Send me home. Tonight was to be my wedding night. I'm sure there is still time—"

"Nay." Merrick's lips came close to her ear. She closed her eyes tight, fighting the urge to reach for him. Her hands balled into fists. In a hot whisper, his lips brushing along her racing pulse, he enunciated his words against her throat, "I will never let you go."

Juliana gasped. Her head fell back, her neck weak. She reached for him, expecting her head to land on his chest. Instead, it fell through air. Merrick had disappeared. She stumbled backward as she fought to right herself. "Merrick, wait."

He reappeared before her, his body solidifying. She looked him over. His blond hair appeared strange in the moonlight, almost glowing against his dark clothes. Her gaze followed the small braid from his temple down to his waist. His arousal strained against his tight breeches. She blushed, quickly turning her eyes from it, moving her gaze back to his face.

"Do you enter my dreams?" Juliana took a step for him. It was torturous not to touch him. "Last night, was that you?"

"You dream of me?" The words were altogether too arrogant.

Juliana frowned. There was no way she'd admit to it, or to the fact that last night wasn't the first time she'd felt him inside her dreams, though last night was the first time she'd seen his face. She turned away. "Must you mock me, sir, at every turn?"

"Sir?" Merrick's hand grazed the back of her neck, sweeping beneath her hair. With one swift movement he pulled her into his arms. His hot gaze moved to her lips, watching them intently. He forced her to take a step, walking her along until her back hit the trunk of a tree. The rough bark scratched her as the solid press of his chest trapped her to it. His body was like a piece of iron, holding her to his will. Her breasts ached, the nipples hardening for him. She parted her lips, panting at his nearness. His words a low growl, he asked, "Why so formal, Juliana? We are past that. You know me too well."

"Know you?" She weakly shook her head in denial. "I hardly know you."

"Aye, you do." Merrick nodded. His lips came closer, teasing her with their nearness but not giving her what she craved. "That's the problem with mortals. You can't see beyond the rational. You can't feel into your dreams. With your kind, everything is literal, logical, either right or wrong, good or evil."

"And how do you see things, Merrick?"

"For what they are." He let her go. But when he tried to back away, her fingers gripped onto his tunic, holding him tight. She forgot every reason why she should push him away, as she waited for him to kiss her.

"Then explain to me why you do this. Make me understand. If your reasons are not rational, then what hope do I have of—? *Ah-a-ah.*" His mouth came forward once more, stopping her words as his lips hovered close to hers. Lightheaded, she sighed dreamily. The world spun around them. She felt like they were dancing, though they didn't move.

"The reason is simple, Juliana. You torment me as I torment you. Only one of us can win this game and I never lose."

What in all the heavens did that mean? Juliana whimpered. Suddenly, Merrick let go and disappeared. She stumbled forward, nearly falling to the ground.

"What's wrong with her?" Halton asked, coming from the trees. "Do you think she's taken to drink?"

"Oh, aye, and where'd she get the drink?" Gorman demanded, sighing in obvious frustration at his friend. "She milk it from the trees?"

"You can do that?" Halton proclaimed, sounding excited.

"Argh, be quiet!" Gorman harrumphed.

Juliana glanced around for Merrick, feeling cold now that he was gone, even as the air got warmer. The flowers' petals were opened, as if they'd never closed. She spun in circles, searching the trees for him. He had truly left her.

"Hum, wonder if she's possessed," Halton answered. "I say we make camp here for the night."

"Good idea." Gorman leapt into the forest, calling cheerfully, "I'll get the firewood."

"I'll get the food," Halton said. "My lady, you just wait right here."

Juliana nodded. She felt numb, empty. A fire sparked when Merrick was near and burned out when he was gone. Falling to her knees in exhaustion, she whispered, "Release me, Merrick. Please, just let me go."

Fire Palace of the Damned, Kingdom of Hades

King Lucien chuckled as he watched the mortal woman collapse onto the ground. Her reflection filled up the divining mirror he held. With a snap of his fingers, he lit the silver hand mirror into flames. It burned, disappearing into nothingness. His voice mocking, he said, "Mm, yes, Merrick, release her. Or, mayhap, I should bring her here and release her for you."

Lucien lounged on his bed, surrounded by the dark grey stone of his castle. Rolling onto his back amongst the dark furs, he held his palm up. His knees were bent and his bare feet dug into the fur coverlet. He normally only wore breeches, and perhaps a cloak, while in his home. Flames appeared in his palm, and he absently danced them around his fingers, winding them like a snake down his arm and over his naked chest. Forming the flames into a ball, he tossed it back and forth between his hands.

Fires burned all around him in his bedchamber—in basins, on candles and torches, in the oversized fireplace. The immense heat didn't bother him. In fact, he welcomed it. It warmed his otherwise chilled skin. Light gauze hung from the ceilings, fluttering noiselessly around the room. Though the material occasionally blew close to the flames, it did not light.

"Why don't you leave them be, Lucien?"

Lucien didn't spare a glance for the beautiful woman chained to the end of his bed. Her tone reeked with a strange combination of anger and indifference.

"I keep you alive, Mia, only because you amuse me. Start to vex me and I'll extract what soul you have left." Lucien crushed the flames into his palm, smiting them. He then rested his hands above his head, letting them lay on the sea of his black hair.

"It's near dead anyway," Mia answered. "What do I care?"

"Obviously you don't. You bartered it to me to begin with." Lucien winked at her. A metal collar wrapped around her neck and two shackles bound her wrists. She lunged for him. The chains rattled, keeping her back. He didn't move as his eyes filled completely black, purposefully frightening her. "Ah, there's the fire in you. Care to come warm me with it?"

She trembled and turned her head sharply away. "I hate myself for succumbing to you."

"Mm, I love your self-hate, Mia. It feeds me."

"Then maybe I'll fall in love with you and destroy you," she spat, not moving to touch him.

"The fact that you love me is why you hate yourself." Lucien chuckled. He rolled over on his side to look at her. Her dark flesh twinkled, shimmering in the firelight. Dark black kohl lined her violet eyes. It matched the black leather and steel of the tiny bodice that barely covered her chest in thin strips. Her shoulders and midriff were bare, as were her legs beneath the short skirt. His voice filled with the sound of demons, as he said, "You look beautiful in chains, my little nymph."

"And these chains would look lovely about your neck, my king," she answered, her voice as dark as his, "choking the breath from you."

"You wish to play?" he asked, smiling. Lucien quickly rolled up on the bed, kneeling before her. Mia growled, striking out at him with her nails. He didn't flinch as she scratched him. Beads of blood trailed over his skin. His head fell back as he moaned in pleasure and arousal. The wounds healed as fast as they were inflicted. His mouth opened and he looked at her, his lids lowered.

"Leave Merrick and the woman be," Mia said. Lucien lifted his hand. A silver dagger appeared in it. Mia's gaze greedily went to it. Her hands balled into fists. "What do you care if they are—?"

His dark laugh interrupted her and she snapped her mouth shut.

"Still such thoughts of others. It would seem I haven't broken you after all." Lucien drew the tip over his mouth, cutting his bottom lip so it bled. "Care to buy the answer you seek?"

"What terms?" Mia demanded. She didn't reach for the knife, but he knew she wanted to. He let the chains dissolve off of her wrists and neck, freeing her.

Lucien reached out to touch her face, caressing her cheek with the backs of his fingers even as he still held the dagger. "I'll answer your question if you yet again succumb to yourself."

A tear slipped down Mia's cheek, even as she reached for him to return the embrace. "I hate you, Lucien."

Lucien felt the demon surfacing in him. He welcomed it and the power it would bring him. Leaning toward her, he moved to kiss her. Before pressing his bloodied mouth roughly to hers, he whispered, "Quite the opposite, my little Mia."

Chapter Five

"It's Juliana's," Hugh stated. He touched the hilt of his sword, resting his hand on the cool metal. Thomas nudged his stallion forward. Hugh glanced at his brother before picking up the cloak from the ground. The material was stiff, the wool burnt, but he still recognized it as his sister's. Turning to Nicholas and Thomas astride their stallions, he grimly added, "I'm sure of it."

"Blood?" Thomas asked, choking on the word. The men were armed with swords and daggers, but carried no armor as it would weigh them down. Instead they wore simple tunics and cloaks. The colors were muted, blending in with the surrounding forest.

Hugh examined Juliana's cloak. It was muddy and damp, but he saw no blood. "Nay."

Thomas let loose a long breath. Hugh glanced at Nicholas. The man wouldn't meet his gaze as he peered off into the distance. He'd been getting a strange feeling off of Nicholas. But, taking into account that the man had just lost his father and was now in a magical world none of them had ever before known existed, Hugh dismissed his worry. They were all trying to cope the best they could with what was happening. Not knowing why Merrick took Juliana was almost as bad as her being taken to the Otherworld in the first place.

The three men traveled non-stop, but Hugh felt as if they made slow progress. They'd searched endlessly for a sign of Juliana—riding continuously in the immortal realm for three days, sleeping and eating astride their horses. Aside from the occasional bird, they hadn't seen anyone or anything. They were all tired, but none thought of stopping while his sister was still missing.

Until now, they hadn't seen a trace of the noblewoman. The tattered cloak was hardly reassuring. William had sent them in the most likely direction to find her, giving them a list of hurried instructions as they took off into the forest. At first, they thought themselves mad, as the Otherworld looked like Bellemare's property. However, when they glanced to look back at the castle and found it gone, all doubts were put to rest.

Hugh had brought the best of Bellemare's stallions with them. Fittingly, the breed was known as Bellemares. They had a distinctly simple chestnut coloring to their coats with a dark stripe down the back from shoulder blades to tail. The horses' hair and eyes were also dark chestnut, making them nearly invisible at night.

The horses were an ancient mix of bloodlines, a crossbreeding of French trotters and hunters for stamina, with the intelligence of a Holstein Warmblood and the jumping abilities of a Lipizzaner. There was also some Arabian blood in the English stock. To the common ear, it sounded like a hodgepodge, but the men of Bellemare knew horses and took their breeding seriously. There were many more elements to the breeds, but Hugh now understood their "blessing" more than likely had something to do with their breeding luck.

"William said King Merrick lives in the Black Palace," Nicholas said quietly. It was the first time he'd spoken that day. The brothers looked at him. He didn't return their gazes, as he stared between his horse's ears. "I say we find this King Merrick and kill him for his crimes against my family and yours."

"We don't know that he's taken Juliana," Hugh said, with damning rationale.

"You have the cloak," Nicholas said. "It proves that she was here and obviously traveling in a hurry if she were to leave it behind. Either she was running away from someone or she was being forced by someone. Often the most ready explanation is the true one."

Hugh took a deep breath. Though he'd like to weave King Merrick into a villain, the truth was he didn't know the King. He'd never heard of him before this quest to find their sister. William appeared to think the King above Lord Eadward's death. William's judgment, though strange at times, was often sound. He would not dismiss that. "Perhaps we should consider this King Lucien of the Damned?"

"You heard Will. King Lucien cannot enter the human world," Thomas said, adjusting himself atop his horse. Hugh tossed Juliana's cloak to him. He caught it, looking it over before lightly fingering the burn marks.

"What choice do we have? Let us at least meet this King Merrick and then judge his character." Hugh swung atop his mount, seating himself easily. Nicholas made a sound of frustration, but said nothing to contradict the decision. Thomas nodded in agreement and laid the cloak over his thighs.

"When this is over," Nicholas gave a pointed look at Hugh before turning to stare straight ahead. His eyes burned with hate and anger. "I will speak with you about Lady Juliana. I *am* my father's heir."

Hugh shared a look with Thomas. Neither brother answered. Nicholas didn't look as if he expected one. Now was not the time for such talk. Hugh nudged his horse across the valley, galloping through the clearing to the forest.

"King Merrick!" Bevil's high-pitched voice rang over the hall, causing instant silence amongst the goblins. His feet hit hard as he pumped his short legs, running along the stone. His voice was raspy in his urgency, but Merrick didn't move from his place on the throne. He frowned as the music he'd been listening to suddenly stopped with his irritation. "A visitor."

"Where?" Merrick asked, sitting up quickly. His gaze flew down to the goblin before him.

"The gates," Bevil said.

Merrick's body dissolved into smoke as he quickly crossed the hall to stand before the goblin. Bevil skidded to a stop. Eyeing him, the Unblessed King demanded, "A woman?"

"Nay, my king," Bevil's high voice squeaked.

Merrick frowned, not caring to wonder at his disappointment. It was unlikely Juliana could make it to his palace so quickly, even if she had help. He didn't know where she was and he refused to go to the garden basin to watch her, mainly because he so desperately wanted to.

"Then send them away," he said, very distinctly, leaning over to emphasize his words. His hands threaded behind his back as he glared at the goblin. "I don't take uninvited guests in my hall."

"King Merrick."

Merrick frowned, his dark gaze whipping up to look at his hall's main doors, which led to the front entrance of his palace. Seeing the red tunic of Tegwen's guard, he stiffened. His eyes scanned the small group of elves, not seeing his brother amongst them. The five men stared back, their faces grim. They were about as happy to be in his hall as he was to have them there. To Bevil, he hissed, "I will deal with you later."

Bevil squeaked and ran quickly away. Slowly, Merrick straightened to his full height. His voice soft, he said to the leader of the Tegwen guards, "Your manners have not improved since last we met, Commander Gregor."

"I seek an audience," Gregor said. Though he kept his voice calm, Merrick knew he burned inside. He could feel the man's hatred for him.

"Denied," Merrick said, just to aggravate him further. Gregor and he had never gotten along, not even as children. The commander prided himself as an expert swordsman and so Merrick turned his back on him. The insult it implied was very intentional. His goblins laughed at their king's rudeness. The sound was grating, mocking.

"I have a missive from King Ean," Gregor stated, his voice clipped. Merrick heard the man step forward.

"My dear brother writes after so long?" Merrick asked, turning with a purposefully evil grin. "Then, I'm sure I'll take just as long to read it. Set it on the floor and leave."

Merrick again turned to dismiss them, walking leisurely to his throne. When he was seated, the men were still there, having moved closer. He looked down at the guards, reaching his hand through the air to produce a chalice of wine. Taking a sip, he tilted his head back and started to close his eyes. Gregor's quick movement stopped him from shutting them completely. The man threw a vial on the hall floor. Blue liquid spread over the stone and smoke rose from the puddle it made. Merrick frowned, but didn't move. The image of his brother formed in the smoke.

"Greetings, King Merrick," Ean's low, rich voice said. The image solidified, looking as real as the guard behind it. Merrick frowned, refusing to find pleasure in seeing his brother's face after so long. He noted the subtle lines along the edge of Ean's youthful eyes, knowing that stress and little sleep put them there. He felt a connection to Ean, knew his brother felt the briefest of his emotions—though Ean could never know how deeply Merrick's emotions ran. As the Unblessed King, he couldn't help but wonder why Ean didn't just sever the tie. Undoubtedly, it was so he could always track him, just as Merrick could track Ean. No matter what they once were, now they were enemies. "Thank you for seeing to the safety of my men."

Merrick snorted, not bothering to hide his look of contempt. The goblins laughed, this time joined by the loud troll, Volos. The grating, loud noise echoed off the stone walls, making it sound as if three times as many subjects were in his hall. The elfin visitors shifted their weight, their hands instinctively lifting to rest on the swords at their waists. Merrick knew his brother's men had nothing to fear—yet. The goblins would not attack unless he ordered it.

"I wish to extend my hand in invitation," Ean's message continued. "It has been far too long since we last spoke. If you're agreeable, we shall meet in the borderland at Rivershire. I will be there two days hence."

Merrick didn't move. Ean's image bowed and disappeared into a thin veil of mist. Merrick took a sip of wine, saying nothing.

"Have you an answer for my king?" Gregor asked, stepping forward. His face was stiff with anger at Merrick's callous treatment.

Merrick tilted his head back slightly, eyeing the man. "I'm sorry, Gregor, I had not realized you'd gone from commander to courier."

"Your answer?" Gregor was no match for Merrick and he knew it.

"Will not be given to you." Merrick scowled menacingly. "Now, you are in my home uninvited. Go, lest my good humor deserts me. Be thankful I'm in no mood to torture you this day."

Gregor snarled, but slowly nodded. Custom dictated that he obey, as did prudence. The commander had already pressed his luck by entering the hall against the king's wishes. He took several steps back, keeping his eyes on Merrick. When he neared the door to the main hall, he turned on his heels. The Tegwen guards strode from the castle.

Merrick crushed his hand, making the chalice disappear. His eyes scanned the hall. The goblins and Volos went back about their business as if nothing had happened, laughing and plotting their mischief. It had been a long time since he'd seen Ean and against his better judgment he wanted to—not that seeing him would change anything. It couldn't. Fate had seen to it that they were enemies.

Merrick again looked about at his goblin court. There was no one in the hall from which to get council. He thought of Juliana, longing for her nearness, even if his intent would be to torment her. With that in mind, he stood and moved toward the black garden.

Just one look, he told himself. *Just a peek to see how she fairs on her little adventure.*

Juliana stopped walking. She was so exhausted. All she wanted to do was sleep. Oh, and eat something other than nuts and berries. What she wouldn't give for meat—roasted boar, chicken, venison, anything. She moaned and whispered to herself, "Mm, herbed potatoes, fresh baked bread, apple tarts."

"I'll get the firewood!" Gorman called. Juliana flinched at his loud voice.

"I'll get the food!" Halton answered, sounding cheery.

"Sure," she mumbled, finding a log and sitting on it. "That's because they haven't spent the last three days playing cart horse."

Frowning, she watched the two sprights hop off. They looked positively happy to be camping in the woods. It was the same attitude they had each night. Though, to be fair, they didn't know the weight she carried. Her stomach knotted each time she thought of the children, picturing their faces in her mind. She'd never forgive herself if anything happened to them.

"Please bring back something besides berries," she whispered, letting her head fall into her hands. She suppressed a yawn, knowing she should be thankful for their company at all.

"Sprights don't eat anything but berries and nuts most of the time."

"So I've learned," Juliana answered before the fact that someone other than Gorman, Halton and Merrick spoke to her—not that she'd seen the frustrating man recently. Her head snapped up. "Who said that?"

Suddenly, one of the boulders on the other side of the path began to move. A squat little round man with chubby red cheeks and tiny features popped his head up. His hat, jacket and long beard were the perfect gray of stone and blended him quite well to his surroundings. His beard touched and dragged on the ground as he moved. "Domovoi Djedoesjka at your service."

"Are you a garden gnome?" Juliana asked, studying the little man.

"Garden gnome?" Domovoi spat, appearing insulted by the very idea. Gingerly, he threw the beard over his shoulder and waddled forward. "I be not a garden gnome! I be woodland. Does this look like a garden to you?"

"Pardon me, sir," Juliana answered, momentarily forgetting her problems as the gnome inspected her.

"Pardon you for what?" the gnome asked, blinking his little eyes rapidly. "Did you do something to my mud?"

"Mud?" Juliana asked.

"Aye, mud," he repeated. His tiny hand reached to grab hers. Before she knew what he was doing, he jerked her down and inspected her hands. Seeing a dirty smudge on her palm, he scratched at it then sniffed. "Do you think it was growin' there waitin' for just anyone to come along and take it?"

"You...grow mud?" Juliana asked, having little doubt the gnome was crazy. She looked around for the sprights. They were nowhere to be seen. She couldn't even hear them, which was rare.

"Then how exactly does it get there without someone tending to it? Magic?" the gnome asked with a snort. To her dismay, he tapped his tongue on the dirt smudge and tasted it. He made a face and let her go.

"I'm beginning to believe there isn't much magic, just creatures unlike myself," Juliana said, wiping her hand on her skirt.

At that Domovoi frowned. He shook his head, soon forgetting his anger. "Magic be all around you, child. What do you think this forest be?"

"Abandoned," she mumbled dryly.

His frown deepened, though his eyes softened. "Abandoned? With all the creatures here now?"

"There are more of you?" She shivered, looking around her for other signs of life. She saw nothing.

"Aye, you don't bother us, we don't bother you." Domovoi chuckled. "We be thankful you be keeping 'em entertained."

Juliana frowned. Him or them? She couldn't understand. Did he mean Merrick? Or the sprights? "You're the third creature…ah, fifth if you count Merrick and the dragon, I've actually seen in three days."

"Be it because of 'em you've been traveling around in circles?"

"Aye." Juliana stiffened, rising to her feet. "Wait, circles? What do you mean circles?"

"We've watched you for three days, making two circles a day through the forest with the meddlesome sprights on your shoulder." Domovoi shrugged and moved as if to leave. "Seems like a waste of time if you ask us, but you haven't, so we didn't."

"Wait, please, sir," Juliana said, tensing. Nausea grew from the pit of her stomach. She clutched her waist, taking deep breaths. How could they? Tears welled in her eyes, burning her nose. She refused to cry. Her voice shaking, she asked, "Are you saying that I've just spent the last three days walking in giant circles?"

"Aye." Domovoi took off his hat and scratched the back of his head. "I'd heard humans were slow creatures. But, that be all right. I'll just have to remember to talk slower so you can understand me."

Domovoi again began to turn. Juliana took a step for him. "Please, sir, can you tell me how to find King Lucien? Am I anywhere close to his palace?"

"Sure. You be wanting the Fire Palace. He spends his time there. Don't come out much that I know of."

Did he say Fire Palace? Wasn't she supposed to be going to the Black Palace? She was so tired, she couldn't be sure anymore. Juliana took a deep breath, fighting the torturous ache in her head. "Are you sure King Lucien wouldn't be at the Black Palace? I was told to find him there."

"Aye, he might be, but you'd really have better luck at the Fire Palace."

"Can you tell me how to get to the Fire Palace?" Juliana insisted when he again turned to leave.

"Now, why would a thing like you want to get to a place like that?" Domovoi frowned. His face scrunched up with worry. Juliana was in no mood to explain. She wasn't sure she understood it herself.

"I don't have a choice. I have to ask the king something." Juliana swallowed. The way Gorman and Halton talked of Lucien nonstop for three days, she was pretty sure she knew what she'd have to ask. She'd have to ask him to take her soul in exchange for the children's freedom. No doubt Merrick was a demon who worked for King Lucien. On many occasions, she'd wanted to ask them about Merrick, but something stopped her. Maybe she didn't want to hear the truth of him—not when he was so much in her thoughts. And maybe she was scared they'd see through her—see that she desired Merrick. It was too shameful.

"Come on, then. I'll get you where you be goin'. But we had better hurry. The dew-beetles have been singin' off pitch and the grass blows in three different directions. It be going to rain in a week and three hours, give or take a minute, and I have a new crop of mud to harvest."

Juliana looked at the forest for Gorman and Halton. Did she follow the gnome? Or did she wait for the sprights? Obviously, she couldn't trust either of them. The sprights had led her in circles for days. She knew they were worried about her selling her soul, but she couldn't help that.

It turned out she didn't have to decide. The gnome walked excruciatingly slow and had only gone past five trees by the time the two sprights hopped in front of her. Their arms were laden with sticks and nuts.

"Where you going?" Halton asked cheerfully.

"Apparently in circles," Juliana quipped, glaring down at him. He flinched, looking at Gorman with his tiny bundle of sticks.

"She knows!" Halton whispered loudly.

"I got this," Gorman answered, before turning to her. He tried to blink innocently, but she wasn't fooled. "Whatever do you mean, my lady giant?"

Juliana raised a brow, placing her hands on her hips.

"Oh," Gorman said. "That."

"That," Halton repeated. "Oh."

"Aye, that!" Juliana fumed. "How could you lead me in circles? Do you know what you have done? What you have cost me?"

They shrugged, blinking their big eyes.

"Don't be mad, my lady giant," Gorman said.

"We only meant to save you from harm," Halton added.

Juliana shook her head and stomped off. It was getting late and she was exhausted, but she couldn't stop to rest now. She'd already wasted too much time. These two obviously weren't as helpful as they seemed. She'd have to try her luck with the gnome. It didn't take her long to catch up to him and at the rate Domovoi walked, she'd end up carrying him as well.

❦

When Lady Juliana was out of sight, Gorman looked at Halton. "She's a touchy one, eh?"

"All we tried to do was save her." Halton leapt up to a branch and craned his neck to see her. "Poor dear."

Gorman joined him on the branch. "Good thing we didn't tell her about that group of human riders."

"How do you know they were humans? They didn't smell like humans."

"I met a human once," Gorman said, nodding.

"When?"

"It was a Tuesday." Gorman's chest puffed up with self-importance. "I know they're human because of their horses. I'll warrant those men are up to no good. Their eyes are too shifty as they look through the forest."

"Aye, no use worrying her about that. We've led her around and back away from them. They've gone on ahead toward King Merrick's. No good could come of humans going to King Merrick's."

"Aye, good thing she has us to look after her. Come on then, let's follow her and keep the simple creature out of trouble." Gorman hopped down.

"Aye, good thing." Halton followed him. "Though, let's stay out of her sight. She appears to want and try things on her own."

"Ah, poor simple creature." Gorman shook his head.

"Poor, poor simple creature."

Juliana followed Domovoi for about a half-hour. The air had cooled, but was pleasant. They didn't make it very far at the gnome's pace, but she didn't pay attention, using her time to think. Thankfully, the two deceitful sprights stayed away. She wasn't in the mood for them at the moment. Hearing water, she stopped and looked up from her place on the path.

"Well, I got you where you be going," Domovoi said.

Juliana's brow furrowed. It just looked like more forest to her. "The Fire Palace?"

"Nay, why would I take you there? My instincts, and my nose I might add, told me to take you here." Domovoi waved toward a shrub.

"To a shrub?" Juliana asked.

"Nay," Domovoi scowled and waddled over to the bush, pulling it aside, he showed her a clearing. Juliana gasped despite herself. Stars sprinkled the night. They almost seemed to dance around the full moon. A large pond reflected the heavens, as if the stars were caught within the water. "To bathe. You be startin' to offend the woodland creatures. They be already edgy, being as the snow only lasted one day. They didn't get their rest and be right testy at that. I don't know what the wizards be doing."

"Is it safe?" she asked, feeling a little breathless.

"Aye," Domovoi answered. "It be deep for me. For you, not as much."

"I mean…is there anything in it?"

"Like what?" Domovoi waddled over to the water and looked in. She saw his reflection looking back at him.

"Nixies," Juliana said quietly, joining him at the water's edge. If a little gnome wasn't afraid, she wouldn't be either.

Domovoi laughed. "Nixies? Whoever heard of a Nixie?"

"Oh." Juliana sighed. She tapped the surface with her hand. It was warm and inviting. "Nobody will see me?"

The gnome frowned, looking her up and down with a careful eye. "Who'd want to?"

"Ah, good point," she said, nodding slowly. She was too tired to care.

"There you be," Domovoi said, waddling away.

Juliana watched after him as he disappeared. Belatedly, she called softly, "Thank you."

There was no answer. She glanced around. It really was too beautiful to resist. Sitting on the ground, she took off her boots. The ground was moist under her bare feet and it felt good to stretch her toes. Slowly, she pulled out of her overtunic wishing she had a change of clothes. With another look around, she assured herself that no one would see her and tugged the thin chemise over her head.

Merrick watched the basin with rapt attention. Knowing the sprights had run her in circles brought a smile to his face. She still searched for King Lucien and that bothered him for some inexplicable reason, but he didn't wish to be the one to correct her. It wasn't like she'd find the Demon King. He debated on whether or not to tell her he was the King of the Unblessed, but something kept him from getting involved. Let her find her own way. It was her adventure and he could do little to protect her. That was the bargain they'd made, whether she knew it or not.

Or was it that he *would* do little to protect her? Merrick frowned, not liking the doubts that plagued him. He didn't want to be conflicted.

Merrick leaned forward with interest. His body stirred to life, his shaft erect with desire. He'd seen her change, had watched her do so many times, unabashed, but there was something erotic to the way the pale moonlight caressed her skin. Or maybe it was the fact that she was alone, in his world, within his control. He could go to her, touch her, kiss her—how he'd dreamt of kissing her.

Juliana made her way into the water. The surface rippled, undulating around her thighs. Moonlight reflected off the water, dancing on her stomach and breasts. She looked thinner from her travels, a small change to be sure, but she was still beautiful. Her breasts were ripe, the perfect size for his hands. The nipples hardened like beacons, calling to his lips. How sweet it would be to feel them. He wanted to taste her, drink the sweet water of the pond from her flesh.

Dark hair fell long over her back, touching her hips. A thatch of dark nether curls drew his attention. It was almost unbearable agony. He thought of relieving himself, but a strange sense of pride and self-loathing kept him from dipping his fingers down the front of his breeches. His heart tightened in his chest. Looking made the heartache worse, and yet he couldn't turn away.

◆◆◆

Juliana shivered with pleasure as she stepped into the pond. Slowly, she lowered herself into the water. It felt wonderful and she ran her hands over her body to wash. Shivering again, she felt like she was being watched. But as she looked around, calling out softly, she detected nothing in the forest. Domovoi had hinted there was no one interested enough to watch her. Gnomes and sprights were probably as attracted to her as she was to them. The thought gave her some comfort.

A soft moan tried to escape her, but was cut off by a sudden howling. Juliana stiffened. She stood, crossing her arms over her breasts as she looked over the rocky shoreline surrounded by forest. She took a deep breath and then another. The howl sounded again, but was farther away.

Juliana tried to relax. She felt something brush by her leg and stiffened once more. A fish? She tried to see beneath the glassy surface. Nothing.

"How did I get here?" she whispered. She closed her eyes and thought of Merrick. She tried to hate him, but couldn't—not completely. Oddly, she missed him.

Shivering, she imagined feeling his hand on her leg, fingers running lightly up the back of her calf to her knee, before moving along the outside of her thigh to her hip. Every fiber of her being reached for him, as heat washed over her. She was no fool. She knew what happened between a man and a woman. Why, after all her years, she'd desire that something to happen with Merrick was beyond her. The touch skimmed her stomach, a soft brush of lips, gliding through the beads of water on her flesh.

"Merrick," she whispered dreamily, as the touch moved between her breasts to her throat. Her imagination had always been so real that she didn't stop to consider anything else. She wanted to wrap her arms around his neck and beg him to carry her away from it all, to a soft, warm bed where she never had to wake up. In her fantasy the children were safe and she didn't have to marry Eadward. She was free to do as she will. The dream felt amazing and real and Juliana had no desire to fight it. Fingers tipped her face, holding gently beneath her chin. Her limbs were heavy, lethargic. "Merrick."

"Aye," came a soft answer.

She gasped, her lips parting as she struggled to open her eyes. When she did, she saw him before her. His dark eyes met hers, narrowed, predatory. His mouth lowered, gently brushing along her lips. The unique smell of his body roused her senses, lighting a flaming trail that torched its way through her blood. She moaned softly, keeping her lips parted as she discovered the texture of him, the heat.

Juliana lifted her hands, resting them on his chest. His long, wet hair was pushed back, but her fingers managed to twine in a long strand as she touched the smooth, toned flesh. He wasn't wearing a tunic and she didn't hesitate to spread her palms flat over his naked chest. Not a measure of fat marred his taller frame. His heart beat against her hand, sure and steady. Fear and nervous anticipation knotted her stomach, as she tentatively lifted her knee to brush alongside his leg. It was with a strange mix of relief and disappointment that she found he wore breeches. The material was wet and oddly slick to the touch. She let her leg fall back down into the water, away from him.

Somewhere in the back of her mind, sanity tried to take root. She pushed lightly at his shoulder, though the gesture was barely hard enough to be considered an adequate protest. His hands didn't touch her, save for the light finger to her chin, tilting her face up for his kiss.

Merrick didn't heed her gentle objection, as he deepened his kiss. He slid his tongue into her mouth, snaking it around her teeth as he probed her depths. Soft noises came from the back of her throat, both natural and accepting. As her fear of him lessened, he was fed with a new kind of power—a power that did not belong to the King of the Unblessed, but to a man starved for the arms of a woman, for contact beyond that of fearful submission.

He'd been a fool to think he could stay away as he watched her bathe in the moonlight. Water had beaded on her flesh like stars, glistening in silver trails, calling to him. His intent had been to frighten her, to push her away from him, but as he rose up from the water and she didn't scream, he couldn't help but kiss her. Her lips didn't move with expert skill and still he felt her as he had no other woman before her. The sensations took him by surprise and he abruptly pulled back.

"Merrick, don't go. Not yet," she pleaded, her lips pursed for more.

Merrick tried to resist, tried to leave her, but couldn't. She asked him to stay by her own free will. He ached to possess her. Why should he deny them both? It's what they wanted. She admitted it by her own words, even if she believed him to be a dream.

He glided his fingers over Juliana's wet skin and she didn't move to stop him as he kneeled in the water. Merrick watched her closely as he leaned to kiss her thigh. Her full lips trembled and he groaned, sensing the heady scent of her need. Unable to resist, he dipped his tongue into the slick folds of her sex, parting them as he briefly tasted her. She grabbed his hair with shaky fingers. The trembling was so bad it vibrated against his skull as she weakly tried to pull his mouth back. Her thighs tightened beneath his searching hands. Merrick kissed along her stomach, slowly standing as he made his way up, only stopping to pull an erect nipple into his mouth.

He became more aggressive in his urgency, letting his breeches dissolve to leave his body naked and ready. Merrick knew he would make love to her, taking his time, weaving a web of his magic around them. He let his own pleasure radiate onto her and she took it willingly.

Juliana gasped. Her eyes fluttered open with a soft moan. A strange mist surrounded her senses. Her body was alive with sensations so potent they made her knees weak. Her nipples ached and it felt as if her whole body was being burned alive.

Why did she beg for him? He was the enemy, wasn't he? He'd kidnapped the children. He made her go on this journey, possibly facing death. Despite this, she couldn't stop. God forgive her, she wanted him to touch her.

All thoughts left her as she felt his fingers along her back. His heat wrapped around her from behind, drawing her to his chest. He pressed his body to hers. The naked, hard length of his desire was unmistakable.

Juliana jerked in his arms. Merrick's hands glided over her chest, rubbing her breasts from behind. He ran his fingers down her stomach, rocking his hips into her. He kissed her neck, licking a trail from her earlobe to her pulse. Pleasure coursed through her at his touch. He nudged her from behind, parting her legs with his thigh so he could run his fingers along her center.

Juliana arched into him as he intimately caressed her. Moisture that had nothing to do with the water gathered between her thighs, welcoming him. The heat of his touch was so real, felt so good, that she couldn't help but wiggle against his exploring hand. She wanted more of him. She wanted it all.

"Ahhh," he said into her ear, the vibrations of his voice causing her to shiver.

"Please, I don't want to wake up, not yet," she whispered, knowing none of this could be real. Merrick wouldn't touch her like this. His hands wouldn't be so gentle. His body wouldn't be so close. He liked to torment her too much to give her what her body craved. She turned in the water to wrap her arms about him, but Merrick was gone.

A derisive laugh escaped her. It was only her imagination. It had always been so vivid, even in girlhood. But this time was different somehow, more real. She touched her lips, which still stung, still tasted unlike her own. When she started to step from the pond, her stomach pulled in protest. Her sex ached, nearly pulsing with sensitive jolts. Now was not the time to take care of such a private thing.

As she stepped, her leg hit flesh. She glanced down to the water. Merrick knelt before her. What was happening? Why was her mind tormenting her? Perhaps none of this was real—this world, Merrick, her feelings. Had she finally imagined too much and gone mad? Nothing made sense. Her world was turned upside down. Looking down into Merrick's eyes, she shivered. Juliana tried to resist him, tried to stop. It was no use. She wanted him. Whatever madness this was, she wanted it to happen.

Merrick grabbed her hips, lifting her up. She naturally wrapped her legs around him for support. Water caressed their skin, hitting upon them in small waves. She felt like she was in the stars. Nothing else mattered right now. Somehow, she knew that first moment she saw him they would come to this.

Juliana ran her hands over his strong chest and back. She kissed his throat, enjoying the taste of him. His erection probed her from underneath, making her stomach knot in a mixture of anticipation and fear. Every time she would try to think, the mist would surround her senses once more, drawing her under the euphoric spell.

"Ah, Merrick," she said softly against his mouth. Their wet bodies slid, molding together as he pulled her closer. "Merrick."

Then he lifted her, angling her body to accept his. His thick arousal probed her sex. She tensed, waiting for the pain that was said to come. He let her hips slide from his grasp, her own weight impaling her on him. The size of him stretched her, but the fullness felt too good to resist. When she thought she could take no more he pushed deeper. She squirmed, naturally drawn to pull off him. Suddenly, he gripped her hips and thrust her down, hard and sure, taking her maidenhead in one painful stab.

Juliana gasped, her eyes opening wide at the discomfort. Merrick groaned, leaning forward to kiss her. She felt him inside her, not only his arousal and his tongue, but his power. She felt his pleasure as he took away all lingering pain. His satisfaction heightened her own until all she could do was beg him for more. His voice was in her head, drowning out her thoughts. "Ah, aye, Merrick, please, please."

Fearful that they'd fall over into the water, she gripped his arms tight. He lifted her, thrust his body into hers in shallow strokes. It seemed his hands were everywhere at once. Her skin tingled as she accepted him in. Learning his rhythm, Juliana followed his lead. He quickened the pace as tension strained his body, pushing himself into her. His fingers slid from her hips to her butt, supporting her as he squeezed her cheeks, pulling her open to him. She felt the end coming, welcomed it. Her body jerked. She couldn't stop and he wouldn't let her.

Suddenly, she tensed, her body convulsing around him as she climaxed. A light scream of surprise left her throat as she clung to him. His body jerked within her, signifying his release. Dazed she took a deep breath and closed her eyes tight. A tear slid over her cheek, not because she was sad, but because she felt so much. He lowered her back to her feet, kissing her for a long moment. Slowly, flesh was replaced by water, his lips by air.

She opened her eyes, still breathing hard. Merrick was gone, but the aftermath of his intense pleasure was still there. What had she expected? It was only her imagination, right? None of this was real.

Juliana laughed, shaking. The mist was gone and she felt strangely tired. She pulled her heavy limbs onto the shore and reached for her clothing. What just happened? Her gown was gone. She gasped, her gaze darting around the dark forest. She found a pair of horse legs, then another. Frozen in fear, her gaze moved slowly up to the riders.

"Hugh?" she gasped, blinking in surprise. She instantly hid her body from view, mortified that they should see her naked. "Thomas?"

"Aye," they said in unison, their voices gruff. They didn't look at her. Thomas tossed down her wool cloak. She caught it and quickly wrapped it around her naked body. It was stiff, caked with mud in spots, but she didn't care. That's when she saw Nicholas. His hot eyes were on her, burning and passionate. She instantly blushed. He was like a brother and she didn't relish the idea of him seeing her bare any more than she wanted Thomas or Hugh to.

"What? How?" she asked, shaking in embarrassment to be caught fantasizing in the pond.

"Where are your clothes, Juliana?" Thomas asked.

Thomas' stern voice was nothing compared to the grave tone of Hugh's. Hugh's dark eyes turned to her in outrage. "Are you compromised?"

"What?" Juliana gasped. "What do you mean? I was bathing. Alone."

Nicholas snorted. She turned her round eyes to him, confused. He didn't look away.

"Is this any way to greet me?" Juliana asked. "What are you doing here? How did you find me?"

"We saw you," Thomas said quietly.

"Saw me what?" Juliana swallowed, nervous. Her lips trembled.

"We saw you kissing him," Thomas elaborated.

"Who is he?" Hugh demanded. "Is that why you left? Why you ran away from you duties? Your family?"

"Who is who? And you know I'd never run from my duties. I will marry Eadward. I…I just can't yet. There is something I must do first." Juliana took another step back. All three pairs of eyes bore into her. Hugh swung from his horse, landing before her on steady feet. He towered over her, his look dark and protective, yet tormented at the same time.

"We saw you, Juliana. Who was the man you were kissing? Have you been compromised?" Hugh asked.

Juliana paled. Her knees weakened and she fell to the soft ground. It was real? Merrick had been there? What had she done? "Nay, I only imagined—"

"Do not!" Hugh growled. "I will have none of your stories. The truth this time. Who was he? And where did he go? We saw him disappear."

Juliana cringed as Hugh lunged for her. She expected him to strike. Instead, he pulled his arms around her, hugging her so tight she could barely breathe.

"Did he force himself on you?" Hugh whispered in her ear, patting down her wet hair as if by wrapping her in his arms he could protect her. He was shaking terribly. So that is why he and Thomas looked at her with such grim eyes. They thought she'd been ravished.

"Nay, I'm pure," Juliana lied, knowing by her brother's questions that he hadn't seen everything. Her voice was barely audible, but Hugh heard her.

Hugh instantly relaxed, letting her go. He cupped her face. "We thought the worst when we saw him holding you…"

He gave a brief glance at Thomas and Nicholas. Both men seemed to understand for they too loosened the grip on their reins. Thomas swung down from his horse. Nicholas soon did the same, keeping his distance from the siblings.

"Who was he? The one who brought you here?" Thomas' words were soft as he glanced at the pond.

"His name's Merrick. I can't tell you why he brought me here." Juliana looked away, embarrassed anew. It was bad enough knowing her shared passion hadn't been a dream, but to have her brothers see her kissing him willingly? It was mortifying.

"You don't know?" Thomas prompted.

"I can't tell you." Juliana still couldn't meet their eyes.

"Do you protect that murderer?" Nicholas hissed. Juliana's round gaze darted to his. Nicholas' green eyes burned with a deadly passion. She trembled, never having seen the brooding man in such a rage of emotions. "Do you give yourself to him?"

"I have given myself to no one," Juliana whispered. She couldn't look at them. Surely he only asked for his father, since she was to be Eadward's bride.

"You were missing and after Lord Eadward's death we feared the worse," Thomas admitted.

Juliana paled. Nicholas' words about a murderer slowly sunk in. "Eadward is dead? Thomas?"

"I'm sorry, Juliana," Hugh said.

"Thomas?" she insisted, looking at him. He could never lie to her. She'd read the truth of it if he did. A sinking sensation consumed her chest. Tears threatened, not so much that she loved Eadward, but because she'd known him as a friend for so long. "What has happened?"

Thomas couldn't meet her gaze. That was never good. His mouth opened and shut several times. In the end, it was Hugh who answered, unwilling to give the details of it to her. "He's been murdered."

"Nay," Juliana shook her head. "Nay."

"By your lover," Nicholas spat.

If she felt bad before, Nicholas' words positively ripped her apart. She sobbed once, a loud, echoing noise. She turned to the water. The pond was empty, but the memories it held were branded on her skin. Merrick had murdered Eadward? She didn't want to believe Merrick capable of such a thing, but how could she do otherwise? Had he not said he'd see to it she never married? Thomas, Hugh and Nicholas would not lie to her. She shook violently.

"He's not my lover, Nicholas," she said weakly, clinging to her lie. The words tore at her. What else could she say? How could she admit to what she had done? A tear slipped over her cheek. "How could I ever love a demon?"

Merrick crossed the empty hall. Suddenly, a pain seized his gut and he fell to one knee. One hand braced the wall, his nails digging into stone, as the other gripped below his chest. The memory of Juliana's sweet touch had been on his flesh until that moment. Now all that was left was raw, numbing pain. It radiated from his chest to his stomach, swirling through each limb, climbing up his neck to his head. He couldn't escape it and it refused to lessen.

Faint words, her words, echoed in his mind. With much effort he stood, ignoring his discomfort. He breathed hard, knowing his eyes darkened to a deadly black. He didn't care. He welcomed the beast in him. The beast would feed off the pain, grow powerful from it. It would kill his emotions until he was dead inside.

I swear to you, her voice whispered in his head, I could never love him. I would rather die than feel his touch.

Chapter Six

Merrick stepped into the Black Palace's great hall only to see the King of the Damned sitting in his throne. Lucien's eyes lifted, his long nails idly tapping against the stone arm of the chair. Merrick had felt the Demon King before entering and wasn't surprised to see him. He bowed his head in slight acknowledgement. It had been a long time since they'd met, but neither one of them needed a reintroduction.

Grinning indolently, Lucien took in the blackness of Merrick's eyes before rolling lazily over his unlaced overtunic. Since Merrick's coronation, the two kings had felt more than they ever needed to say with words. Being different types of evil, they shared an undeniable bond. The Demon King stared at Merrick's blond hair for a moment, as if contemplating the color. Merrick quirked a brow. Lucien shook himself slightly.

"Let me introduce you to my new pet, Mia," Lucien said, sounding bored. He motioned his hand to the side where Mia sat in chains and strips of leather. She didn't bother to look up. Merrick in turn ignored her. There was nothing he could do for her. Already, he could tell her soul was half gone. Why Lucien didn't take it all the way was a mystery Merrick didn't wish to solve. Lucien grew a ball of fire in his hand, twirling it about his fingers. "Mia, where are your manners?"

"King Merrick," Mia mumbled dutifully, tilting her head at him, though her eyes stayed turned to the nearest fireplace. After a pause, she moved to look Lucien in the eye without flinching. That was a feat in itself. "Where are your manners? You're in his seat."

Merrick couldn't suppress his small chuckle at that. Lucien shrugged, as if to say, *what can I do?* Unfortunately for the obstinate woman at his side, Lucien could do much. Merrick's smile died and he pitied the creature, just as he contemplated doing the same thing to Juliana. At least then she'd be marked by him, publicly claimed, chained to his side. Just as quickly, the idea left him. He wanted her willing. Lucien would never comprehend such a thing, but Merrick wanted Juliana bound to him by her own resolve, her own honor. He would never chain her thus. Well, Merrick did consider chaining her to a bed, but for a whole other purpose.

Instead of standing, Lucien lazily motioned his hand to the side of the throne. From the stone another throne chair grew, twisting and spiking to match the outside of the castle. Merrick took a seat, reaching his hand to produce a chalice of wine. He handed it to Lucien, who took it with a sly grin. Merrick produced one for himself as well.

"What honor is this?" Merrick asked.

Lucien sipped the drink once before giving it to Mia. She took it, gulping heavily until it was gone. Merrick unconsciously refilled it for her. She blinked in surprised, but didn't thank him. Lucien frowned slightly at the action, but didn't comment.

"King Ean plots your death for taking his ward from the mortal realm," Lucien said. Mia choked on her wine. They ignored her. "I can see by your face you didn't know. Lady Juliana of Bellemare I believe she is called. My spies tell me she is beautiful, though I have not seen her. The entire Bellemare family is blessed. I've been trying to get at them for decades, but they just don't seem to corrupt like most mortals do."

"You wish for me to corrupt them?" Merrick asked, swirling his drink in feigned boredom. Lucien's dark presence drew upon his emotions, which he carefully hid under a wall of complete indifference.

"Nay," Lucien said to his surprise. Merrick stopped to study him. "My interest in them has been merely a diversion. I really don't care one way or the other. Eventually, every bloodline calls upon me. Theirs will too. And what do we immortals have if not time to sit and wait?"

Merrick didn't answer.

"King Ean has sent you a dispatch, has he not? To meet him on neutral ground?" Lucien smiled, though it hardly looked like concern that brought forth the question. Mia tried to slide away from his seat. Without looking at her, he lifted his hand and stopped her. She struggled against his power, but had no choice other than to give in. Nearby, goblins laughed, pointing at her. She ignored them, again staring into the fireplace.

"Aye," Merrick answered, sipping his wine.

"Will you go?"

Merrick shrugged.

"Merely a warning." Lucien chuckled.

Merrick nodded once, the gesture brusque.

"Ah, as I said, I'm bored." Lucien waved his hand. "Methinks King Ean loves the mortal and seeks to marry her. I hear he watches her or did before you took her from him."

Merrick stiffened, as Lucien tried to hide a smile behind his hand. Mia made a weak noise, but didn't speak.

"Strange that he would marry a powerless mortal rather than an immortal," Lucien continued. "Then again, the blessed always did choose with their hearts and not their heads."

Merrick didn't move. If what Lucien said was true, and he saw no reason for the Demon King to lie, then Ean's message made sense. With Juliana under unblessed protection, Ean wouldn't be able to find her as easily. Juliana knew nothing of Ean's supposed affections, but she also knew nothing of his.

Merrick let his lips curl at Lucien's expectant look. "How very interesting. My diversion just became more diverting, didn't she?"

Lucien chuckled, low and dark. His black eyes lit with pleasure. "You can understand my interest in Ean never finding love, can't you?"

"Aye," Merrick said. "You think I'll help you?"

"Oh, I'm betting on it." Lucien smiled, gesturing with his hand. He disappeared, taking Mia with him as he left Merrick alone on his new throne.

Lucien's motivations were apparent, but it didn't mean Merrick completely trusted them. Lucien would do anything to keep Ean from happiness. Happiness would only make the King of the Blessed more blessed.

Merrick frowned. If Ean loved Juliana, it was a pure emotion. Merrick's heart wasn't so pure, couldn't be because of who he was, yet he'd never step aside. Juliana was his, more so now than ever before. Such a blow to the heart, as lost love, would hurt his brother's power, weaken him. It was an odd coincidence that Juliana was one of Ean's blessed wards, though not completely improbable. Perhaps that was what drew Merrick that first night. Perhaps he'd sensed her goodness like a light in the darkness that was his existence. Perhaps he'd known somehow that she was blessed.

It wasn't really improbable that Ean fell in love with a human. It had happened oft enough in the past between the elfin and humankind. It was said, if the love was pure and the elements right, the mortal would change and live forever. Since he saw no immortal humans living amongst them, he could only assume they were rumors.

Merrick sighed. There was only one way to discover what Ean and Lucien were about. He'd have to accept Ean's invitation. His gut tightened. It had been a very long time since he'd faced his younger brother and he wasn't sure he wanted to do so now.

***

"Why did you lie to him?" Mia stared at Lucien from the end of his bed, her fists planted on her hips. He rested on the bed, looking very pleased with himself. She shivered, hating him for what he was capable of and unsure as to how to stop him. His naked body drew her even now. She wanted him. That was her curse to bear. Some days she just wished he'd let her die, take her soul and be done with it.

"What, in your entire knowledge of me, makes you think I'd ever tell the truth?" Lucien asked, grinning. "Unless it suited my purpose. Confess it, Mia. It will be fun to watch what comes of this. Can you not see the humor? Ean wishes to know why his brother kidnapped an unknown ward. Even now he's convinced it's an act of war and will be on the defensive. Merrick, the fool, is enamored with the girl."

"Nay, he loves her," Mia interrupted softly.

Lucien frowned, eyeing her. "You're sure, nymph?"

"As sure as I can be with only half a soul." Mia turned to the fire. It blazed orange over her skin. It heated her in waves and she knew Lucien made it hotter so she'd draw closer to him. She knew his games well. Taking a deep breath, she did move closer to him and away from the fire.

"Hum, no matter. Merrick can't really love anyway—not in the way that you think of the emotion. He's like me in that regard," Lucien said, not sounding upset. "As I said, Merrick's enamored with the human, Lady Juliana of Bellemare. He now believes his brother feels the same. Did you see the possessiveness in him when I mentioned it? Oh, he'll claim her for his own very soon. That is if he hasn't already."

Mia visibly swallowed, edging closer still to Lucien on the bed. She stood by his head, gazing over his muscular body. Just the sight of him aroused her. Figures made of fire danced over his naked chest like a play, their flaming, miniature arms twined together. Then, suddenly, the figure of the man tossed the woman down onto her back before falling on top of her. It looked like rape and the faint echoing of a scream sounded as if from the back of her mind. Mia reached her hand out and squashed the flame couple, resting her fingers on the chilled flesh covering Lucien's beating heart. Too bad the organ was black, just like his soul. Lucien furrowed his brows as he studied her hand, his fire play interrupted.

"And Juliana?" Mia asked, her tone soft. "What is your plan for her? Is she merely a pawn?"

"They're all pawns." Lucien tilted his head back to study her, even as his fingers moved to trace the outline of her hand on his chest. It was a rare moment that he didn't look full of contempt. "Lady Juliana no less so. Right about now, her brothers are explaining to her how Merrick killed Lord Eadward, her betrothed. She'll believe them, because she is human. Before long, she'll realize that it is Merrick she seeks in his little adventure, not I."

Lucien didn't take his eyes away as heat grew under Mia's palm. She jerked her hand away as the flames once more grew on Lucien's chest. His mouth curled up at the side. He didn't look at the flames, but instead studied her face as she watched. The flame man had the woman on her hands and knees and was taking her from behind in rough, angry thrusts, as her tiny orange hands dug into Lucien's flesh.

"I thought the Bellemare souls were what you were after," Mia said, pulling her gaze away from his sick little fire show. "Why not let her come here?"

"It is so much more fun this way." Lucien chuckled. He lifted a finger to Mia's breast, running it along the bottom edge, tangling it in the leather strips. Her nipple budded and her breath deepened with her arousal. "Besides, you should know. The soul can only be given if the asker begs me to take it in trade. Merely coming here is not enough. They need to be desperate."

"Why do you watch such things?" Mia motioned to the burning couple, changing the subject in exasperation. Lucien had shown her many things with his fire and she never could tell what was real and what was part of his sick imagination.

As if reading her thoughts, he answered, "Usually, I do not make the fire but merely watch the cruel actions of others with it. You cannot condemn me for what others do." There was a mocking to his tone. She knew he had the power to control the fire to his will, should he so choose. Again, as if reading her, he whispered, "This was not one of those times."

"You sound so sure your plan will work," Mia said to get back to the topic at hand.

"It's what I do." Lucien's face became marred with the beast inside him. He drew his finger over the flames, rolling the couple together into a ball before pulling the flames into his fist, smiting it. When he opened his hand, a little puff of smoke was all that was left. "It's what feeds me. Merrick's convinced her he's kidnapped the human children—ingenious really. She'll think the worse of him. When she rejects him, he'll come to me for help. Rejected lovers always do."

Mia gently stroked Lucien's dark hair, listening.

"After I deliver the woman to him, the Unblessed King will be my ally. Merrick will sever all ties to his brother." Lucien grabbed Mia by her top and pulled her down in one swift jerk so her breasts hovered over his face. Her hands fell flat against the mattress along his waist as he breathed deeply. His voice gravelly, he said, "Darkness will rule."

"Methought Merrick already on your side." Mia frowned. She didn't push up as Lucien slowly licked the valley of her breasts. Her heart leapt in her chest. "He is the King of the Unblessed."

"The unblessed will always cause mischief and mischief can be fun." Lucien drew his tongue to encircle a nipple. She gasped as pleasure shot through her body. She was a nymph and it was a sin for her to find pleasure in his arms. He kept kissing her, tempting her to sin with him yet again. As he spoke, he kept his lips moving over her flesh, pulling at her bodice so she was forced to crawl slowly forward, over him. "But until Merrick finds his hate, embraces it completely, he'll always be torn between good and evil. Right now he can feel Ean and me both." Lucien licked a fiery trail down to her belly. Flames teased her skin, following his tongue, but didn't burn. "Ean's refusal to sever their tie is what has kept him from slipping, because the lingering of his former self is in that tie. Regardless, he was falling into despair, so close to joining me until he saw the human. Juliana is his balance. When he loses Juliana, he'll belong to me."

Mia gasped as Lucien's mouth worked between her thighs. She straddled him, helpless to crawl away as he kept her chained to him with his will. His hips wiggled beneath her, tempting her to his arousal. She tried to resist, but the need in her was strong. His breeches dissolved into mist, leaving hard, naked flesh. His erection poked up at her. Lucien dipped his tongue beneath her short skirt, finding her naked sex wet and ready.

"Come Mia," she heard the whisper in her head. "Succumb to me."

Mia obeyed, for she could never resist. Lowering her mouth, she kissed his shaft, rolling her tongue over the sides. Lucien adjusted his hips and moaned, urging her on. Sin or no, she couldn't reject him. His embrace was dangerous, dark and she wanted more of it—always more. She rubbed her hips against his face, moaning softly at the pleasure he gave. As always, the pleasure was mixed with pain. He bit her, hard, making her squirm. She rocked faster, taking him deep into her mouth.

Lucien tensed. With supernatural ease, he slipped from beneath her to stand on the side of the bed. She didn't move as he grabbed her hips firmly in hand. With a thrust he was deep inside her, riding her hard. Mia made soft noises, the sound clashing with the harder, demonic sounds of his grunts. She knew without looking that the beast was coming out. His body expanded inside hers, almost painfully large.

Lucien came with a jerk, bringing her to the edge, but not letting her fall over. She was so close. She panted, squirmed, wanting release.

"Tell me," the Demon King ordered. So long as she always gave him what he wanted, always submitted, he'd give her what she wanted.

"I love you, Lucien!" she screamed, hating herself for her need, her weakness. Lucien chuckled darkly behind her. He thrust his still hard shaft again, letting her meet her climax.

<hr />

Juliana looked across the campfire to her brothers. It was late, but none of them felt like sleeping until their situation was understood. The three men were having a hard time meeting her eyes. She couldn't blame them for being disappointed in her. She was disappointed in herself.

Domovoi had taken her clothes, only to return them clean. The men stared at the gnome, but handled it better than Juliana thought they would— especially Hugh, who'd never given her stories much credence. He depended on the rational and nothing about this world fell into that category. Halton and Gorman didn't come back for her, and she secretly worried about them—even if she was mad at them for leading her in circles.

The men told her about William's abilities. She wasn't shocked so much as surprised. He'd never let on about them. A sinking feeling came over her as she was told of Rees. By the description, she vaguely remembered "imagining" him as a young girl. The stories she knew were not made up with her imaginary friends. They were actually told to her by her invisible friends. As a young girl, she'd been told so many times that Rees, the faeries, the goblins, the whatever else she saw, simply weren't there. In time, she'd stopped believing they were, convinced she had a vivid imagination. Their conversations had turned into stories. As she grew older, she told the stories to other children, embellishing them and making more up.

No wonder she'd thought Merrick wasn't with her in the pond. How foolish she was! It turned out that her imagination wasn't vivid at all. If her childhood friends were real, then she'd truly given herself to Merrick completely. She shamed her family's name, as well as her honor.

"And that is how we came across you in the pond," Thomas said, finishing his tale. "Now it's your turn, Juliana. What has happened? Why are you here wandering about the forest?"

Juliana quickly told them about the children and of her task to get to the King of the Unblessed. A knot formed in her gut, but with Eadward dead, most likely killed by Merrick, she knew she didn't have much choice. She needed her brothers' help. "I have to find King Lucien or Merrick will—"

"Don't you mean King Merrick?" Nicholas demanded, his eyes burning.

Juliana swallowed, trying to force down the heat in her face. "Methinks I'm not explaining this well. King Lucien controls the demons. Merrick is the man from last night. I believe he is one of King Lucien's demons."

"Juliana," Hugh said softly. "I believe you mean King Merrick of the Unblessed. According to William, Merrick is the Unblessed. King Lucien is the Damned."

"King Merrick?" She repeated, feeling like a fool. She hugged her cloak tighter to her body. Her limbs still ached to hold him, even as she hated him. "I'm such a fool. There he was, right before me. All I had to do was ask him to free the children and this would have been over."

"I don't think it's that simple," Hugh said. "He said you needed to go to Valdis. I'm assuming he wants you to journey to his palace and ask there."

Thomas nodded his agreement. "Aye."

"Why? To what purpose? I don't understand it." Juliana buried her face in her hands before glancing through her fingers at Nicholas. "I'm sorry. This is all my fault."

Nicholas studied her with his hard, silent eyes. She wanted for him to yell at her, condemn her for Lord Eadward's death. Without comment, he stood and walked into the forest.

Thomas sighed. "He's taken his father's death hard. I don't think he's slept. At night I've seen him pacing the forest."

"I should go talk to him," Juliana said, standing. Her brothers didn't stop her. Finding Nicholas easily in the dense trees, she made sure he heard her footsteps. "Your father was a good man, Nicholas."

He nodded, not looking at her.

Juliana swallowed. She couldn't blame him if he hated her. "He would have made me a fine husband and yet I brought about this. I asked for an adventure. It's my fault King Merrick…" She took a deep breath, brushing a tear off her cheek. "It's my fault. I foolishly begged him to come. I just wanted something to happen before my marriage, before becoming a wife. You're a man, so I don't expect you to understand it."

Nicholas didn't move.

She took a hesitant step toward him and placed a light hand on his shoulder. Nicholas was stiff beneath her palm. "You always warned me to be careful what I say lest the devil hear me and answer. I should have listened."

Slowly, his hand covered hers. He pulled her in front of him.

"Nicholas?" She blinked, seeing his intense stare.

"I was so worried," he said, his voice hoarse.

Juliana didn't have time to think before he pulled her to his chest. His lips crushed down on hers, instantly smothering her with a hard kiss. She gasped in surprise and he took entrance, moving his tongue along hers. He rocked into her, pulling her body tighter against his.

Juliana felt the press of his hard arousal against her stomach. She was too shocked to do anything but let him kiss her. It wasn't unpleasant and, as his lips softened their claim, a warmth stirred inside her. She inched her hands up his shoulders, resting them on his neck.

Nicholas pulled back to look at her. There was so much desire in his gaze that Juliana shivered in the wake of it. Merrick's body taught her what could come of touching, but this was Nicholas. She'd never seen such passion in his eyes. What had happened to the moody boy she'd carried in her head? For a long moment she didn't move, confused, torn. Part of her wanted to kiss him again, to see if what he felt for her could be returned. His warm taste was on her mouth, his hands on her arms, holding her close even as they gripped her. Another part of her wanted to pull away, shamed that she should kiss him after sinning with Merrick, worried that he would taste Merrick's lips on her and know what she had done. Just as she tried to pull away, her hands slipping down to his chest to push out of his embrace, he kissed her again.

Juliana moaned in surprise. This kiss was gentle, probing, tempting. He nipped at her with his teeth, pressing her back into a tree. She touched his face, moving her mouth to his. A piece of bark stabbed her back, jolting her once more to reality. She tore her mouth from his, gasping. "Nay, Nicholas, we cannot."

He instantly pulled away. His hands left her and his face became a blank mask. When he spoke, it was as if the kiss had never happened, only her mouth was still warm from it. "Do not blame yourself. I, too, prayed for there to be no wedding."

Juliana frowned at his words. She was so confused, couldn't think. Nicholas had just kissed her and she'd let him. There had been so much need in him that she couldn't resist. But what of Merrick? She'd kissed him as well, wanted him so desperately her entire body begged him to take her. He had, too.

With Merrick it was a rush of emotion. With Nicholas it was a gentler feeling, an old friendship, a connection to the familiar. What was happening to her? Surely what she felt for Merrick was just a spell he wove around her, a dark temptation to confuse her. Maybe all it had been was a kiss. Maybe the rest didn't happen. It was a fool's dream, but she clung to it nonetheless. With Merrick, how could she ever be sure what was real?

And Nicholas? She shook her head. It made no sense why she would kiss Nicholas. He was a friend, just a friend. She'd known him forever. He didn't feel for her beyond that friendship, did he? No, Nicholas was just confused, lost after his father's death. Then why was her body stirring for him? Why was her mind considering him?

"It's because of you that I begged for there not to be a wedding." Nicholas reached for her and she stepped away. He dropped his hand. "It's because I didn't want you to wed my father. I lo—"

"Nay," Juliana said to stop him. There were so many reasons why she should consider him over Merrick—their families, their homes, the fact that they were both mortals. "Don't Nicholas. You're grieving. Words like that cannot be taken back. They change everything."

"I want everything to be changed. You look so surprised. Has my heart truly been hidden so well from you? Have you been so blind as to how I feel?"

"You never said," she began, shaking. She didn't deserve him, not after what she'd done. "Nicholas, we...we grew up together. I look upon you as a brother."

"Don't you think you have enough brothers, Juliana? I'm not your brother. You have never looked on me as a brother. You respected them. Me, you taunted. You called me Sir Humphrey the Foul. Oh, how those words stung. But I dared to hope that if I played ignorant, you would come to see me for me. I waited and said nothing. I will not be silent any longer. I must tell you how I feel."

"Nicholas, we were children. It was so long ago. I'm sorry if we hurt your feelings. Truly, we did care for you as our friend."

"We are children no longer." He took a step toward her, reaching for her face. Cupping her cheek in his palm, he said, "You felt it, too. I know you're scared, but you don't have to be. You kissed me back. You felt it."

"Nicholas," she whispered. She couldn't do this, not now. She needed time to think. Panic struck her as he spoke.

"Juliana, I stand before you a man. I—"

The sound of footsteps stopped his words, much to her relief. He pulled his hand from her and stepped away. Juliana was stunned, thankful for being interrupted. She quickly swiped her eyes before turning to look at Hugh. He glanced at Nicholas and then back to her. Lifting his hand, he gestured her to his side.

"Juliana?" Hugh asked.

Juliana mustered a weak smile before turning her eyes down. She rubbed her arms as a chill swept over her skin. In a few short days her world had been torn apart. Nothing made sense in it.

"Come," Hugh said. "It's late. We should rest for—"

Hugh stopped talking. Juliana looked up at him. The temperature dropped drastically, cold and bitter. Her breath puffed white as she saw her brother. Hugh was frozen solid. Horrified, she glanced at Nicholas. He was staring at her, his face forlorn. He too was as still as carved marble.

"Merrick?" she whispered, glancing around the trees. Icicles hung from the limbs, reflecting moonlight until the small alcove sparkled with the blue diamonds of frost. "Are you doing this?"

"Tsk, tsk, tsk," Merrick said, walking from the forest. The ground crunched under his feet. Life seemed to drain around him as he moved— leaves withered, blossoms hid. Standing by Hugh, he placed a hand on the man's shoulder. Her brother didn't change. "Juliana, what is this I find?"

"They came after me," she said quickly. "I didn't tell them."

"You didn't tell them of our little bargain? After I warned you I wouldn't be pleased?" Merrick asked, arching an eyebrow. She shivered and again lied as she shook her head in denial. His eyes looked darker than usual—blacker. He was livid. How could she even compare this dark creature to sweet Nicholas? She did her best to meet his steady gaze. "I can tell when you lie to me. I don't like it."

"Nay, I didn—"

Merrick lifted a finger to Hugh's temple. Lightly drawing his finger over her brother's cheek, he studied Hugh's features. "I can learn what he knows easily enough. If you won't tell me, I'll get it from him."

Juliana didn't move.

"Very well." Merrick drew his finger between Hugh's eyes. The earl's features instantly grayed. His tone flat, the king recited, "King Merrick? I'm such a fool. There he was, right before me. All I had to do was ask him to free the children and this would have been over. I don't think it's that simple. He said you needed to go to Valdis. I'm assuming he wants you to journey to his palace and ask there. Ay—"

"Stop it!" Juliana cried, easily recalling her conversation with her brothers. She ran forward, striking out. Merrick caught her hand in his fist, squeezing. Whimpering, her knees weakened at the pain. He pulled his finger from Hugh, but the earl's face remained gray. Taking her along with

him, hauling her by her fist, Merrick went to stand before Nicholas.
"Merrick, please!"

"And him, Juliana. What did you say to him?" Merrick held up his
hand. Juliana's jeweled dagger appeared in his palm. He squeezed her fist
tight as he drew the blade to Nicholas' throat. He let the blade's pointed tip
dance over the man's neck.

"Nothing," she whispered. It was so cold, she couldn't stop shaking.
Her feet were going numb from it. Merrick was unaffected. His eyes burned
with rage. It poured off of him. She cringed in horror.

Merrick drew the blade down to Nicholas' chest, right above his heart.
It would be nothing for the Unblessed King to plunge the blade in—her
blade. He angled the knife. All it would take was a single push and Nicholas
would be dead. Juliana weakly shook her head in denial, willing him to
stop. "I warned you about lying to me, Juliana."

She couldn't meet Merrick's eyes. He was her tormenter, a murderer
and still she felt guilty for kissing Nicholas, as if that was what made her a
whore. "I just told him I was sorry for his father's death."

"Is that all?" Merrick twisted the blade tip back and forth, digging it
into Nicholas' frozen tunic.

"More or less." She made a move to take the knife. Merrick held her
away with her fist in his. A chill crept down her arm and she watched as her
fingers began to freeze within his palm. Her flesh turned blue, so numb she
could no longer feel them.

"And what did he say to you?" The knife disappeared and Juliana felt
its weight back in her boot. She sighed with relief, but the feeling did not
last long. Merrick's blade hand instead gripped her by the throat,
dangerously holding her. He brushed his thumb over her pulse, but did not
squeeze.

"Nothing of importance," she whispered.

"Nothing," he repeated, his brows rising, "of importance?"

"Nay," she said.

"He didn't say he loved you?" Merrick's tone mocked the words. "He didn't ask you to be his wife? Didn't promise to wed you in his father's place?"

"Nay, he said none of those things." Juliana tried to pull her hand free. Her fingers stung, throbbing where his hold cut off her circulation. "Ah-hah, I swear, Merrick. He didn't. He said none of those things."

"Tell me, Juliana, did you tell him about us?" Merrick stroked up to her cheek, reminding her body just how familiar he was with it. Even now, she wanted him. She couldn't answer. "He has nothing to do with us. Does he, Juliana? He's not important to us, is he?"

"Nay." She sniffed. Her fist warmed as the ice crept back up her arm. Feeling returned to her hand, a deep ache where he gripped into her.

"He's nothing to us, is he Juliana?"

"I said nay. Nay, he's nothing. He's not important."

"Then I could kill him, right here and now." Merrick's thumb pressed over her bottom lip, pulling it down to part her lips to him.

Tears streamed over her cheeks. She damned herself for her attraction to Merrick. He was cruel, evil, and still she wanted him.

"You cry for him?" he spat, squeezing her fist so tight she expected the bones in her hand to break.

"Nay, aye, nay, please Merrick." Juliana shook his hold from her face.

"Please?" Merrick frowned. "You beg for him?"

"He is my friend. Only my friend. A brother. Nothing more. Please, you're misunderstanding."

"I will hold you to that statement, my lady." Merrick jerked her into his arms. His eyes flashed with warning as he leaned into her face. His nose brushed alongside hers. "For if you ever kiss another man again, I will not only kill that man, I'll kill you and every child set in my path for all eternity. Your life is mine. You are mine."

"You already killed Eadward." Juliana didn't know why the words slipped out. She leaned back to look at him. She hated him, desired him, feared him. "Why? You didn't have to kill him. Eadward was a good man. He—"

"Lord Eadward, your betrothed?" Merrick's eyes darkened by degrees. She wouldn't have thought it possible. The black centers drew to the sides, blocking out more of the white. "You dare to talk to me about him? You dare to mention another man's name to me now? At this moment?"

"Aye. I know you killed him. How could you? Eadward was innocent in all this."

Merrick laughed, a dark, wicked sound. Taking her chin, he forced her to look at Nicholas. "And what of this man, Sir Nicholas? Is he a killer Juliana? Is he a bold knight? Does he love you enough to kill for you? Would he rearrange the very heavens for you? Is he the man you want to give you an adventure?"

"Nay, he's…he's only my friend."

"I hold you to that still, my lady," Merrick said, whipping her face back. "You are mine."

"—tomorrow we ride early," Hugh finished. Juliana blinked, stumbling forward. Merrick was gone. Hugh moaned and grabbed his head. "Juli…? How did you get over there?"

Juliana didn't answer. She glanced at Nicholas. He slapped his neck, absently scratching at a thin trail of blood that appeared beneath his ear. His eyes met hers, softening some in question. He made a move as if to touch her. She pulled away from him, shaking her head as she went to Hugh. Hugh's color had returned, but his eyes were red.

"Juliana, you look pale," Hugh said.

"It's nothing," she managed. "I just need to rest. I'm so tired."

Hugh nodded and placed his arm about her shoulders. Giving her a brief hug, he walked her back toward the fire. "Aye, methinks I need rest as well. My head is suddenly pounding like it's been trampled by horses."

Chapter Seven

The morning sun shone over the long valley as Juliana, her brothers and Nicholas rode out of the forest. Juliana was behind Thomas on his horse, watching the endless lines of trees pass by them. They'd traveled most of the late morning in silence. Guilt weighed her thoughts, keeping her from speaking.

Hugh slowed his mount, joining their side as they journeyed down into a valley. Nicholas came up from behind. Both men turned to study her. Thomas leaned slightly to glance over his shoulder.

"What?" she whispered, refusing to look at Nicholas. All three men turned instantly away, not answering.

Nicholas' eyes had lingered on her most of the morning. Juliana felt them boring into her. He wanted answers, but she had no answer to give him. She was sorry for it. Even if she had an answer for him, she couldn't tell him or encourage him in his pursuit. It was odd to think he loved her, for surely that is what he'd been about to say. She didn't know how she missed it before. His love was in his eyes. He was sick with it and it was all her fault. Or maybe now he just let her see it.

But when she thought of herself, her heart, she thought of Merrick. Would she love Nicholas if there was no Merrick? Did she even love Merrick? Her mind told her she couldn't. Maybe it wasn't love at all. Maybe she only wanted to call it love to justify what she'd done. The Unblessed King was a liar, a trickster, a murderer, a kidnapper. He tormented her and yet she was drawn to him. When he was gone—like now—she thought of him. His dark eyes, though deadly, haunted her. She wanted to touch him, wanted to kiss him. She just wanted him. And because she wanted him, she hated herself.

Hugh and Thomas would never understand. Nicholas would never forgive her. How could she love her intended's murderer? She was alone in this. Her attraction was her burden and she would bear it in silence, even as she prayed to be free from its spell. Too bad William wasn't with them. His advice on the matter would have been welcomed.

Juliana studied Nicholas from the corner of her eye. He was handsome. His short brown hair was only slightly tousled from travel. He was of moderate build, much like Thomas in form, but with a quieter disposition. His gray eyes were an odd color, though they were attractive.

Nicholas had hardly spoken as a child, but he'd followed them around endlessly. They'd thought him to be in a foul mood because he never smiled and only opened his mouth to scold her for her "imagination". She blinked, looking him over as she forced herself to think of him as a man, not the brooding child he'd been.

Nicholas carried himself nobly. His body was fine, muscled. When he did smile, a dimple formed in his cheek. He had a good, proud face. Though he wasn't nobility, he'd inherit property from his father and would undoubtedly come into a title someday. She'd heard tales of how he'd survived in battle when so many around him had fallen. He'd make any woman a fine choice in husband. She'd been a fool not to see the quality in him before now.

Hugh and Thomas would undoubtedly be pleased if she chose him. Bellemare would have their alliance. Nicholas would treat her well, just as his father would have. Juliana closed her eyes. She couldn't think of Eadward now. Not now.

Juliana took a deep breath. The day was warm, the breeze fresh. Clouds dotted the heavens, silhouetted by the glimmering rays of sunlight. She smelled the perfume of flowers, the fragrance of nature. Birds sang nearby. Their songs filled the air with beautiful music.

"It's gorgeous here," Juliana said, sighing wistfully.

"Aye, it is," Nicholas answered. Juliana glanced at him. He stared right at her. She looked away, swallowing nervously.

Before she could speak, Thomas asked, "Is that snow? I swear this land is strange in its seasons."

Juliana looked up. Little rays of light fell from the sky—tiny silver and white sparks. They drifted like the burning ash from a bonfire, though the weather did not change. Soon fifty sparks turned into a hundred, a hundred turned into two hundred, until the sky was filled with specks of light. A spot fell on her arm, tingling the flesh but not painfully so.

"Look," Hugh said, pointing before them. Down in the valley the light hit upon an invisible fortress, outlining a silver palace. The sparkling light clung to the edges of a tower, a gate, the arched windows. "What is it?"

"Is it real?" Juliana grabbed Thomas' arm for support and swung down off the horse. Her legs wobbled as she found her footing. She stepped toward the palace, walking up a silver-lined path that led to the entrance.

"Juliana, wait!" Nicholas dismounted from his horse and joined her. He touched her elbow.

"Can you hear it?" she asked, pulling away from Nicholas. Closing her eyes, she heard singing and began to hum along.

"Juliana?" Hugh asked.

"Juliana," Thomas stated, louder than his brother.

"Follow her," Hugh ordered as Juliana walked down the path toward the castle. "Whoever lives here must be inviting us in."

As they neared, the silver walls became less translucent. One of the specks of light flew forward as Juliana passed under the front arch, through the gate. She saw it was a winged faery. The creature's pale skin was perfect, as were its wide blue eyes and long blonde hair. She wore a shimmering gown of silver on blue. Soon others joined the first—men and women, all graced with pale beauty. One by one, the faeries poofed into a shower of light only to stand tall before her. She curtseyed at their attention.

The humming didn't stop, and Juliana was drawn past them to the entrance of the palace.

Hugh watched his sister walk through the gathering throng. A soft smile graced her features. He rested his hand on the hilt of his sword, ready to defend her if need be. The crowd parted to let her by. The men followed her but didn't touch. He felt a hand on his sword arm and looked down. A woman smiled up at him, her eyes full of invitation. His body responded, though he refused to be drawn into her lovely spell. Another hand slipped onto his forearm, another still onto his hip, his thigh, his backside. He was urged by the gentle touches to follow Juliana.

Thomas and Nicholas walked ahead of him. They too were being led by lovely winged creatures into the palace. Small hands tousled their hair, rubbed up beneath their tunics, teased the line of their waistbands. Hugh took a deep breath. Being caressed by so many beautiful women was making it hard to concentrate.

"Welcome, my lord," a faery whispered into his ear, rimming it with her tongue. He tried to focus, tried to fight the sudden arousal growing beneath his breeches. A hand slid down his stomach to boldly stroke him. "We hope you find your stay pleasurable."

Rivershire, Clishmore River, Neutral Territory

Rivershire was a thriving marketplace that stretched for miles along the ancient Clishmore River. The city was special, for it was the only place in the entire immortal realm that fell under no one king's domain. Lord Griffen, elected noble of the city, officially controlled it all. The city was neutral ground, often the trading place of black and white magic. Blessed and unblessed alike came to trade wares. Hopefuls came to Rivershire to apprentice in wizardry and magic.

Boats of all shapes and sizes were tethered to the docks. Merfolk crawled from the water onto the shore, drying off their fins to form legs. Almost every creature in the immortal realm could be found along the Clishmore banks. Merrick didn't have to look hard to find his brother in Rivershire as he slipped through the crowds like mist, unnoticed by most except for a chill. He was drawn to Ean's side like a thread pulling him to his own blood.

He found Ean to be in a small pub. The wood tavern was hardly fit for a king, but Merrick didn't care. As children they'd loved Rivershire for its roughness. Merrick didn't wish to think of such things so instead he quickly took in his surroundings before showing himself. Wizards gathered in a dark corner, stroking their beards as they drank tankards of ale. The old men were quiet as they watched a group of dwarfs and gnomes negotiate over a slip of parchment. Tiny fists hit the tabletop in small thuds as the gnomes spoke. Overhead, a faery couple sat in the rafters, holding hands and gazing adoringly at each other. Merrick even detected a cloaked human.

The only true ally the Unblessed King appeared to have in the place was the troll who drank alone in a corner. As Merrick collected himself on the threshold, gasps erupted over the patrons. His name was whispered amongst them in awe and fear. *Merrick, King of the Unblessed.* The troll bowed his head in respect and made a move to stand. Merrick lifted his hand to stop him.

Without comment, Merrick went though a door in the back and up the narrow steps. He was surprised his brother didn't have guards with him. If what Lucien said was true, Ean would be a fool to try and kill him on his own.

Abovestairs, the hall was empty, nothing but a long row of doors. Placing his hand on the fifth door from the stairs, he pushed. The room within was dusty and small. A pitcher sat on a wooden table next to a goblet. Two chairs sat next to the table and a straw mat was tossed on the floor. Merrick smiled faintly as he looked at the table. Ean was there, stroking his bottom lip thoughtfully. It was an action he'd seen the man do oft. It meant he was thinking.

"I felt you," Ean said softly.

"I let you," Merrick answered. He waved his hand, slamming the door behind him without touching it.

"You're early, brother."

"Am I?" Merrick moved and took a seat. He stared at Ean from across the table. "Your brother?"

"Aye," Ean said. "Such things cannot be undone."

"Death and fate can undo much, King Ean."

"Is that a threat, King Merrick?"

Neither of them moved toward the other. They didn't touch, merely stared. Ean looked tired, but was still as youthful and handsome as Merrick remembered him. Ean had been the youngest of four brothers. Merrick had been the oldest. Even so, they had been close at one time. Seeing him, Merrick knew they were close no longer.

"I'm here. Speak." Merrick crossed his arms, leaning back in his chair. He pretended to be bored.

"Lady Juliana of Bellemare," Ean said.

Merrick closed his eyes briefly. Maybe Lucien had told the truth. His voice purposefully nonchalant, he asked, "What of her?"

"Why did you take her?" Ean studied him. The Blessed King had hardened some with his reign.

"I wanted to." Even now Merrick tasted Juliana's lips, smelled her fragrance, felt her body on his. His blood stirred to claim her, but his anger kept him from her. He'd felt the moment she let that man touch her. Nicholas. How hard it had been not to stab the mortal through the heart when he had the chance.

"Did you know she was my ward?"

Merrick said nothing.

"Her family is blessed and under my protection. I want you to free her from whatever game it is you play." Ean sat forward and took a drink. "Please, for me."

"Why do you care?" Merrick chuckled darkly. "She is mortal."

"She is my…"

Merrick narrowed his eyes, stopping Ean from finishing his answer. He studied his brother. Merrick knew he had changed quite a bit, knew he no longer looked as he had last they met. His face was older, his body stiff, and it had been a long time since a full, happy smile crossed over his features.

"She is under my protection," Ean said softly.

"I see." Merrick chuckled again, a purposefully cryptic sound. "Then tell me, where is she?"

"You know I can't detect her. You have her imprisoned."

"Then it would seem, dear brother," Merrick yawned, continuing to feign boredom, "that the lady is under my protection, for I can tell you exactly where she is."

"And where is that?" Ean challenged.

Merrick closed his eyes, as a small smile curled his lips. "Feia."

"She's with the faeries?"

"Aye."

"What are you up to, Merrick?" Ean shook his head. Standing, his voice rose by small degrees. "There are those who claim you wish to be at war. Is that what you want? You wish to fight me? Do you take Lady Juliana to provoke me?"

"As you fought Ladon and Wolfe?" Merrick taunted. He remained seated.

Ean closed his eyes. "I had no choice. You know that. How dare you mention our brothers' names to me? If not for you, they wouldn't have left Tegwen. If not for you, they—"

"This conversation is old, Ean," Merrick interrupted. His heart squeezed to think of the past and seeing Ean was only a reminder of that. "If you have nothing new to say to me then I shall go."

Ean sighed, but said no more on it. "Will you release Lady Juliana?"

"Nay."

"Then there will be war."

"If you so wish there to be," Merrick answered, his voice calm. "I am not afraid of war. I could use the diversion."

"You would fight those you loved in boyhood?"

Merrick merely smiled. "But who have no love for me now. It is you they see on their throne. I am but a dead man to them."

"You're not dead to all of us, Merrick," Ean whispered, his eyes studying him.

Merrick knew his brother searched him. He felt Ean's desperation as if it were his own. "Aye. I am. Sever your tie to me, Ean, for you will do so someday, regardless of how you feel now."

Ean reached forward, gripping his brother's arm. Softly, he swore, "Never. You are still my blood. I feel the goodness in you, Merrick. Give up your throne. Come back to Tegwen."

"You know it cannot be so," Merrick said, still not rising from his chair. "Only death will free me."

"I've looked through our scrolls. Lady Juliana is not one of us. I'd hoped you sought her for some greater purpose. I'd hoped she was special, sent to free you from your dark prison. But she's just human, the many-great niece to our Aunt Alyssin by human marriage. Alyssin had no children of her own."

"What makes you think I wish to be free from my throne?" Merrick tugged his arm and Ean let him go. He couldn't stand the Blessed King touching him. It only made his existence all the more cursed. It made the pain inside him ache until he wanted to scream.

"Don't you?"

"Nay, I haven't even tried." It was the truth. Merrick didn't try to end his reign, had never tried. The power had entered him at his coronation, weaving with his life until all his body fed off that power. He understood then as he knew now—death was the only way to end it. He did not wish to die.

"But—"

"Enough, Ean. If you wish for a war, then fight me. I care not. My goblins will answer the call to arms, as will the trolls and the dark elves. Lord Kalen's knights alone will crush your army if I were to call upon him."

"Kalen is a madman! You would threaten him and his Berserks on me?" Ean frowned. "Do not say such things. My love for you will not surpass my duty to my people."

"They are not threats, but warnings." Merrick finally stood. "My reasons for taking Juliana are my own. You'd do well to stay out of it. She is lost to you. If you would see blood shed for one mortal woman, then the blood is on your hands, not mine."

"She is blessed. You know I cannot turn away."

"Then do what you must and I will do what I must." Merrick bowed, leaving his brother's room. When he climbed down the stairs, the tavern was empty. He stopped. Without looking around, he said, "Gregor. Have you been demoted from courier to barkeep?"

"My king may be blind, but I know what you really are," Gregor said behind him. "I've always known."

"And what's that?"

"Evil."

"I could have told you that much." Merrick chuckled. His eyes darkened in rage, but his voice was calm, mocking. "You're still going on about that woman, are you? Shyra was hardly faithful to you, Gregor. I was not the first she gave pleasure to, nor have I been the last. Would you like me to show you what I know of her?"

Gregor hissed, tossing two daggers at Merrick's back before he could turn around. Merrick sensed the attack and tried to block the knives. One blade sliced into his arm. Bouncing off him, it fell to the floor. The other stuck in his shoulder. Growling, Merrick ripped the dagger from his flesh. He stumbled on his feet, lightheaded. Sniffing the dagger, he cursed as he recognized the scent of dragon's blood.

"Get him!" Gregor ordered. Knights wearing the red tunic of the Blessed Guard came from behind him. They wielded their swords, all soaked with the blood of a dragon. Such an amount wouldn't kill Merrick, but it would weaken him.

Merrick growled, throwing power onto his attackers. Many flew back, hitting the wall. His legs weighty, he forced his way through the tavern doors and into the crowded streets. Blinking heavily in the harsh sunlight, he waved his hands through the air. The dragon's blood was laced with magic. Seeing two thick arms coming for him, Merrick collapsed, falling into a dreamless sleep.

Silver Palace of the Faeries, Kingdom of Feia

"I am Queen Tania. Welcome to the Kingdom of Feia." The tall faery waved her small hand to encompass the sparkling great hall of her home. She was slender with dark blonde hair parted in the middle. The locks fell to her waist in silken waves, held down by a silver and diamond crown. Her white wings were threaded with silver veins. They fluttered behind her back, making her body hover down the stairs from her throne to the main floor rather than walk. "And welcome to my court."

The tips of her toes barely touched the ground as she flew forward to study the humans. She glanced over Nicholas and Thomas, only to stop when she got to Hugh. Juliana watched as the queen studied the Earl longer than the others. To her amazement, Hugh looked at the faery queen just as intently. A smile started to curl on her brother's lips when suddenly the queen slapped him. Those in the hall gasped. Hugh touched his cheek. His face hardened and he didn't move.

Finally, the queen came to Juliana. The faery smiled. "You are the one who travels to King Merrick?"

"Aye," Juliana answered. Not wishing to get slapped, she averted her eyes. The faery fluttered before her face. Juliana turned her face the other direction. The faery queen again tried to catch her eyes. Juliana made a move to turn again when the queen grabbed her chin and turned it up. Juliana hesitantly looked at her.

The queen smiled. "Much better."

Juliana frowned and glanced at Hugh.

"Ah, that. Well, Lord Bellemare shouldn't have such thoughts without invitation to do so," the queen explained. Hugh's jaw tightened.

"How do you know who we are?" Juliana asked.

"My dear, everyone knows who you are. You're the human who kisses the King of the Unblessed. You can't go about kissing kings without everyone in the realm knowing you did it."

Juliana paled. The queen laughed. Soon those in the faery hall joined in. Guiltily, she glanced at Nicholas. His eyed burned into her.

"We thank you for your hospitality, but we must be going," Hugh said, tight-lipped. He grabbed Juliana's arm and tried to lead her away.

The queen fluttered over his head and landed before him. Scowling, she said, "I didn't dismiss you."

"I didn't wait to be dismissed." Hugh pulled Juliana around the queen and stormed for the door. The faeries poofed into smaller form and scurried out of his way.

"I can get you to the Black Palace," Tania called, sitting cross-legged on her throne.

Hugh stopped. He was breathing hard. His hand tightened and loosened on Juliana's arm.

"Maybe we should listen," Juliana whispered.

"She's right," Thomas said quietly from behind them. "Do you really want to walk out on a queen's hospitality? Do you want to risk her anger? Perchance she can really help us. Maybe she knows the way to the Black Palace."

"We don't have much time left." Juliana pulled from Hugh's grip and turned to the queen. Louder, she stated, "We welcome your help, Your Majesty, and are grateful for it."

"I don't trust her," Hugh growled under his breath.

Juliana gave her brother a helpless look at the comment. Nicholas tried to stand next to her, but Tania smiled brightly and fluttered forward to take her arm. The queen pulled Juliana before the throne once more before dropping her arm.

"First you bathe and relax. Then, tonight, we will dine," the queen announced. Tania clapped her hands and lively music drifted over the hall. The faeries cheered, clapping their hands. Several winged women rushed forward, leading the human guests from the hall.

Juliana stretched her arms over her head. The faery queen stayed true to her word. She was given a private room and a warm bath. Every luxury she could have ever asked for was before her—lavender soap and hair rinse, a large white bed with a thick feather mattress, a beautiful tunic gown of soft blue material that shimmered when she moved. It was almost perfect, marred only by the reason she was at Feia in the first place.

With a sigh, she poked her head out of the door. No one was there. Thomas, Hugh and Nicholas were led to chambers just down the hall from hers. Only problem was she didn't remember which room was whose. Tiptoeing down the hall, she stopped at the first door. A woman laughed on the other side and there was a loud splash followed by a moan.

Juliana giggled, covering her mouth. She assumed the room belonged to Thomas. He always was the charmer. She wouldn't want to interrupt anything in there. Tiptoeing to the second door, she paused. A low masculine moan sounded from that room.

Nicholas or Hugh?

Juliana listened, pressing her ear to the wood. Furniture creaked. The man moaned again. He was joined by a feminine sigh. Juliana pulled away. It must be Hugh.

"Juliana?"

Juliana stiffened. She turned to Hugh who stood by the third door. He was dressed in a clean blue tunic and black breeches. His wet hair clung to his forehead.

"If you're here..." Juliana frowned and pushed open the door to Nicholas' chamber without stopping to think.

"Juliana?" Hugh asked. She ignored him. Nicholas was on a bed much like the one in her room. He was naked, his hips thrusting between the parted thighs of a blue-winged faery. Her tiny hands pulled his mouth to her breast and he was sucking it like a man starved. Worse still, there were two more naked faeries behind him—one with green wings, one with yellow. They pressed along his back, their hands rubbing along his length.

Nicholas groaned, thrusting harder as the green faery pinched his nipples. Juliana paled, backing away. Hugh caught her in his arms and she yelped in surprise.

"Juliana, what...?" Hugh looked in at Nicholas, who stared out his room with an expression akin to horror.

"Juliana," Nicholas said loudly. She heard a scuffle then footfall as Nicholas tried to get off the bed. A faery protested his going. Juliana wiggled away from Hugh.

"Don't let him near me," she yelled over her shoulder to her brother as she ran down the hall.

"Juliana!" Nicholas called. There was the sound of a struggle as Hugh held him back. "Hugh, let me pass. I must—"

"She doesn't want to see you."

Juliana ran faster. She didn't hear the rest of what Hugh said. The shock of seeing Nicholas in the arms of other women tore at her. She knew she had no right to be jealous, but she was. It wasn't like she loved him. But had he not said he loved her? Or in the very least almost said it? Is that how Nicholas showed his love? By fornicating with a couple of scandalous faeries? At least when she was with Merrick, she had been under a spell. What was Nicholas' excuse?

A shower of sparks burst in front of her, stopping her thoughts. Queen Tania appeared before her on the stairwell. "I don't know why you're upset. You don't love him."

"I might," Juliana answered, moving to brush past the queen.

Tania grabbed her arm and squeezed with surprising strength. "You forget your manners, mortal. I am still a queen and you have not been dismissed. Like it or not, you will listen to me."

Juliana pulled back. "I apologize for any rudeness, Your Majesty, but—"

"Ah, apology accepted. Now, see, that wasn't so hard." Tania threaded her arm through Juliana's and led her away from the bedchambers. "By the by, we've found two sprights hidden on Lord Bellemare's stallion. They claim to be yours."

"Halton and Gorman?" Juliana asked in surprise. "They're here?"

"Where else would they be but with their mistress?" Tania asked.

"Oh, I'm not their mistress." Juliana shook her head. She glanced up to make sure Nicholas hadn't followed them. She felt sick to her stomach, not to mention hurt and betrayed.

"Mm, you see, sprights tend to bond and I believe they have bonded to you. Like it or not, they're yours until you die." Tania laughed, the sound like ringing bells. "I've given them a warm bed and a fire. They are pleased enough with it."

"Thank you," Juliana said. They stepped down a narrow row of steps, winding in circles as they descended.

"You want to ask me something," Tania said.

"Aye, many things." Juliana nodded. The queen's mood seemed to change with each flutter of her wings.

"Please." Tania motioned her hand through the air as they continued down the stairwell. The way was lighted, though she could see no torches. "Ask."

"What did my brother think to make you slap him?"

Tania giggled. "Ask something else."

"How do you know so much about me?"

Tania nodded. "I wish I could say it's because I am all knowing, but alas, it is because my kind loves gossip and you, my dear, are the latest gossip. It's why I wanted to meet you. Now, you must tell me. Are the rumors true? Are you in love with King Merrick? Is that why you journey to the Black Palace?"

"What?" Juliana gasped.

Tania frowned. "It's not true? You don't love him? Pity."

"Where did you hear that?"

"Ah, then you do. I hear everything that happens from my faery ladies. They have spies all over the forest. There isn't a thing that can be said without them finding out. Gossip has it that you fell in love with the King of the Unblessed and begged him to give you a chance. If you get to his palace on time he'll accept your suit because you'll have proven yourself worthy. We all thought it terribly romantic. It's why I offer to help you. I should like to tell the story at the Feia court with me in the ending."

"That's not exactly correct." Juliana took a deep breath. "But I do need to get there right away."

"Then you do love him?" Tania stopped on the stairwell. She sighed, her wings quivering.

"Well, nay—"

"You don't love him?"

"Aye," Juliana said.

"I see." Tania resumed walking. "You don't know you love him. But we all saw the mark on your head when you walked in. That's why none of the faery men touch you. He's claimed you as his. How very interesting. Tell me, why are you going to the palace, if not to prove your love?"

"King Merrick has kidnapped children from my home. I go to save them."

At that Tania laughed so hard tears came to her wide eyes. Juliana frowned.

"You say King Merrick has kidnapped mortal children?" Tania demanded, grabbing her waist as she bent over. Her wings fluttered, pulling her up when she would fall over in merriment.

"It's not funny. He'll hurt them if I don't get to his palace and ask him a question." Juliana put her hands on her hips, scowling at the insensible woman. Why was she laughing?

"A question?" Tania shook her head, calming to a chuckle. "What game is this? You must tell me everything. Why would you believe Merrick stole children? The very idea!"

Juliana took a deep breath. Hoping she was doing the right thing, she quickly told the queen how she asked for an adventure and Merrick popped up out of nowhere to give her one. "I looked. The children were gone. I know he has them."

"My dear, dear woman," Tania said. They came to the end of the long stairwell. Pulling Juliana through the narrow door, she said, "Come, let us see about these children of yours."

The round chamber was intricately carved from silver like the rest of the palace, only the walls were decorated with ancient symbols. In the center of the room was a round pool of water. In the center of the pool was a stone island. Tania took Juliana's arm and, wings fluttering, she flew her over the water to the island. Juliana gasped as a strange hairy fish jumped from the water to nip at her feet. It had long, sharp teeth and seemed to snarl.

"Hold still," Tania scolded. "They can't jump this high."

"I'm sorry." Juliana nearly screamed as the fish jumped again, nipping close to her toes.

Landing on the stone island, Tania plucked a strand of hair from Juliana's head and sat down on the floor. She motioned for Juliana to join her and tossed the strand of hair into the water. When they were both seated, legs crossed, Tania said, "Now, let's look for these children, shall we?"

"But—"

"Ah, here we are," Tania said. A wall of light flashed up over the water in several colorful squares. "They look safe enough to me. I knew Merrick wouldn't be bothered with human children."

In each square was one of the missing children from the prisons. A couple of them played, one worked in the garden, two petted a Bellemare colt, another ate with his family outside. "But how? I saw them disappear. I went to look for them. They were gone."

"Glamour. He only made it look like they were gone. Honestly, it's child's magic to make things disappear from sight. These are the children at this exact moment. They're fine. The unblessed do play nasty, wicked tricks, don't they? It makes them great lovers, or so I've been told. Still, I can't believe you fell for this one. Whoever heard of a quest to ask a question? Even mortals have nobler pursuits than that. At least they search for holy relics, or journey to worship their gods."

"Why would he do this?" Juliana asked.

"Because he loves you." Tania sighed, clearly thinking it romantic. "That must be it. You asked for an adventure and he gave you one. Though, it's quite a foolish wish. Wouldn't it have been much simpler to just ask him for a pretty dress? Or perhaps hair ribbons? Aye, ribbons."

"Nay, he...nay. I saw with my own eyes." Juliana took a deep breath. "Can you show me Lord Eadward of Tyrshire?"

Juliana bit her lip. If the children really weren't kidnapped, then maybe Eadward really wasn't dead.

"Who's he?" Tania asked. The children disappeared and the light darkened. Eadward's face appeared as large as a castle gate. It was bloated and rotted in his coffin. The eyes were gouged from his head, oozing with fluids. Tania screamed and made the image go away. Jumping to her feet, she screeched, "Why did you ask for that? Why look at a dead man? Wretched, wretched mortal! Don't you know faeries must only see pretty things?"

Oh, Eadward, nay! Juliana gagged. "I didn't know."

Tania studied her for a moment and slowly sat back down. "Who is he?"

"Nicholas' father. He was my intended." Her voice strained to say the words.

"Nicholas? The one you ran from?" Tania asked. Juliana nodded. "Why did you react in such a way? Your heart isn't for him. He thinks to love you, but you don't return the feelings. Why pretend to be affected by him in bed with others? Only your mortal pride is stung."

Juliana frowned. She wasn't pretending. It had disturbed her to see it. What did this woman know about it anyway?

"Is there anything else you'd like to see?" Tania asked, happily changing the subject as she wiggled in her seat. "I do like to look at pretty flowers. Or we could spy on mortal lovers? I've learned a great many delicious things from... Nay?"

Juliana shook her head in denial. Even if Merrick didn't take the children, that didn't change the fact that Eadward was dead.

"Ah, then you must promise to tell me how it turns out." Tania hopped to her feet. Juliana was slower to rise. "He's going to love that dress."

Juliana started to answer, but the faery queen pushed her into the water. She screamed as she splashed into the pool, waiting for the first bite of the hairy fish. Instead, she fell through the water, only to land on hard stone. Moaning, she lifted her head, feeling oddly dry for having gotten soaked. Her head spun and her eyes blurred. All she saw was strange blue firelight on black stone before passing out.

Chapter Eight

Merrick shot up in his bed. He was weak from the dragon's blood, but thanks to the loyal troll in the tavern he wasn't captured. Reaching behind his back, he winced as he felt the puckered wound on his shoulder beneath the long length of his hair. He brushed the locks aside to get a better feel. It had stopped bleeding but it would be several days before he was up to his full power.

Frowning, he thought of Ean's deceit. His brother had set him up with talk of love and family, only to try and take him down when his back was turned. If he ever crossed paths with Gregor, he'd kill him. In fact, if he ever crossed paths with Ean, he might just kill him as well.

His bedchamber was black to match his mood. Tapestries hung along the dark stone, no designs embroidered into their dark surfaces. His bed posts, his coverlet, even his fur rug were all black. Only the blue fire, burning brightly from the fireplace, gave any relief to the solemn chamber.

Merrick swung his feet off the side of the bed. He was naked, but didn't bother to materialize clothes quite yet. He frowned. There was a pile of shimmering pale blue in his sea of his blackness. It must have been what woke him. His gut tightened and he knew who she was even before he saw her face. Juliana. She was in his bedchamber. But how?

As his feet touched the floor, tight breeches appeared on his legs. He stepped closer to her. Her body faced down and the long, dark locks of her hair covered the side of her face from view. Kneeling, he held his breath, waiting for the rise of her back to show she breathed. She was alive. His tension eased by small degrees.

Merrick touched the edge of her gown, lifting it. The material sparkled like stars. Frowning, he grumbled, "Faery magic. Queen Tania."

Queen Tania and her faeries liked to meddle. He hadn't been surprised that Juliana had caught the faeries' attention in the forest, though he was surprised Tania chose to help her come to his home. Closing his eyes, Merrick sensed his palace. The queen had sent her alone. Her brothers and that man, Nicholas, were not with her.

The beautiful material withered in his hand. He watched the blue turn to hard black as the material changed, growing out from his hold. The faery gown disappeared leaving Juliana clad as he would have her. Her hair twisted, piling onto the top of her head, revealing her face, as dark kohl lined her eyes. Merrick smiled, watching with a sense of fascination as her features turned from girlish innocence to smoldering seductress. She was in his palace, under his complete control. Now there would be no escape. Juliana was his for all eternity.

◆◆◆◆◆◆◆◆◆

Juliana looked at herself in the long mirror, stunned. The woman staring back at her could not be her reflection, but it was. Her gown's bodice pulled tight, pushing her breasts up high and pulling at her waist until she could barely breathe. Her shoulders and arms were bare. The floor-length skirt was narrow, hugging her hips. It split down each side to give peeks of her thighs and calves when she moved. Black leather boots traveled high over her legs, stopping mid-thigh. They were so tight to her flesh, she didn't know how on earth she'd get them off. The whole gown was positively indecent.

A black coil wrapped around her arm, almost as if it was drawn on her skin with a quill. She touched it, smearing an ink-like substance with her finger. As soon as she drew her finger away, it fixed itself, melding back together. It was the same with the dark lining around her eyes. She couldn't wipe it off, though she tried.

"Queen Tania?" she whispered. Juliana didn't expect an answer. She looked over the bedchamber, from the bed she'd awakened on to the colorless walls. Everything was black and the fire burned an eerie blue, casting her skin in what looked like moonlight. Juliana was certain the faery queen had kept her word. She'd sent her to the Black Palace. Closing her eyes, she asked, "King Merrick?"

All was quiet.

Juliana took a deep breath, staring at her reflection. What now? Merrick didn't kidnap the children. Her whole reason for leaving her world had been a lie, and that was only if she believed Queen Tania. If the children were indeed safe at home, as she suspected they were, then her quest was over. So, what now? Why did Merrick want her at his palace? Was her journey ended? Did she simply need to ask to go home and that was the end of it? And what of her brothers? Of Nicholas? Dare she ask the Unblessed King to send them home as well? Would he let her ask him anything?

Life had become complicated.

Once home, would she marry Nicholas? Could she love him more than a brother? Seeing him in the arms of other women had hurt, but did it affect her heart? Such actions were the way of men, she knew that. Did it really matter what she thought? Marriage wasn't about love, but alliances.

Juliana turned away from the mirror, unable to look any longer at what she'd become. Perhaps it was fitting that Merrick dressed her as the whore she'd become. Her gaze fell upon the door and she went to it. If fate waited for her, she'd face it head on. Refusing to cower, she threw open the door, not knowing what to expect. What she found was an empty passageway.

Beyond the black passageway was another black passageway, beyond that another. She supposed it didn't matter if she got lost. She had a feeling King Merrick would be able to find her anywhere. He might even be watching her now.

Merrick looked up from his throne as the fireplace surged. Borc was again on fire and Iago was rolling around on the floor in a fit of grating laughter. His rasping voice echoed loudly over the hall, causing others to join in. Borc jumped around, not finding a water bucket to sink into. Finally, he managed to pat his head and smother the flames.

The joke was old, but Merrick found himself smiling slightly at his subjects. At the subtle gesture, the goblins gasped and turned to look at him. He quickly hid his expression behind his hand, pretending to yawn. Much quieter than before, the goblins went about their business, whispering amongst themselves as they plotted their endless mischief. Merrick wondered if all they ever did was plot. They didn't seem to do much else.

Merrick's gaze traveled up over the ceiling, as he pretended to stare at the arches. Juliana was awake, walking his castle. He felt her, knew exactly where she was, as he did all things in his home. Easily, he could picture her in the black dress. She was beautiful, dressed like a dark elfin lady. Merrick gave a small smile to think of it. She'd fit into the unblessed court nicely. He expected her to be more frightened than she was. Her bravery would serve her well.

Let's just see how brave she really is. Let her look upon the whole of my subjects. Merrick's smile widened, this time not bothering to hide it from his minions.

"A celebration," Merrick announced. The goblins turned to him, their wrinkled face lit with interest. What better way to welcome Juliana to her new home? What better way to bring his people to him? Besides, he needed to talk to Lord Kalen about the probability of an upcoming war with Tegwen. "We shall bring all of the unblessed court to these halls. It will be a great and monstrous feast like no other. I feel like celebrating."

The goblins cheered in excitement. The uneven sound rasped loudly over the hall.

"Iago, send dispatch to Lord Kalen," Merrick ordered. Iago's dark, wrinkled face turned to him, listening. "Tell him I command him to bring his knights and the ladies of his hall three days hence. That should be enough time for him to get here."

Iago nodded eagerly. "Yes, my king."

"Also send invitations to all unblessed creatures. I want this hall filled." Seeing the large troll, Volos, crouched in the corner by Bevil, Merrick ordered, "You two, go find me three nymphs to sing and a wizard to perform wondrous magical feats. I will be entertained. And capture me a dragon, whose very breath will light this hall."

Volos looked at Bevil for guidance. Bevil motioned to him. The troll picked the goblin up and placed him on his shoulder as he hobbled out of the great hall.

Merrick lounged back in his throne, grinning as he looked at the ceiling. Juliana was lost, wandering in circles. That was because he let her into a hall without end. It would turn, twist, change in décor and circle around for an eternity if he wished it. She'd never make her way to a door unless he willed it. Let her wander awhile in a place he could watch over her. He had a celebration to plan.

※

"Where's my sister?" Hugh demanded, struggling against his chains. The prison may have been a bed decorated with silk coverlets and feathered pillows, but it was still a prison. The faery queen had mesmerized him somehow and he'd awakened with his wrists in shackles and his shirt missing. Glaring at Tania, he demanded, "What have you done to her?"

"Lord Bellemare, such a temper," Tania scolded, fluttering just out of his reach. Her gown shimmered beautifully, but he didn't see it. Her gaze drifted over his chest and she affected a pout. "Don't you know we faeries don't like tempers?"

Hugh continued to glare. It was a good thing they had him chained. If he was free, he'd be sure to strangle the aggravating wench.

"Your sister is well. Your brother and Sir Nicholas are being attended by my ladies of the Feia court. Trust me, they are well looked after."

"Trust you? You hold me prisoner and then ask for my trust? Are you mad? What are you up to, woman?" he growled, thrusting his arms angrily against his chains.

Tania leaned over the bed and slapped him. Hugh's face didn't move, not even to flinch. His eyes stared into hers as she withdrew her hand. "Mind your tone, mortal. I am a queen."

"Nay, you are an aggravating wench." Hugh ground his teeth as Tania gasped. He wanted to say more. Only the fact that she was a lady kept him from turning the full force of his words on her. Infuriating or not, there was some things a man didn't say to a woman.

Tania pulled away from him. Tears outlined her eyes, but Hugh couldn't say he was sorry for it. She lost his respect the moment she slapped him in her hall for no reason. Besides, queen or no, the woman was frustrating and something inside him strove to annoy her.

Tania turned from him, her wings fluttering so fast she hovered above the ground. Her body was slender and she was taller than the rest of the females of her kind, even some of the men. Still, with her feet on the ground, her head only came to his chin.

"Stop thinking those things," she demanded, trembling. Her lip pushed out with an adorable sulk. Hugh didn't like it. He didn't want to think anything about this woman was adorable. Right now, she was the enemy. Her tone was hard and she looked at him in complete frustration, as she added, "I have not given you permission."

"I don't need permission to have my own thoughts," Hugh said. "Besides, how can you possibly know what's in my head?"

"When you have those thoughts I see them too." Tania hovered closer to him, getting in his face. "You do not have permission to think of me in such a way. You must cease at once."

Hugh snapped his teeth, as if he would bite her. She gasped and instantly drew back. Tilting his head back, he laughed.

"Cease at once!" she demanded, pouting her lip and tapping her foot in the air.

"Do you mean these thoughts?" Hugh grinned, instantly imagining Tania naked. Even though he was mad at her, she was a beautiful woman and it wasn't too much of a stretch to fantasize about her. He watched her face as she paled.

"Nay," she demanded, crossing her arms over her chest. She was still clothed so the gesture was pointless.

Hugh's grin widened. He licked his lips, imagining that she straddled him on the bed and that her small hands were on his body, slowly stripping him of his clothes even as he was chained. Closing his eyes, he imagined himself naked, her soft lips on his neck and chest, her hands reaching down to the erection growing between his hips. He imagined her wings to flutter as she drew her kisses lower, down his stomach to wrap around the hard length of his...

"Argh!" Tania screamed.

Hugh opened one eye. He'd only had the fantasy to annoy her, but succeeded in giving himself a very uncomfortable mass between his thighs. Forcing a frown, he asked, "Do you mind? I wasn't finished. It was just getting good. That is unless you'd like to..." He nodded down his body, arching a brow in invitation. If the pretty faery queen wanted to give him pleasure, he'd not deny her. Although, right now, she looked mad enough to bite.

"You are an uncouth barbaric mortal," the queen announced. "How dare you?"

"I dare much." Hugh narrowed his eyes, giving her his most intimidating look, a look he reserved for the practice field when disciplining his men. She flinched, actually looking scared of him. "I'll imagine this and so much more until you let me go. I'll imagine you in ways you've never dreamt possible."

"I'll let you go, but not just yet. We must give your sister time, Lord Bellemare," Tania answered, her voice small.

"Then slap me all you want, but I'm going to finish what I started." Hugh closed his eyes, letting his mind pick up where it left off. Tania gasped as he envisioned her lips sucking him into her mouth. Hearing a flutter of wings, he opened one eye. The faery queen was gone. Hugh chuckled to himself. Never did he think such a tactic would serve him in a fight. Then, looking down at his arousal, he sighed. This plan would pain him greatly as well.

King Ean looked up from his throne as Gregor stepped into his palace hall. They were alone. Ean had banished all creatures of his court from him so he could think, so it was quiet. Seeing Gregor's face, he sighed. "Any word from King Merrick?"

"Nay, my king," Gregor answered, bowing his head. "He doesn't let us pass beyond his castle gate, but met me alone outside the walls. I gave him your missive, but he has no answer. He merely laughed at you and called you a fool."

Ean sighed. He'd hoped for another meeting with Merrick, another chance to talk reason into his brother about Lady Juliana. "Why would he attack my men at Rivershire? We were peaceful. We let him pass."

"He wants a war," Gregor answered. "It is the only explanation."

"Tell me Gregor. Is a mortal woman really worth starting a war over? Mortals are so temporary, their lives so short." The melancholy would not leave him and had only grown worse since his talk with Merrick. He felt sick, weak. His powers weren't what they should be. Ean said nothing of this to anyone. "Perchance, Lady Juliana wants to be with Merrick."

"My king, no blessed mortal would choose King Merrick, of that I am sure. Regardless of why she is there, this is not about Lady Juliana. This is about your kingdom. This is about King Merrick wanting a war with

Tegwen. If there is to be a war between the blessed and unblessed, it would be started over a mortal but it would be about so much more. By taking your ward, he laughs in your face. If we do not act, word will get out that we are weak, that you, my king, are weak. King Lucien will strike."

Ean watched Gregor carefully.

"I fear he seeks to reclaim the throne that was lost to him," Gregor said. "He would be both ruler of Valdis and Tegwen."

Ean nodded slowly. Gregor's words made sense, but the idea that Merrick could be king of both was absurd. He looked at his hall, a hall that would have been his brother's had fate not intervened and turned him dark. "Leave me, Gregor. I need time to think."

"There is more," Gregor said, not meeting his eye. "There have been rumored from the countryside that King Lucien visits the Black Palace."

Ean nodded once. "Leave me."

"My king." Gregor bowed and quietly walked out of the main hall.

"Lucien and Merrick?" Ean whispered, resting his forehead in his hand. It wasn't unheard of, the unblessed and the damned joining forces. Is that what Merrick had meant when he said Ean would sever their tie someday? "Why come for my throne now after so many years? You know as well as I that a man cannot be both King of the Blessed and Unblessed. Have you gone mad? Unless you are not after my throne at all, but seek to destroy it. Perhaps you seek to destroy all of Tegwen and the blessed with it."

Ean sighed. Time and rage were lethal combinations. Merrick had plenty of one and many reasons for the other.

Looking over his empty hall, he whispered, "What are you doing, brother?"

Juliana lifted her head from her hands, sitting against the wall of a passageway that would not end. Touching the design on her arm, she repeatedly smeared the ink, watching as it collected itself. With her shoulders left bare and the slit up the sides of her skirt, it was chilly.

Juliana walked for what had to be hours, endless hours spent going nowhere. The hall turned an impossible number of times until she had to be going around in circles, but the décor changed. Sometimes she'd pass a statue, sometimes a tapestry, sometimes a chair. She'd even tried to turn back around and walk the other way. That is when she discovered the hall shifted and changed. When she turned around, backtracking, the statue she'd passed was no longer there. In its place was a large vase sitting on the floor. She was imprisoned in the never-ending hall.

"Merrick," she said, her flat tone resigned. There was no choice but to call to him. "Merrick, are you there?"

"Aye?"

She looked up from her arm. He stood before her, lounging against the opposite wall as if he'd been there all along just waiting for her to say his name. Juliana quickly stood, smoothing down her skirt to keep her thighs from showing. The fact that it was pointless, that he had seen her naked and felt every inch of her body, was not lost on her.

"I know who you are," Juliana said. "You're the King of the Unblessed."

"It was never a secret," Merrick answered. The corner of his mouth curled up in amusement.

"You let me look for King Lucien. You made me believe—"

"Tsk, tsk, tsk, I told you I was Merrick and that Lucien controlled the demons. You only assumed that damned and unblessed were the same. You never asked me, so I made you believe nothing." Merrick took a step closer, crowding in on her. "It was you who assumed that my goblins were demons. Trust me, they are quite a different race."

"And the children?" she asked. "Queen Tania showed me the children. They're not kidnapped, are they?"

"Now, what would I want with a bunch of mortal children?" Merrick laughed.

147

"You lied to me."

He shrugged. "That is a matter of perception. You should have asked me where I was keeping them."

"You tricked me."

"I'm unblessed. It's what we do." His gaze moved over her face. She felt the look all the way to her toes. There was something almost reverent in the way he eyed her.

Juliana shivered. She didn't want to feel anything for him. Remembering Eadward's face rotting in his grave, she swallowed, overwhelmed with the sudden onslaught of nausea. "And murder? Is that just something you do?"

Merrick stepped forward, forcing her to stumble back into the wall. The hard stone pressed along her spine, making retreat impossible. He caressed her cheek, his touch gentle. "I only did what you asked of me."

"I never asked you to kill Eadward." Juliana closed her eyes, balling her hands into fists at her side. She wanted him so desperately, wanted his touch, wanted more of him than he could give her. In spite of what she felt, she knew he was bad for her. He was evil, the king of evil. Whatever she thought to see in him, those facts remained. He controlled the goblins. He twisted her fate. He brought her here. He killed Eadward.

Merrick had all but admitted to the crime. He promised her that first night that he would see to it she never married and he kept his word. For what other way to assure that she never married Eadward than with the finality of death?

"You mortals look with your eyes and hear with your ears, but you are blind and deaf," he said softly. His hand stopped moving. Juliana's breath caught at his tortured expression. His gaze roamed over her face, studying her intently. She felt no better than a prize mare, or a pet dog. "All I ask is that you see me for what I am, hear me."

She didn't understand what he wanted from her.

"Desire me." His voice was hard, commanding, yet his expression pleaded with her, as if he could make her obey him with his look. He drew his hand down her throat to her naked shoulder. The corset's laces pulled tighter against her chest, causing her breasts to lift up against the bodice's top as she gasped for breath. His fingers settled on the top of her heaving chest, lying over the mounds. He was so warm. It was strange that when he came to her she felt the cold only to find his body warm. Desire flowed through her at his touch. "Touch me as you did in the water. Beg me to touch you. Ask me not to go."

When she didn't speak, his hand slid up and tightened on her throat. His fingers flexed as if he wanted to strangle her but couldn't. He didn't hurt her. His lips parted and he breathed as hard as she.

"Beg me," he ordered, though the words were soft. He hooked her bottom lip with his finger, pulling open her mouth. He was close. With one sweep, his finger could brush her skirt aside and press intimately into her. There was no material blocking him. Speaking into her ear, he demanded, "Say the words. Submit completely to me."

Juliana tried to resist, but it was hard. She did want him. Even now she felt damp beneath her skirt and her nipples ached where they pressed into the tight material of the bodice. She did want to submit to him.

"I don't have to wait for your compliance, Juliana." His eyes darkened. "I can take you now. I can force you. I can control you. No one will hear your cries. No one will save you."

Juliana looked at him. She knew he was powerful, had seen the things he could do. For all his threats, he hadn't forced himself on her. His eyes bore into hers. And, for all his threats, he was waiting for her words.

There were so many reasons why she shouldn't be there with him. At the moment, she couldn't think of them. She touched his waist, her fingers gliding over the black linen that hid his muscles from view. "You may command my body to you, but that is all you get. It is all I will freely give."

Merrick closed his eyes and slowly nodded. Juliana made the first move, even as she knew it was madness to give in. She pulled his waist forward, drawing his body to hers. He was as aroused as she. Groaning, he kissed her hard. The onslaught of his demanding mouth only excited her more, as he drew a hand over to her bodice, cupping a breast. The part of the bodice covering her breasts disappeared. His hand was on her naked flesh, kneading. The corset was still tight to her waist, pushing her breasts up from underneath.

Her hand kneaded his shirt, pulling at it. The material dissolved from her grasp. She looked at his chest in awe. "How?"

"Everything in this castle is mine to control," he answered. "Even you."

Juliana wanted to protest, but he again kissed her so passionately she couldn't think. His hands seemed to be everywhere at once, roaming over the formfitting bodice that pushed her breasts high. His mouth moved to her chest, licking and sucking a fiery trail. The material from her skirt softened, closing along the sides, baring her legs to him. It split up the front, revealing her thigh high boots and naked sex. She felt the material against her butt, so light it tickled the backs of her thighs as she moved. There was something sensual in being thusly attired.

Merrick reached into the skirt's front slit, pushing the material back as he grabbed her naked hips. He left her dressed in the strange outfit. With one firm pull, he lifted her up against the wall as if she were no heavier than a feather.

Juliana's booted legs dangled behind him as he pressed forward, crushing her against the stone. Merrick's breeches dissolved, leaving him completely naked. His arousal pressed into her thighs, rubbing along her sex without penetrating as he rocked himself against her.

Juliana remembered all too well what it was like to have him take her. The heat of him teased her flesh as he rocked faster, refusing to thrust up inside her willing body. She moaned, gripping and pulling his flesh, scratching him in her urgency.

As she kissed him, she demanded, "Merrick, take me."

"I want to hear you beg for it," he answered into her mouth. "Tell me you want me."

"Please," she obeyed, mindless. "Please, I want you."

With that, he thrust into her. Juliana cried out softly. The hard stone softened and when she opened her eyes they were in his bed.

Merrick consumed her with every inch of his body, thrusting hard and deep and slow. Her thighs spread as he pulled his knees forward. He stretched her legs wider, gripping the boots along her thighs to control her body on his as he fell onto his back. Juliana moaned softly to find herself on top of him, but didn't stop the rhythm he'd set. Every inch of her reached out to him. It was impossible to deny what her body so desperately wanted.

Juliana rode him, touched him, leaned over to kiss him. His firm lips felt good and when he touched her, she felt protected. The tension built within her and she was mindless, wanting, needing. Nothing mattered but Merrick—his touch, his smell, his sound.

Juliana stiffened, crying out in soft surprise as her climax finally hit her. She felt him jerk, his body tensing beneath her. He let go of her thighs. An animalistic sound of pleasure escaped his throat, primal and raw. She fell forward on his chest, breathing heavily, caught between fulfillment and fear.

Her eyes widened and her whole body tensed. The full extent of what she'd done overwhelmed her senses. She didn't dare move.

Merrick lay sated. Juliana's body pressed into him and he knew he should be satisfied that he could control her willing body, but he wasn't. He wanted her complete submission, wanted her to enslave herself freely so he could rule over her. Even now, he could feel her spirit resisting him.

She pushed off him and crawled backward to the head of the bed. When she looked at him it was an expression of misery that crossed her features, not pleasure. It tore at him to see it. Her round eyes looked first at him then down at herself. Juliana hid her body from him, pulling the sheer skirt he'd given her and crossing her arms over her chest. "Why do you do this? Why me? Why this?"

Merrick didn't move. He turned his head to watch her, forcing dispassion into his gaze. Tears gathered in her eyes. His heart tightened to see them.

"Let me go, Merrick. You've gotten what you wanted. You've proven I am nothing more than your whore."

Whore? Merrick wanted to scream at her, hit her. He wanted to hurt her as she hurt him. They come together and she dared to say she was a whore? As if being with him cheapened her somehow. Not lover, not friend, but whore. Instead of lashing out, he buried it all inside. "You're trapped here, Juliana. I will never let you go. You are mine."

"I will never belong to you," she whispered. "No more than this. I despise you."

Her cold words were like a slap across his face. He had not forced himself on her. She came to him willingly and yet here she was staring at him, her eyes accusing. Why was she not pleased? She wanted him. He smelled it, felt it, answered her call when she said his name. She had summoned him to her and he came. He gave her what she wanted and still she blamed him, hated him.

As if to confirm his thoughts, she said, "I will never love you, Merrick."

Her stinging rejection ripped through him. He would never be good enough for her. He knew that now. She had denied him to her brothers that same night they'd come together in the pond. She went to Nicholas, let him kiss her without a protest. Juliana used him, took her body's fulfillment and then tried to toss him aside. Nothing he did would ever please her. What had he expected? He was king to all that was unblessed. Why would he not be unblessed in this?

Merrick slowly sat up. "Make no mistake. You already belong to me."

Merrick disappeared from her sight, hearing her gasp as he left her. Rage simmered within him and he was unable to look at his tormenter a second longer. She could fight him all she wanted, but he vowed that in the end he would rule her completely—willing or no.

Chapter Nine

"My king, Lord Kalen's army marches."

Ean looked up in shock at Gregor's words. He was in the center courtyard. Expansive gardens stretched within the protective embrace of the castle walls. The air was sweet, filled with the fragrance of flowers warmed by the sun. Like all days in the Golden Palace, the weather was perfect. The sunlight shone on the crystal wall making the palace appear gold in color, casting its light over the garden. Fruit trees grew, always bearing ripe fruit no matter the season, outside the palace. White cobblestone pathways led in harmonious design through the shrubbery.

Ean took a deep breath and held it. He had spent many hours in the courtyard with his brothers and it pleased him, even as it saddened him, to remember the days long passed. However, seeing Gregor's face, all pleasure faded. "You're sure?"

Gregor nodded. "Our spies have seen the Berserks marching from the mountain fortress of Taranis. Lord Kalen leads them toward Valdis. They don't even try to hide themselves from view. It can only mean one thing. We must prepare ourselves for battle."

Ean's gut tightened and he thoughtfully rubbed his bottom lip. First Lucien and now Lord Kalen at Merrick's palace. What was Merrick up to? Surely it was too soon to call up arms. He did not want to fight over a mortal woman. "Have the men readied, but do not lead them from their homes just yet."

Gregor bowed. He turned to do as he was ordered.

"Gregor," Ean said, his voice stern. "We will not strike the first blow. Am I clear?"

Gregor nodded once. "Yes, my king."

Ean waved him away. He no longer saw the gardens as he stared at his hands. At one time he'd considered starting a war to ease his boredom, but they were just thoughts. He would never intentionally put his people in harm's way. Closing his eyes, he whispered, "Ah, Merrick, what are you up to?"

Juliana stepped through the doorway, drawing attention from some of the goblins in the main hall. A couple days had passed since she'd succumbed to Merrick. He had not seduced her again. She knew it was for the best, even as she longed for his touch.

Merrick had come back to her, granting her freedom to roam his palace with the promise that none of his subjects would harm her. The first time she stepped into his main hall, she wasn't so sure. She watched the horrific looking unblessed goblins staring at her with both disgust and curiosity. It had taken all of her resolve to walk across the hall with her head held high. Merrick had watched her from his throne, his challenging look giving her strength.

Each morning she awoke, it was to the same room but the décor always changed with Merrick's moods. Mostly it was black, but sometimes there would be a display of color amongst the dark. When she asked about it, he said it was an unconscious changing, like her clothing. The castle merely knew what he wanted and changed to suit him.

Along with the room, each morning her gown would be different. The material was always dark, usually black. Aside from that first time where her hair had been coiled on her head, her locks were left loose about her shoulders. At night, her clothes seemed to disappear, leaving her to sleep in the nude. It was disconcerting to see her clothing just dissolve from her limbs as she lay down for the night.

Today her dress was more like she was used to, though the bodice did show a great amount of cleavage. The upturned collar framed her face, dipping down the front in a long V. The long, trailing sleeves touched the floor, but were short enough on top that her hands were not covered. The bodice formed directly into a full skirt with no belted waist, just formed pleats. The gown lacked petticoats, but it was long and no slits showed off her legs. The black material was soft, accented with the briefest touches of silver embroidery along the hems. Her thigh-high boots had been replaced with more sensible short boots.

Almost every comfort she desired, she was given. The morning after they came together, she awoke to find a long table with every imaginable toiletry at her disposal. If she wanted to bathe, Merrick would materialize a bath for her, steaming with hot water. If she was hungry, Merrick would materialize food. If she needed anything, all she had to do was say his name and he would hear her. He never came to her on his own, always waiting to be summonsed. Occasionally, their paths would cross in the great hall. It was for this reason alone she spent so much time there, though she would never admit it.

This time she had reason for going to the hall. Iago, who she recognized from outside her bedchambers at Bellemare, had delivered a summons from Merrick to the great hall. Every time the goblin spoke, she'd see his sharp teeth poking out from beneath his thick lips and want to run for cover. His beady black eyes watched her every movement as if he was just as wary of her as she was of him.

Now, as she took a hesitant step forward, the goblins peeked around the thick Corinthian columns lining the hall to watch her, their eerie faces contrasted by firelight. She paused, eyeing them as they eyed her. A few turned their backs, others continued to stare. The large troll, Volos, sniffed at her. She shivered. Out of all the creatures, Volos scared her the most.

With one strike of his beefy arm, she'd be crushed. When she looked up at the throne, it was empty. Glancing at Iago, she inquired, "Where is he?"

The goblin frowned, tossing out his hands. Juliana studied him before looking around the others. She'd seen them play pranks on each other, binding each others' ankles together so they would trip, putting pretty flower petals in each others' soups to make the person sick. Strangely they reminded her of very mischievous children—ugly, hairy, smelly, mischievous children with some magical abilities and unlimited imagination in which to use them. Thinking of it, she realized it was a frightening combination.

Iago watched her expectantly. The hall was quiet, too quiet. They were all staring at her.

"I don't suppose you would want to hear a story?" she asked, wondering if she could somehow win their loyalties from Merrick. It was doubtful, but she had to at least try if she ever hoped of escaping. Surely these creatures knew how to get out of the Black Palace. Perhaps she could even convince one to help her find her brothers. If that plan failed, it would be nice to ease their tension around her. She tired of their eyes following her with suspicion.

Iago's ears perked up, actually twitching on his head.

"What kind of story?" Tuki asked. The small, hairy goblin stepped forward on his taloned feet. Juliana trembled, almost sorry she offered as a few of the other goblins drew nearer. Their wrinkled faces turned up to look at her with curiosity. She bit her lip, keeping a sharp eye on them.

"About...a...Nixie?" she asked, remembering how the story had made the mortal children giggle.

"Those old hags?" Bevil shouted in his high-pitched whine. His long arms dragged on the floor as he walked in front of Volos. Volos stuck a finger up his nose. "Why would we want to hear about them?"

"All right." Juliana tilted her head to the side. In her head, she ran through all the stories she'd told to the children. "How about a great human knight and how he fought the beast who was eating the King's men?"

"Only if the beast eats the knight," Iago said, looking interested. The goblins laughed, drawing closer to her. Juliana looked around and finally sat down at their table. She kept her back to the strange rotted foods. They gathered around her, sitting at her feet on the stone floor. She did her best to look past their gnarled bodies and distorted faces.

"Ew, humans are too bony to make a good meal," Tuki cackled

"Funny," Juliana countered, seeing the look they shared. She saw their diets of worms and slugs and highly doubted humans were on it. "We say the same thing about nasty little goblins."

Her comment met with a round of laughter and nods of approval. Juliana hid her smile. Maybe winning over the goblins wasn't going to be so tough after all. She was used to playing with the children of Bellemare. Maybe these creatures weren't so different.

"This beast, what does he look like?" Iago asked. "He sounds like this cousin I once had."

Juliana leaned forward, narrowing her eyes and dropping her voice like she did to the group of children back home. As she spoke, she held their rapt attention. They gasped and nodded and laughed at all the right places in her tale. Only this time when she reached the ending, she made sure the hero knight died and the vicious beast won.

Merrick stopped as he entered the hall, lurking in the shadows so he couldn't be seen. Iago was to bring Juliana to him. The king wished to inform her of the celebration before the guests arrived. He could have easily found her himself, but he didn't want to be alone with her. Besides, she needed to get used to his goblin subjects if she were to live in his palace.

Juliana's soft voice carried over the hall, punctuated by the laughter of his goblins. She lifted her hand, swiping it through the air as she told some human story. The goblins were completely enthralled with her. It would seem she'd adjusted to them quite well. Merrick caught himself smiling as Volos pushed Tuki out of the way to sit next to her on the bench. Tuki went rolling like a ball across the floor. The king chuckled to see the stunned look on Juliana's face as the giant troll stared at her, a bit of slimy drool dripping over the side of his lips. To her credit, she didn't hesitate long.

Merrick waited until she finished her story before making his presence known. He stepped into the hall, quirking an eyebrow at the group. The goblins scattered, looking incredibly guilty. Bevil pulled Volos away. The large troll protested, pouting loudly, but in the end he did as Bevil said. Some went before the fire, others gathered at the table to eat.

Juliana watched them leave before standing to dust off her skirt. Merrick went to his throne. It was hard not to go directly to her and kiss her senseless. Knowing his kisses would not be welcomed kept him away. She came before him, curtseying lightly. "Your Majesty."

Merrick frowned. She'd been doing that a lot lately. If it wasn't "your majesty", it was "your highness" or "my king". She never called him by his name.

"You requested I come to the hall?" she continued, not looking at him.

"Tonight we will have a celebration," Merrick said. Juliana gasped in surprise, finally turning her wide eyes to his. "You will help me entertain my guests."

"Do you mean I'm to…?" She took a step back, frowning. "What do you mean by entertain?"

Merrick scowled in annoyance. Did she really think he'd share her with other men? "You are the lady of this palace now. I expect you to act as such in this small capacity. You will greet my guests and make them welcome. Or just show up in the hall and ignore them. I really don't care who you offend."

"Am I?" She searched his face.

"Are you what?"

"You said I was the lady of the palace," Juliana said. "Wouldn't prisoner be a better title?"

Merrick felt his stomach tighten in irritation. She made it known at every turn that she thought of herself as a prisoner. Was it too much to ask that she thought of his home as her home and not a dungeon? She wanted an adventure, he gave it to her. What was more of an adventure to a human than this? The immortal realm. The Black Palace of the Unblessed. A dark elfin King who came at her very call. He gave her what she asked for and still she was not happy. Lifting his hand, he twisted his fingers through the air and said, "As you wish."

Chains grew out of the floor like snakes, the metal links winding up from the stone and sprouting manacles for heads. The goblins laughed, cheering Merrick. Juliana screamed as a manacle snapped its iron jaws at her foot. She backed away, only to have another snap at her from behind. A manacle clamped her ankle. She screamed, kicking her leg to get it free. Soon the other manacle captured her other ankle as two more grew from the ceiling to capture her wrists. The ceiling chains pulled her up off the ground. She dangled, her arms pointing straight above her head.

Merrick stepped down from his throne and walked to her, eyeing his handiwork. Pointing two fingers at her legs, he spread them apart, making the chains do the same thing. Her legs pulled to the side, holding her firm to keep her from spinning around. She was high enough that he could pass easily under her skirt. It would be an alluring view, but he refrained. "If you prefer to be the decoration, so be it."

"Merrick," she said, her voice trembling.

He was instantly sorry for losing his temper, but he didn't back down now. How could he? She'd openly insulted him in front of his subjects. The goblins liked to gossip. If it was known that a mere woman, and a mortal at that, slighted him in his own home, he'd be attacked for sure. No one could resist coming after a weak king.

"Merrick," she said again, louder. Her voice quivered. "I would be honored to act as a lady in your home."

Merrick smiled. The chains disappeared and she floated slowly to the ground landing on her feet. He came close to her, his voice low. "I care not if you insult every guest that walks through my door. I care not if you sulk in a corner. I care not if you dance with every male tonight. But disrespect me in front of my subjects again and you will be severely punished. I cannot have a guest in my home insulting me."

Juliana nodded. Her mouth opened and he knew she would protest his choice of words. She did not consider herself a guest. Then, to his surprise, she refrained and didn't speak. Instead, she merely trembled before him. He hated that she feared him, but he wouldn't change it. How could he? He was frightening. Besides, she wouldn't believe anything he would say to comfort her.

Merrick leaned next to her ear, not touching her as he said, "Try to convince anyone to help you escape or let them get too familiar and I'll reinvent the word punishment. You belong to me. Am I understood?"

"Yes, my king," Juliana said softly.

Merrick touched her cheek, wanting to do more. But he would not force himself on her. He might threaten and yell, but in the end he wouldn't harm her. In the end, it was she who ruled him.

"Good." Merrick pulled his hand away. He should have just killed her like planned, rid himself of her and been done with it. He must truly hate himself to bring her to his home. The Unblessed King would never find happiness. He would find many things, but happiness and contentment were not amongst them. "My guests arrive tonight."

"Yes, my king." She didn't move. He couldn't take his eyes off her. There was so much he longed to say.

"Juliana," Merrick said softly. He kept his voice calm, but inside his stomach was knotted. "You have nothing to fear from me."

Her wide blue eyes turned to him, eyeing him as if he were insane. "This from the man who murdered Eadward? The man who holds me prisoner, forbids me to leave and threatens to punish me if I insomuch dare to try?"

Merrick withdrew his hand and slowly nodded. It was hopeless. She would never see. Without saying a word, he left her, dissolving into mist to hide alone in his Black Garden.

The dark blue gown Merrick materialized for her was finer than anything she'd ever seen. The sleeves were made from a sheer material, starting just off her shoulder and falling gracefully down past her wrist to hide her hand. The overlay fabric of the skirt matched the sheer fabric sleeves. The gown had a dark satin underskirt and bodice. The bodice was tight like everything else he put her in, pushing up her breasts and showcasing them with a squared neckline. The skirt swept around her body as she moved, hugging suggestively to her curves.

Curls piled high on top of her head, cascading down the back in long ringlets. Blue ribbons threaded through her hair. It was a fashion she'd never seen, but so were most of the clothes Merrick chose for her. A sapphire necklace clasped her neck, pulled tight along her throat. The heavy stones pressed into her. A matching ring graced her index finger and two dainty blue shoes were on her feet.

"The guests arrive."

Juliana shivered at Merrick's low words. She turned to look at him, surprised to see he didn't wear all black. His tight breeches and shirt were still that color, but he wore a long sleeveless overtunic that was much like the first day she saw him in Bellemare's side yard. It hung open in the front, falling to the ground like a cape. The black material was embroidered with dark blue, the front held together by two silver chains that draped over his chest. The upturned collar framed his face. Leather bound back the sides of his long hair, winding down the length from his temples to just above his waist. A band of silver wrapped his forehead disappearing beneath his hair. A blue gem shone from the center of the crown.

"You look beautiful," he said, instantly appearing as if he wanted to take the words back.

"And you look like a king," she answered, finding great pleasure in his compliment. Merrick held out his arm for her to take. She did and he led her to the door. "My king—"

"Merrick," he said, stopping. "You will call me Merrick. You have my permission to use it freely, or whatever it is you humans seek, but enough with this formality. I will not have you curtseying every time I walk into a room."

"Can I have more bodice?" she asked, not realizing she'd curtseyed so much. He looked down at her cleavage and her face heated at his attention. Desire sparked at the look and she had to remind herself that he was the enemy.

"As you wish." Merrick lifted his hand over her chest. He smiled slightly as he ran his fingers over her skin. When she looked down, the bodice was higher, covering more of her chest. "Happy?"

Juliana shivered at the way he said the word. She nodded, unable to continue looking at him. "Aye, thank you, my ki—thank you, Merrick."

Merrick nodded, took up her arm, and silently led her down to the hall.

"They celebrate tonight," Tania said.

Hugh opened his eyes and looked up from his place on the silk bed. He was still bound, but the chains were lengthened so he could move freely about his silk prison. His ankles were crossed and his fingers were threaded behind his head. He'd been resting quietly for some time, bored out of his mind, waiting for Queen Tania to come back so he could torment her. Aggravating her was the only bright spot in his days since his imprisonment began.

Hugh was not a man used to just lounging about. He liked being active—sword fighting, horseback riding, energetic sexual pleasures. Thinking of the latter idea, he glanced over Tania slowly, keeping his face impassive. The faery queen hovered above him, fluttering in the air. Her petite figure paralleled his as she looked down, and her sparkling white gown fell onto his legs, brushing over his thighs. He tried, but he couldn't see her legs under the ample folds of luxurious material.

"Your sister and King Merrick," Tania explained at his blank look. "They celebrate tonight. Together."

"You lie." Hugh pulled against his chains, rising up on the bed. His movement was so swift that he managed to catch Tania off guard. He grabbed her foot, holding it tight. She fluttered back, her wings flapping wildly as she tried to free herself. "Release me now or I'll break your foot."

Tania struggled, whimpering softly. Hugh reached up and grabbed her leg, pulling her down as she tried to fly away. Her wings were strong, but his arms were stronger. When he had her before him, he wrapped his arms tightly around her waist. Her soft body molded to his.

"Release me," he ordered, his tone dropping in a way that made women shiver.

"Nay, not yet. They must have more time." Tania was breathless as she wiggled against him. She was so fragile beneath his hands, so delicate. He'd spent the last several days thinking irresistibly wicked thoughts to annoy her every time she was near and it didn't take long for the passion within him to come surging to the surface. She wiggled again, trying to get free. Her wings fluttered lightly against the backs of his hands, as soft as silk and as light as air. "I cannot let you go. The story is not ended."

"What story?" Hugh demanded, his voice gruff as he tried to concentrate. She smelled sweet, like flowers in the spring. He hardened his resolve against her, refusing to be stirred by the treacherous woman. "What is going on? Why do you keep me here? Why do you send Juliana to him? Tell me."

Tania leaned forward and kissed him, pressing her closed mouth to his. Hugh startled in surprise. His grip loosened and he automatically parted his lips for more. He thrust his tongue into her mouth. She gasped and poofed into a ball of light, shrinking into a small speck of her former self.

Hugh growled in anger, swatting into the air at her. It was no use. She was beyond his reach. Tania flew wildly from the room as if stumbling around in the air, leaving him alone.

The Black Palace was filled with all manner of extraordinary creatures. Juliana gripped Merrick's arm as he led her into the hall. She tried to look regal, but it was hard. Goblins and a few trolls mingled with small faeries. The faeries wore black and crimson dresses and did not have the general appearance of being from Tania's court, though they were pale in complexion. They were more sinister in coloring—dark eyes and black hair, darker clothing.

A torrent of fire flowed over the ribbed vaults of the ceilings like a burning river. It wound around the giant Corinthian columns, edged over the sides of the walls, until the whole great hall ceiling looked to be on fire. Strangely, there was no more heat than if only the five giant fireplaces along the walls burned. The fire stopped, burning out, only to be replaced anew with a great rush of flames. Tracing the fire to its source, Juliana's steps faltered as she saw a large dragon perched in the rafters. His brown, scaled body barely moved as he let out another breath. She gasped, her mouth opening in awe. She was unable to help it as she stared in wide-eyed fascination and worry.

Merrick chuckled, gently pulling her as he continued to walk. Tables had been set, filled with food and drink. The hall seemed bigger, as if stretched to accommodate everyone. The tapestries and banners along the wall were blue with red and black designs. Juliana didn't recognize the symbols, but the blue matched her dress.

The fierce faces of the crowd looked on Merrick with admiration and fear. They stayed back, stepping aside to let him pass, bowing as he did. Eyes turned to her, curious. She imagined seeing hostility there as well. Juliana hugged closer to Merrick's arm. The king glanced at her briefly, his expression unreadable. She swallowed, not even trying to smile for him in her nervousness.

A hag, her white hair frizzed about her head, stared at Juliana with her one good eye. She snarled, showing a set of rotted teeth. Merrick turned to the old woman. Juliana couldn't see his expression or what he did, but the hag instantly lifted her hands over her face and crouched to the floor, turning away.

The hall was loud with laughter and talk. Not all the creatures were hideous. There were several human-like beings intermingled with the fierce. Three pretty ladies sang on a platform. Two stood on legs and one, a dark skinned mermaid, sat on the stone with her purple and silver fins dipping down into a basin of water. Theirs were the most beautiful voices Juliana had ever heard. The song tinkled like bells, not needing instruments. Juliana didn't understand their language, but the melody was spellbinding and light and made her feel like dancing.

An older man caught her eye. Something about him looked familiar. Then she realized it was his dark green robe. It was the same cut as William's when he came home from the monastery. She remembered what her brother had said about William apprenticing to become a wizard. As she watched, the wizard lifted his hands. A ball of light formed between his palms. Juliana gasped. Lightning struck out of the sphere, streaking over the heads of those in the crowd.

"It's just a simple trick," Merrick whispered. His breath hit her ear, causing her to shiver. There was an odd mixture of concern and amusement in his voice. "A glamour. It will not hurt you."

Juliana nodded. Every time Merrick spoke to her, she got a chill. Not unpleasant in nature, but a wave of desire that made her want to forget logic and fall into his arms. Now was not the time for such thoughts. She turned away from him, saying nothing as she again looked at the crowd.

Great, broad warriors sat next to trolls, wrestling their arms in a vast show of strength. By the slight point to their ears, she guessed they were elfin like Merrick, though they wore fur pelts over their clothing and dressed in the tunics of knights. Beautiful elfin ladies, in revealing gowns much like the ones Merrick gave Juliana to wear, cheered on the men. The women were lovely, their olive and cream complexions flawless and their eyes wide and alluring. Juliana looked at Merrick to see if he watched the beautiful creatures. He did not. Instead, he stared toward his throne where a table had been set with a great feast.

As they neared the table, several of the knights stood. Their leader was as tall as Merrick and a little broader of shoulders. The man stepped forward. He had long, wavy brown hair and dark purple eyes. A pelt was cinched over his shoulder with a gold brooch. Though he carried himself well, he did not move like a gentleman. He seemed caged within the palace walls. Juliana imagined she could see the energy snapping off of him. As he neared, she saw a long thin scar wrapping his naked forearm like a snake.

"Lord Kalen," Merrick acknowledged, lifting his hand straight up in greeting.

"My king," Lord Kalen answered, making the same gesture to lay his palm flat to Merrick's. When they touched, Juliana noticed a thin thread of light wrapped their hands. "It has been too long."

"Aye," Merrick answered. "Too long. This is Juliana, Lady of the Black Palace."

Kalen looked first at Merrick, his brow arching, and then at her. He smiled. "My lady."

When Kalen reached out his hand, she hesitated, looking at Merrick for guidance. He nodded. She touched the warrior briefly, fingers extended up, palm pressed flat to palm. She watched for the light. It didn't appear, but his hand was warm against hers, tingling her flesh. He pulled away. Sighing, she tried to relax.

"I will trade for her, my king," Lord Kalen offered. Juliana tensed once more. He winked at her, grinning widely. There was a mischievous impudence to his expressions. "Two of any ladies of my court for this one."

"I am not for trade, you disgusting pig," Juliana ground out before she could stop herself. She gasped, covering her mouth. Where did that come from?

Lord Kalen tipped back his head and laughed. "Make that four ladies. With such spirit, I will not have need of other entertainment."

"With such spirit, I will make you the entertainment," Juliana threatened, taking a step forward. Laughter rose up around them. Aggression ran through her blood, possessing her. She began to shake, not feeling like herself.

"Five ladies," Lord Kalen said. He tilted his head, studying her. "Well worth it for the right to tame such fire."

Juliana shook, glaring at him. She felt words surging forward. She tried to bite them back.

Merrick watched Juliana out of the corner of his eye. She was lovely this night and he was not surprised Kalen had offered for her. But to hear her voice, so harsh and unlike her own, he frowned. Glancing around the hall, he scanned the guests. A familiar presence washed over him, so faint it was as if it was purposefully being kept hidden.

"I will have your head for speaking about me thus," Juliana warned. She turned, motioning her hand to a nearby knight. The sword flew from the man's scabbard toward her hand.

Before she could grab it, Merrick reached out and caught the blade by the hilt. It snapped against his palm. He directed the blade at the old hag. "End it, woman."

The hag shook her head frantically. "Not I, my king. Not I."

"End it," Kalen said, grinning. Merrick turned to Kalen. The man laughed. Juliana blinked, eyeing him in her confusion. "Forgive us, little one, we could not resist the desire to see what our king had found. Your possession is truly to be envied."

Merrick arched a brow at Kalen. What was the man up to now?

"She has much fire in her, my king, and I'm glad to see your instincts are sharp," Kalen continued, loud enough that the whole hall could hear. "I fear she would have run me through had she gotten the blade."

Laughter sounded over the hall. Merrick grinned, tossing the sword back to its owner. Juliana glanced nervously at him. Weakly, she said, "Forgiven."

Kalen laughed louder than before. "She even speaks like a true queen. I shall have to steal this one from you."

Merrick stiffened at the words, keeping an eye on Juliana for her reaction.

"For a dance, of course." Kalen held out his hand to Juliana. Merrick knew the man was teasing him. Out of all of his nobles, he considered Kalen a friend. In fact, he was the only noble ever invited on a regular basis to dine at the palace—though those times were scarce. He watched Kalen take her across the floor, not caring if she danced with the man. Despite Kalen's words, Merrick knew the man would not steal Juliana away from him. In fact, seeing the look in his friend's eyes, he would wager Kalen would die to keep her at the Black Palace.

Kalen was known as a madman and for good reason. He often made what seemed like rash decisions, sometimes calling off his troops on the eve of a great battle they'd be sure to win. He would judge a person with one touch, turning a seemingly great ally away and accepting an undoubted enemy into his home. Other warriors outside his Berserks thought him reckless. But Merrick knew there was much method to Kalen's madness. Kalen was an empath and a clairvoyant, something he didn't tell many people.

When he touched Kalen's hand, Merrick had imparted all Kalen needed to know about the situation with King Ean. Kalen was more than willing to fight. He was also more than willing to read Juliana. Though getting Kalen to say what he discovered would be a true challenge.

Merrick threaded his hands behind his back. Standing still, he watched Juliana as Kalen swept her into his arms. More couples joined them, spinning around, crossing before him as they danced. Juliana and Kalen did not spin as they stayed in the middle of the hall. Their dance was of the human way, keeping their bodies apart. Juliana's eyes met his from across the floor. She was stunningly beautiful and he felt as if he could look at her for hours.

There were many attractive women in his hall—elves, nymphs, mermaids and faeries alike. All such races were known for beauty and grace. But Juliana, a mere mortal, caught and held his attention. Perhaps it was her mortality that made her so fragile to him, so delicate. Yet, out of all the women in this hall, she was the only one who thought to deny him whatever he wanted. If he were to demand obedience, sexual pleasures, even love, from any of the women, they'd give it without question. Juliana was the one woman he'd have all three demands from and she was the only one who'd dared defy him.

Juliana still wasn't sure what had made her threaten Lord Kalen, but he seemed unconcerned by the whole affair. The man smiled at her, appearing friendly. However, she had no doubt that if she were to provoke him, he'd come at her with deadly purpose. Growing up at Bellemare, she knew well the look of a seasoned warrior. Kalen was a fighter, through and through.

Looking around, she felt as if she floated on a surreal cloud. As Kalen led her onto the floor, tables seemed to shift out of their way, as if the stone floor expanded and grew without disturbing any of the guests. She glanced back at Merrick, knowing he cleared the floor for them. It saddened her to see he didn't appear jealous at all that another man danced with her. Instruments sounded, drawing her attention back to Kalen as the music accompanied the singers.

"I am not familiar with your people's dances," Juliana whispered.

"Luckily, I know yours." Kalen swept her into the first step, bowing gracefully over her hand. The crowd grew quieter as elfin couples joined them on the floor. Hints of orange lighted them from above as the dragon's breath fanned across the ceiling. When she glanced up, she saw fairy couples floating above her head, twirling erratically. The other dancers held each other closer, moving their feet in odd steps and spinning around in fast circles. As per human custom, she kept her distance from Kalen, touching only with her hands and not her full body.

Kalen was a good dancer, especially for being such an obvious warrior, but Juliana found herself looking over his shoulder for brief glances of Merrick within the spinning crowd. Picking up on Kalen's steps, she closed her eyes. She imagined that it was Merrick holding her hand, twirling her, bowing to her, touching her.

Suddenly, the music stopped, breaking her spell. Kalen bowed once more, as she opened her eyes. Then, pulling her hand to his arm, he led her back toward Merrick and said quietly, "It's a good thing I like my king, or else I might take offense to you dancing with him and not me."

Juliana gasped. Heat flamed her face. How did he know she imagined Merrick? "How…?"

Kalen's dark purple eyes sparkled with mischief and he merely winked. "I relinquish her to you, King Merrick."

Merrick touched her and she felt a spark. She looked at her arm. The dance had quickened her pulse and imagining him had only made her want him more. Her lips tingled and she wished she had the nerve to kiss him. The creatures surrounding them faded away as she stared at his lips.

Merrick did kiss her, but it was a bruising, hard kiss. His fingers pulled her jaw, keeping her face upturned. The action laid claim to her, but for some reason she didn't care. His mouth didn't move and his eyes didn't close. Laughter invaded her thoughts. When he pulled back, he said, "Come. Dine with me."

Merrick watched as Juliana danced with yet another of Lord Kalen's Berserks. Her flushed cheeks added a rose to her features and her shoulders weren't as tense as before. Each warrior kept their distance from her, respectfully not touching too often or too much. He'd called her the Lady of the Black Palace, claiming her as his own. To insult her would be to insult him.

"Tell me," Merrick said softly to Kalen. They were alone at the head table, so Merrick spoke freely to his friend. "Why have Juliana possessed to scream at you?"

Kalen chuckled. "To save her from being tested this night. My head swims with the thoughts of our elfin ladies."

Merrick glanced around in surprise. He felt their discontent but didn't dwell on it. He was king. They would do what he willed them to do or pay the price.

"They aren't happy to have a human set above them," Kalen said.

"What do I care? They cannot threaten me." Merrick took a drink. "They wouldn't dare."

Kalen sighed. "Ah, my king, you forget the delicate ways in which women can make each other suffer, not to mention us men. Women are delicate things—roses with thorns. Give it sunlight and pretty things and she'll be happy and blossom. Touch one wrong and she'll prick you. The wound will not kill but it will irritate for many days. They may not threaten a life or a crown, but they can make misery for those they choose to hate."

"You sought to protect Juliana?" Merrick asked. "You didn't know her."

"You chose her, my king," Kalen said. "You put her above all others, even if she doesn't know it."

"Then I thank you for making her stay in Valdis more tolerable for her."

Kalen smirked and took a sip of wine to keep from answering.

"So then tell me this, my friend," Merrick studied him, "if you are so sure Lady Juliana will remain here long enough to warrant protecting her. What is it you see?"

"Many things, my king," Kalen answered, grinning. He wiggled his fingers at the three beautiful singers. "Right now I see that pretty little mermaid singing for your hall. Methinks she likes me."

Merrick laughed. "Why am I drawn to Lady Juliana? What is it about her?"

"She is blessed," Kalen said, taking another sip of wine. "You have said so yourself. Perhaps you are drawn to the trace of power over her that came with the blessing."

"Then you see nothing more?" Merrick asked.

"I told you, my king, I see many things," Kalen answered. "But to know the future is to know madness. There are things that cannot be changed. Sometimes it is better not to reveal."

Merrick watched Juliana. She smiled and he felt jealousy that he was not the recipient of that smile. Kalen sighed, drawing his attention back. He could understand his friend's point, but he would still like to know what would happen. Merrick would have used the divining basin, but the future didn't appear clearly to him like it did with Kalen. To see something so muddled in confusion was worse than not knowing.

"Then do not tell me the future, tell me why I am drawn to her," Merrick said after a pause. "And do not tell me it is because she was blessed. I know that is not the only reason for it."

"The reason you are drawn is part of the future, my king." Kalen took another sip of wine before setting the chalice down. Merrick continued to stare, watching Juliana's eyes to see if they lit with promise of interest as she looked at her dance partner. Leaning to Merrick, Kalen whispered, "It's because she can bear you a son."

Merrick's heart thumped hard. No. It couldn't be. He looked at Kalen. The man wouldn't meet his gaze. No. It was impossible.

Chapter Ten

A son? Merrick took a deep breath. A son? He could not have a son. In the history of the unblessed throne, the Unblessed King could not have an heir. The kingdom passed from one king to the other with death. Whoever killed the old king became the new. It was the same for the damned.

Mating was hard enough for the elfin race, but for him? With the power he held? It was impossible. Wasn't it? Only the Blessed King had children to whom he passed his rule. Merrick understood it the moment the power of his reign entered his body, as he understood it now. Kalen had to be mistaken.

Almost desperate, he watched Juliana. A son? A family? He'd lost his family. Wolfe and Ladon were dead. Ean was his enemy, made so by an eternity of battle between blessed and unblessed. There could never be a true peace between the kingdoms. The unblessed, by nature, sought to undo that which was blessed. The blessed sought to mend what was unblessed. The blessed creature gave birth to nature and light. The unblessed took nature and shadowed light. The blessed gave hope. The unblessed created fear. Only death would relinquish Merrick of his throne and without misfortune and suffering, he would cease to be. Without the unblessed, the blessed would cease as well. They were two very different sides to the same world.

No matter how fortunate he started his life, the fear and hatred would eat at his spirit. Merrick was a necessary evil, but in the end he was still evil, held prisoner on the edge of darkness. He was feared, hated, blamed.

The wicked thoughts that people carried, their sickening deeds, this was his burden to bear. His very power fed off fear and misfortune. Ean's power fed off happiness and pleasure.

Out of the three great kingdoms, Merrick had it the worst. Ean would always know love. Lucien was not affected by hate or death. The Damned King drew pleasure from both. Merrick would know hate but crave love. His reign was made all the worse because he had known what it was like to feel the power that came from happiness, the energy that came from sexual pleasures, from being desired not feared. The Unblessed Kings before him had known mischief and fear and continued to know it after their coronation. But Merrick had known happiness and contentment. He had been loved by his people, his family. To have had it and lost it made his suffering all that much worse, for he would never be content again. That is why he would never know happiness. That is why he would never have a son. His suffering made him a powerful king.

Merrick leaned his mouth against his fist as he stared at Juliana. But if there was a chance that he would be allowed a bit of happiness in his dismal world, didn't he have to take it? And Juliana? Already she fought him, resented him. Was that to be the price of his son? Her hatred and disdain or worse, her mortal death? Everything in his rule came with a hefty price. What would be the price of this? Would the fates make him choose between his son and his Juliana?

"See, madness," Kalen said sadly, interrupting his thoughts. "Now you will be plagued by the unknown. Be careful that you don't squeeze her too tight, my friend, lest you crush her."

"I cannot free her from this. I cannot let her go," Merrick said softly, so only Kalen could hear. He watched Juliana dance. Just the idea of losing her tore at him. "I never could."

"Perhaps you were not meant to free her," Kalen assured him, though his face did not give comfort. "Fate chose for her as it chooses for all of us. It may not decide the outcome, but it sets the rules in its favor."

"A son." Merrick closed his eyes. Kalen was right. With just one small piece of the future Merrick could drive himself into the well of insanity. Yet, knowing this, he couldn't stop himself as he lifted his hand to the ceiling, pushing back the stone arches of his hall. The brick fell apart, floating up into the night sky, spreading so that he may see the stars. The torches blew out, leaving the hall to the blue moonlight streaked with the glow of the dragon's breath. His guests stopped, looking up in awe at his great magic.

Merrick stepped down from the table to get to Juliana. The wizard he made entertain them blocked his path. His old eyes looked up in worry. "My king, a moment of your time, please. I have come to plead with you. You cannot keep rearranging nature. You cannot know the cost of your whims. Already you have ended the seasons. Without the snow we see the forest—"

"Then bring back the snows," Merrick said, dismissing the man. Most wizards were zealots, forever worrying. They served their purpose, but would never know the things Merrick did.

"But, the stars here," the man persisted, "you cannot rearrange the heavens without consequence."

"Kalen," Merrick said. Kalen stood. Merrick gestured to the man. "Do not question my whims again, wizard. If you seek my council then you will ask for an audience."

"But, my king, you do not take audience. We have tried. Please—" The wizard gasped as Kalen took his arm and escorted him from the hall.

Merrick ignored him. Juliana stared up at the stars, her mouth agape with amazement. He liked the look of awe on her features, everything he took for granted was so spectacular to her eyes. He found he liked performing small tricks just to watch her face. Lightly, he touched her arm, drawing her pretty eyes to him. The blue was much like that of the nighttime heavens. Her smile fell slightly. Merrick motioned to the singers, ordering them to sing. The hall was quiet as he took her into his arms.

Juliana shivered as Merrick touched her. He was looking at her intently, in a way she'd never seen before. His hand lifted, taking her fingers up as he pulled her close to his body. She struggled, trying to pull free. He didn't let go and she was frightened by the way his closeness made her feel.

He slowly circled, taking her with him in the elfin dance she'd seen the others do. Only when he moved, it was slower, more seductive. One hand gripped the small of her back, holding her close, the other pulled along their sides. She felt his body pressing into hers, swaying against hers in little caresses. She glanced around, seeing the eyes of the hall on her. Merrick lifted her hand with his, using his finger to tip her chin up, drawing her gaze back to him.

"They do not matter," he said so only she could hear. "You dance with me now."

Her fingers dug into his hand as he turned her. The ground beneath her feet shifted and the stone slowly lifted them above the others. She trembled, glancing down at the hall floor. The dragon's breath grew closer, surrounding them as it passed like they were inside a bubble. Juliana gasped, hiding her face in Merrick's chest as she clung to him. The fire did not burn but she felt its warmth. When she pulled back, he was studying her intently.

"You still don't believe I will protect you, do you?" he asked.

Juliana didn't dare answer. She stared at him, worrying her lip with her teeth, as she tried to peek at the dragon. Another gush of fire surrounded them. She tensed, unable to help it.

"Am I your enemy, Juliana?" Merrick's voice was so gentle she barely heard him.

"Yes," she answered. "You hold me prisoner, so that must mean you're my enemy."

"Then it is done," he said.

"What is done?" Juliana shivered.

"All that you've asked of me."

Juliana was quiet, unsure as to what she should say.

"I've done what you asked of me. You controlled me. I let you. You commanded me. You called to me. Do you see what I have done for you, Juliana?" Merrick asked, studying her face. He pulled her hand with his to her cheek, caressing her. His arm tightened along her waist, forcing her tight to his chest. "I have done everything you wanted of me."

She bit the inside of her lip, breathing hard, as she glanced down again. The floor was far away, the people below them so small.

The stars were bright, close, breathtaking. The light of the dragon's fire surrounded them in flames and her world alternated between fire and night. It was the most beautiful thing she'd ever seen. She looked at Merrick. No. He was the most beautiful thing she'd ever seen.

"I have been your hostage, Juliana. You wanted me to rescue you from your fate. I *have* rescued you, for your fate has changed since that day in Bellemare's garden. You asked for an adventure, I gave it to you. You wanted me to take you away to foreign lands. I have done that. You asked me to show you the castles of your enemies. You call me an enemy and here is my castle. You asked to dance under the stars by the light of a dragon's breath. There is your dragon, my lady, and there are your stars. I have done everything you asked. Now I would have you do your part."

Juliana's whole body shook. She had said those things, but she thought she was alone in the gardens. The words were merely the wistful daydreams of a silly girl. She didn't know he listened. "I did not ask you to hurt Eadward."

Merrick let her go. His eyes narrowed, boring into her. She stumbled back and he took an aggressive step forward. To her amazement, her foot landed on stone. As she walked, a path materialized under her feet. She shook, her steps hesitated by fear. The fire continued to light the night, weaving snakelike paths around them.

Merrick stalked her, almost desperately, gesturing wide as he spoke, "I gave you the adventure you begged for. I had the wizards end the snow. I kept the dragon from attacking you again. I protected you. I did all this for you. I have done what you asked and still I am your enemy. Do you think I summon the very stars for everyone? I do not rearrange my world for just anyone. And yet I have rearranged it all for you. I'm exhausted, Juliana."

"Free me from this, Merrick." Juliana looked down. There was no escaping the high perch.

Merrick stepped to her, pulling her once more into his dance. "You haunt me. I can never let you go. Don't you understand that? I gave you what you wanted and now you must give me what I asked for. I'm tired of you fighting me. I have kept my part of the bargain."

"My undying loyalty for an eternity," she said, recalling his words.

"Yes," he whispered, drawing her closer, spinning faster until everything but his face blurred. "Love me as your king. Fear me. Obey me. Stay here with me and I will give you everything you desire so long as it does not go against my will."

"I'm mortal. I cannot stay an eternity." Juliana looked down to the spinning floor. Merrick cupped her chin, drawing her eyes back up to his.

"Here," he said, "here you can. I can suspend time for you. You will look as you do now, forever. Promise me you will never leave the Black Palace without me. Swear it to me. Give me your word. Let my powers feed off your fear of me. Let me have all of you, Juliana."

Live forever by Merrick's side? Why? It wasn't as if he loved her. Did he? Could he? What was he asking of her? "Why?"

"I can give you everything you desire, but you can never leave me," he said. "You must belong to me. You have only me to fear, if you so wish. My subjects will not hurt you. I will protect you."

"Why?" she insisted.

"Do not seek those answers. They will not be what you wish to hear." He spun her faster, pulling her to his chest. The stars made white streaks across the fiery heavens. "I have my reasons."

"I must have an answer." Dizzy, she closed her eyes. He slowed his spins, stopping completely. She felt weak. As her knees gave out, he held her up.

"I would have you ease the burden of my days. I want you to be here, ever faithful by my side, no matter what I do, as trapped as I by my life." Merrick's voice was pained. The loneliness in him called to her.

"You tricked me," she accused. "You said you took the children."

"I gave you the adventure you asked for." Merrick's grip on her arms tightened. "You walked out of the palace. I compelled you, but I did not force you. You accepted my offer by your actions. For that alone I can bind you to me, but it will not be pleasant. Do not make me force you, Juliana. Choose on your own."

"I did foolishly ask for those things and you did give them to me. I will not go back on my word. You will have loyalty Merrick, but loyalty does not mean I have to stay with you. I can be loyal from afar." His heart beat against her cheek and his body warmed her. Juliana wasn't sure why she agreed, but she was compelled to do so. Honor dictated that she keep her end of the bargain, but there was more to it than that. She felt connected to Merrick and the thin thread of hope that he could come to love her made her say the words. "I will never betray you to another, but I cannot promise to stay."

He pulled back, his eyes looking deep into hers. His mouth came to hover close. When he spoke, she felt his warm breath against her lips. "Promise me you will never let another man touch you. Give me your word that your body is mine and mine alone. Say you belong to me and will never deny me my pleasure when and how I seek it."

Her breath was ragged. The brush of his lips as he spoke filled her with longing. She wanted him, wanted the sinful pleasure she found in his arms. At the moment, Juliana didn't care. She wanted to be Merrick's, wanted to belong to him. If she did leave him, she would never be with another. He'd done something to her.

However, just because she thought to love him, didn't make it right, didn't make the emotion pure. It was a sin to lay with a man who was not her husband. Clinging to her sanity, she said, "I cannot give you that."

Merrick needed her to say the words. If she was to bear his son, he needed to know that it was his son and only his son her body would carry. He could not risk losing this chance because she'd given her body or her heart to someone else. Besides, he did not want to share her. She was his, had been since that first time he saw her pretending to slay a dragon.

He knew what he asked of her. He knew the life he offered and still he insisted. "Say it and I promise always to give you pleasure when we come together. I can make you feel for me. All I ask is that your body is mine alone, that you come to me willingly and do not deny me. If you will not give yourself over completely, then compromise and let me have rule over your body."

"You must never hurt Nicholas or my family."

"Done." Merrick held his breath, knowing if she pledged to him she would keep her word always.

Closing her eyes, she breathed, "Yes.

"Say it," he demanded.

"I pledge my body to you to use as you will. There will never be another lover in my bed. But I will escape you, Merrick. I will not be your prisoner forever."

Pleasure exploded in him. He could tell she was scared. He drew strength from her fear. "There is no escape from these walls. You have given your word. You are bound to me."

Screams echoed over the great hall. Merrick looked down to his subjects, watching as they scattered.

"My lord! The enemy threatens the gate," Lord Kalen shouted from below. His voice was almost excited at the prospect of a fight. Several of the Berserks cheered.

"Are you at war?" Juliana asked him, clinging to his arms as she bent to look over the side of the stone path. Her fear grew, empowering him even as he hated seeing the worry on her face.

Merrick eyed her. It was curious that he would be marched upon the moment she bound herself to him. Caressing her cheek as he willed the stone beneath their feet to lower them to the ground, he said, "I am now."

"Why?" Juliana gasped as they were once more on the hall floor.

Merrick looked at her and smiled. Kalen came up to him, holding a gold arrow between his fingers and wiggling it back and forth. The arrow was a sign of war from Tegwen. "It was found before the main gate."

Merrick nodded. To Juliana, he ordered, "Stay here. Do not try to leave the palace. I will not be pleased if I must stop you."

Her whole body shook as she nodded in agreement. Merrick wanted to touch her, reassure her, but he held back, instead forcing a look of dispassion to his face. He couldn't be seen as weak. He motioned to Iago, ordering him to stay with her. The Berserks joined him as he strode from the hall.

Merrick climbed to the high round window, looking through the carved stone depicting the silhouetted head of a dragon. It was a larger version of the window overlooking the entry to the Black Garden. Outside his palace, down the long, rocky path, he saw a single bonfire.

"Things are not all that they seem with this war," Kalen said thoughtfully. "But I will gladly take my men into battle for you."

Turning to Kalen, Merrick said, "Send your men out."

Kalen nodded, grinning down at his men. He jumped off the high platform, landing on his feet down below. "Come, men. Let's play."

Merrick watched the warriors run from the palace. He knew he could join them, was not scared to, but there was no point. The real war had not started. Let Kalen's men have their fun this night.

<hr>

Juliana watched Merrick leave her in the crowded hall, followed by Lord Kalen and his barbaric looking warriors. When she glanced up, the ceiling was back to normal and the tapestries had turned to a blood red, embroidered with the scene of a battle. Surely, that was not a good sign.

"You show your fear too plainly, lady." A weathered voice broke into her thoughts. Juliana looked to her side. The old hag stood close. She smelled of curdled milk and rotted meat. A scar slashed across one of her eyes, closing it beneath a flap of skin. "He gains power from your fears."

Juliana tried to edge away from the woman, but the hag's bony hand gripped into her arm. Trying to get free, Juliana demanded, "Unhand me."

"It is you who caused this," the hag said before Juliana could step away.

"What do you mean?"

"You were blessed by Merrick's brother, King Ean, and Merrick took you from it. You were to live a happy life and now you are bound to darkness. King Merrick only wanted you to start his war. He cannot love you."

Juliana stiffened. Merrick didn't want her. He wanted to start a war with his brother. It made sense. It wasn't out of tender sentiment that he did those things for her. The war started the moment she bound herself to him. That could not be coincidence. She tore her arm from the hag's grip. Without speaking, she numbly walked through the crowd, making her way abovestairs to the bedchamber. There was much she had to think about.

"My king." Gregor bowed low before King Ean in his throne. His red tunic stood out amongst the lighter clothing of the creatures of his court. They were celebrating, for no real reason except to alleviate Ean's tension. It wasn't working. "Lord Kalen's army joins King Merrick in Valdis."

Ean closed his eyes, sighing heavily. So much for trying to relax.

"We found this at our gate," Gregor said. He set a black arrow on the floor at Ean's feet. Those gathered in the hall gasped. "A lone bonfire burns beyond the gate."

Ean stood, nodding slowly. He looked at the faces of his people, turned to him in worry, needing his wisdom and guidance. But who was there to guide a king? Ean took a deep breath and let it out slow. "Call the men to arms and summons our wizards. It has begun."

Mia looked up from Lucien's bed where he'd left her chained. A thin trial of fire came from beneath the door, snaking over the stones. The light gauze hanging from the ceiling fluttered away from the flames, parting to let it pass. The fire grew, forming into the shape of an old hag. The woman came toward the bed, reaching a bony hand to stroke Mia's throat down to her stomach.

"You look hideous," Mia said, her voice hard. She wore a red silk chemise that barely covered her body from view, as it molded to her skin. Even so, she was warm from the fire that burned in the oversized fireplace. Though the dark furs were soft, she was numb from lying in the same position for hours.

The hag's face shifted into a frown, as she waved her thin arm past her face. Her body shuddered and the glamour faded from Lucien. The bony hand on Mia's stomach was replaced by his dark flesh. "Better?"

"No," Mia said, turning her face away.

"You're still pouting over our fight?" Lucien laughed.

"You left me here," Mia said, quietly. "Tied to the bed."

Lucien trailed his fingers over her, teasing her flesh buried beneath the red silk of her gown. Mia squirmed, but she couldn't get away from him. "And so beautifully tied you are."

Mia didn't move as Lucien lifted his hand. A fiery rose grew from his upturned fingers. Lucien took the flower and drew it over her gown, burning the silk. Her breath caught. There was something seductive to his dangerous games. Smoke wound into the air, curling and twisting from where his rose touched her. He parted her gown, brushing it aside so she was left naked. Her body ached for more. Not touching her further, he stood, smiting the rose.

"Where did you go?" Mia asked.

"To a celebration," Lucien said, grinning. He laughed to himself, looking more at the floor than at her.

"Where?" Mia asked, her tone accusing.

"Valdis. Lady Juliana pledged her loyalty to Merrick tonight." Lucien glanced at her, motioning to free her arms. She pulled them to her side, sitting up. Tugging the chemise, she hugged it over her breasts. Along the floor, small figures made of fire fought each other. It looked like a human battle. Flaming arrows shot through the air at a blazing castle, and a knight fell down into the fiery moat, clutching his gut. The sound of death echoed faintly, punctuated by the clash of metal and stone.

Mia turned her attention to the bed, tired of watching his plays of death and destruction. She untied her legs while he was preoccupied with his battle. Standing on the bed, she turned her back on him and stretched her arms over her head. Her gown flopped to the side and she tried to pull it together to hide herself. The sounds of battle didn't stop. Warm arms wrapped around her from behind, pushing the torn chemise apart once more.

"Ask me what happened. I find I like telling you," Lucien said.

Mia closed her eyes, hating how he made her feel. "What?"

"Lady Juliana pledged her loyalty. She thought Merrick might care for her, but I let her know differently. She knows she's the cause of a war that has started between Tegwen and Valdis tonight."

"Merrick marches on Tegwen?" Mia gasped.

"Nay, the arrow of war was shot at his gate," Lucien said. "It has begun."

"You started a war?" Mia asked, pulling away from him. He let her go. "How could you?"

"Nay, I didn't have to start it. I merely influenced others." Lucien touched her cheek, caressing her with the backs of his fingers. "All the pieces are falling together so perfectly. An arrow was shot at Tegwen tonight as well. No one will ever know who started the war and why."

"Why Lucien? Just let them be. Stop this," Mia begged. She searched him for a sign of compassion. Every once and awhile she saw a glimpse of something more in him, felt a conflict between man and beast.

"It is too late to be stopped. Merrick will send his armies to conquer Tegwen. King Ean does not yet know there are forces in his own home plotting against him. He will believe Merrick started the war. I will let Juliana be for now. Her anger will simmer and she will torture Merrick in a way only women can torture." The floor changed. The human battle disappeared, the flames growing to illustrate Lucien's words as he spoke. A figure of Juliana appeared before a fiery Merrick. The Unblessed King pulled her arm as she struggled to be free. "As soon as the damage is done between them and cannot be repaired, she will run away. Merrick will come to me to get Juliana back."

Mia watched Lucien's face. He was staring at his own creation. Merrick disappeared, turning into a miniature castle.

"Lord Bellemare will trade his soul for his sister's safety," Lucien continued. "Bellemare will fall into ruin, its blessing ended. My demons will rule Bellemare and I will control its armies. Darkness will spread throughout the mortal realm until it is so thick I can pass through the gates and claim it as mine. I will rule both realms, Mia. It will be a glorious time of death and pain. Mortals will worship at my feet, sacrificing each other to appease me. I'll be a god."

Mia didn't move. Lucien studied her strangely, in a way she'd never seen him do.

"You will be by my side to see it all," he said softly, almost tenderly. "I will make mortals worship at your feet."

Mia shook her head in denial. She could barely whisper the words, "No, Lucien."

"You reject what I offer you?" he asked, his eyes filling in with red. They still stood on the bed. Mia jumped off the side, running for the door.

Lucien was there when she reached it, blocking her escape. Angry, he yelled, "You came to me. You asked me to take your soul. I only took part of it and now you reject my offer?"

"Lucien, please." She touched his arm, gently patting him. Frightened, she reached her arms around his stiff neck, hugging her body to his. Her naked skin touched his chest from where the gown parted. He didn't move. She stroked his dark hair, trying to calm him. He breathed heavily, not moving to hold her. Mia rubbed her cheek to his, running her hands over his neck and shoulders. "Sh, Lucien, please."

"Love me," he demanded, his voice demonic.

"I do," she whispered. A tear slipped over her cheek.

He grabbed her chin, his fingers bruising as he pulled her face away from his chest to look at him. There it was again, that look. He was torn. "Prove it."

With a hard toss, he threw her to the bed. Mia closed her eyes, trying not to cry. She was in love with a demon. No, not just a demon. She was in love with the king of all demons.

***

"You tricked me into giving my word. You manipulated me, Merrick."

Merrick sighed, looking at Juliana's back. She lay on his bed. The room was his, but he'd been letting her sleep there. Now that she had pledged her body, he would not be staying away. He'd been up most of the night with Lord Kalen and his men. After the guests had left, they sat around talking, strategizing. The bonfire was abandoned. It was just a simple warning that Ean's men had been there.

"You look uncomfortable." Merrick motioned his hand, giving her a nightdress. Her gown changed to a loose-fitting silk chemise with sheer sleeves. She'd already taken off the jewels and he saw them on the table next to her toiletries.

She tensed, pushing up from the bed. "I'm tired of you doing that. I want to dress myself. I want to pick my own clothes. I'm tired of looking like a..." Juliana's mouth worked as if she tripped over the words. "Like a woman of low morals."

"I dress you in the materials of an elfin queen," Merrick stated. As he lay down, his clothing disappeared, leaving him naked. His crown faded into nothingness. He rested on his back, folding his hands behind his head. "Whores have no need of clothing."

Juliana's mouth worked, as she eyed his naked body. He winked at her, smiling. Fighting the urge to laugh, she asked, "Are you...saying you're a...?"

"Man of low morals?" he prompted. "Most definitely. It comes with the crown."

Juliana giggled, covering her mouth. She hit him lightly on the arm. "I'm angry with you. Stop making me laugh."

"What is it I have done now?" Merrick sighed. Would she never be pleased?

"That old woman tonight, the one with the missing eye. She said that you kidnapped me to start a war."

He said nothing.

"So it is true?" she said.

Merrick reached for her. She was always so quick to think the worst in him. But could he blame her? Everyone expected the worst out of him. He'd long ago stopped explaining himself, knowing it would do no good. For some reason, even as he resolved to let her think what she would of him, he found himself saying, "A war has started because I've taken you. I did not take you to start a war."

"Then why did you take me?" She moved closer to him. Her hair spilled over her shoulders in a messy array of curls. She'd taken it down on her own, but he found he liked the messy imperfection and did not change it.

"Kiss me," he said instead of answering. He expected her to refuse, but she didn't. Crawling over to him, she lightly brushed her lips onto his, making a soft noise as they touched.

"I shouldn't want you," she said. "I don't want to want you."

"I know."

"You killed my intended." Juliana didn't open her eyes. Her hair spilled along his face. "You've tricked me and manipulated me."

"Don't look to the past. It will never bring you peace." Merrick closed his eyes. His body was aroused, but that was nothing new. He was always aroused by her. Her smell surrounded him, so sweet, so soft. She was so beautiful, the one thing he enjoyed looking at in his world of goblins and trolls. "Touch me, Juliana. I want you to make love to me."

Merrick wanted her to get used to him, wanted her to touch him when she had the urge to do so, to not hold back. Juliana feared her feelings for him. Humans were strange creatures when it came to passion. They treated it like a curse. How could something that felt so wonderful, so completing, be a curse?

Juliana trembled, understanding what he was asking of her. The soft glow from the fireplace cast over them. She slowly touched his chest. It was late, but somehow the second he walked into the room, she wasn't tired. Exploring with her hands, she ran them over his flat stomach, along his sides. He was in top physical shape and, as she looked at him, she knew that would never change. He would always be as beautiful as he was now. If she didn't stay with him, her body would grow old. She would die a mortal death. His offer of eternity was tempting, but would his beauty fade from her eyes even as his body stayed the same. In a year, ten years, fifty? What would she think of the choice? What would he? What if someday he looked at her, or became angry and decided to take the gift back? Would she then wither and die within seconds?

"Make the flames blue," she said softly.

Merrick didn't move. The orange fire turned to blue, casting a darker light over them. She continued to touch him, rubbing his skin, exploring and memorizing him as thoughts swam in her head. His breath deepened and he closed his eyes. Leather straps wound out from the headboard as he crossed his wrists. Juliana's eyes rounded as he bound himself for her. The leather pulled his arms over his head, straining the muscles in his arms, trapping him.

She ran her hands to his throat, wrapping her fingers around his thick neck. "I could strangle you."

"Aye, but I am not frightened."

"You trust me?"

"More than you trust me."

Juliana leaned over and kissed his neck, nudging his chin up with her head as she replaced her fingers with her lips. She made love to him slowly, exploring every inch of him. Her fingers shook as she stroked his arousal, the two globes beneath. Even that part of him was strong, commanding. Merrick groaned, tensing and shuddering at her movements. His arms pulled the binds but the leather straps did not disappear.

When he didn't cause the nightclothes to disappear as he had before, she slipped them over her head. Merrick's dark eyes watched her, staring at her stomach and breasts as she came over his body. His wrists stayed bound, though his strong arms pulled tightly against them. Juliana relished the control as she moved over him.

Guiding his body to hers, she took him in. There was something powerful in controlling the pace and depth. She moved gently over him, raking her nails on his chest. Merrick groaned in loud approval. She kissed him deeply, writhing against his body. The tension built between them, rocking through her until she was thrusting harder and deeper. Their climax hit them at the same time, exploding in weak moans and heavy breaths.

Only after they finally came down, gliding into a state of numbing ecstasy, did the ties unravel from his wrists, freeing him once more. Merrick wrapped Juliana in his arms, neither one of them speaking as they fell asleep.

Chapter Eleven

Thomas moaned in contentment, his body more than sated by the faery ladies in his bed. Their small hands stroked his chest. They'd made love to him endlessly for days, until he could barely remember his own name. They fed him, bathed him and slept next to his side. It was a pleasant euphoria and he never wanted it to end.

"It is time to let him go."

Thomas heard the words through a fog. He groaned as the hands left him. His vision was misty, like a dream. He wanted them back, wanted them to touch him, hold him, kiss him. The faery queen appeared before him. Her wings shimmered like star trails as she moved. He blinked, trying to listen to her words.

"It is time to wake up," Tania said. "It is time to continue your journey, Sir Thomas."

"Journey?" he asked, not wanting the pleasure of the dream to end. His limbs were heavy, too difficult to move.

"Aye, Juliana awaits you in Valdis," the queen said. "You must go to her now."

"Juliana?" Thomas blinked, instantly sitting up on the bed. He grabbed his head, trying to clear it. "Juliana. Juliana needs me to go to her. We need to find Juliana."

"Get dressed, Sir Thomas." The queen laid a dark blue tunic shirt and black breeches on the end of the bed, neatly folded. Thomas reached for them. The material was softer than anything he'd ever owned. His boots

Michelle M. Pillow

were on the floor, cleaned. "Hurry, Sir Thomas, so that you may dine before you go. Sir Nicholas and Lord Bellemare await you in my hall."

Hugh glared at Queen Tania as she sat next to him on her throne. She'd barely even looked at him as he came into the hall, instead choosing to ignore him. The wench didn't even act like she'd done anything wrong. When he awoke that morning, he was unchained. A bath had been set out for him along with a change of clothes. The soft material felt nice against his skin, but he refused to find any pleasure in it. Its dark green color mimicked the color of evergreens. The brown breeches matched the color of bark.

A feast was prepared in their honor before they left. Soft music played. He was given a seat of honor at Tania's side, as if that made up for his imprisonment. Nicholas stumbled in first, looking sleepy. He wore a reddish brown tunic matching the color of earth and black breeches. Apparently, while Hugh was captured, Nicholas had been sleeping with nearly every faery in the Feia court. Next, Thomas came in a tunic of dark blue to match the night sky, looking just as sated and tired as Nicholas. Hugh glared at Tania. He was chained, tortured, tormented, his body denied and all the while Thomas and Nicholas were getting pleasured in ways too many to count?

"Tell me Queen Tania," Hugh said, his voice low and hard. "Why imprison me, but pleasure the others?"

He smiled when she paled, choking on her wine.

"Thomas, Nicholas, we're leaving," Hugh announced, standing before his meal was even finished. Both men nodded and stood without question. Thomas grabbed two pieces of fruit. Nicholas took a handful of nuts.

"You cannot leave," Tania said. "We're dining. You're being very rude, Lord Bellemare."

Hugh looked at her. Then, forcing a lopsided grin, he grabbed her face and kissed her for everyone to see. The hall was instantly quiet. The music stopped. She slapped at his arms and neck, trying to get him to let go. Even as she protested, her lips opened to him ever so little. It was a grim victory, but he took it, slipping his tongue between her teeth. Her lips were as sweet as he remembered and he couldn't help but intensify the kiss, thrusting his tongue deeper inside. If he had his way, he'd pull her into his arms and cart her away to a bed to finish what had been started between them. When he pulled back, he swore hoarsely, "First I rescue my sister. Then, I'll be back to settle with you."

Tania's mouth was open, but no sound came out. Hugh motioned at Thomas and Nicholas to follow before stalking out of the castle, intent on leaving the Silver Palace and the aggravating queen behind him.

❖❖❖❖❖

The morning was bright and the sun warm as the three men left the Feia. Their horses had been well tended by the faeries, but were restless to stretch their legs. Thomas watched Hugh, knowing his brother's mood to be sour. He didn't hear what Hugh had said to the queen, but the look on her face had been one of complete bewilderment. Or maybe it was the kiss that paled her already white skin. Thomas could well guess the reason Queen Tania did not let Hugh seek his bodily pleasures with the other faeries, but he wisely kept his mouth shut on the matter. Hugh would not want to hear it.

Thomas' head cleared by small degrees, aided by the coolness of the morning air. They didn't speak as they rode from the valley within the forest. Nicholas looked as grim as Thomas felt. The enchantment the faeries had woven over him was like the finest mead, making him forget everything important. To his shame, he'd forgotten Juliana, his sister, his blood. Even as he resented the faeries hold over him, he missed it.

Juliana was at the whim of King Merrick. It could only be assumed what the king would want with her. His sister was beautiful, smart, young. She'd make any king a fine prize. Already, Merrick had kissed her in the pond. Was it likely, now she was within his grasp, that he would leave it at a kiss? Thomas dared to hope his sister's virtue was intact, but he was not a fool to believe it. The only thing he couldn't reason was that King Merrick had made his sister travel to him instead of just stealing her away.

"Why shouldn't I make myself known? I know where we should be going and this way is not it."

The voice was faint. Thomas frowned, twisting in his seat to look back at Nicholas. Nicholas met his eyes, his brow arching slightly. Shaking his head, Thomas again turned forward.

"Oh and where might we be going?" a second voice said, slightly louder than the first. Thomas glanced around the trees, looking up at the limbs. The voices didn't stop.

"North."

"North?"

"Aye, north."

"And how do you figure that? The Black Palace is south."

"The muse told me last night in a dream. King Ean's armies are north and we're to go to him."

Stopping his horse, Thomas concentrated, trying to locate the voices.

"Shh, we've stopped."

"I know we've stopped!"

"Thomas?" Hugh called softly. "What is it?"

Thomas motioned his hand. Looking down by his leg, he slowly peeled back his saddle pack. Two small creatures sat inside.

"Oh, good day, sir," one said, tipping his head. Big, blue eyes stared up at him.

"Fine morning, sir," the other added, grinning, though his expression appeared a little nervous. "Gone for a ride, then?"

The first looked at his friend. "Well of course he's gone for a ride, Gorman. We've been on a horse for nigh an hour."

"You're sprights?" Thomas asked. They looked very similar to Rees.

"Aye," they answered in unison.

"I'm Gorman," Gorman said, "and this is Halton."

"That's right, I'm Halton." Halton pointed at his chest, puffing it up.

"I just said you were Halton." Gorman frowned, pushing his friend's arm.

"Thomas, who are you talking to?" Hugh asked, slowly backing his horse.

"It appears that I am infested with two sprights," Thomas said.

"Oh, nay, we aren't your sprights." Halton scratched his head, looking properly apologetic. "I know you want us, but you can't have us."

"We're spoken for." Gorman motioned between the two of them. "Both of us."

"We belong to Lady Juliana," Halton said.

"She's a little giant." Gorman laughed. "Poor dear, thinks she's a lady."

"Lady Juliana is a lady." Thomas reached into the pack and pulled out Halton by the back of his tunic collar. "And that lady is my sister."

"You're all little giants?" Halton asked, kicking his feet in the air. He tried to swing around to look at Hugh.

"We're human," Hugh said dryly.

"Ah, hum, that would make more sense," Halton said. Then, yelling down to his friend, he added, "You hear that. Lady Juliana is a human, not a giant."

"That's what I've been telling you," Gorman said, shaking his head. "She's too small to be a giant."

"But, you just said she was a giant," Halton argued.

"Did not."

"Did to."

Michelle M. Pillow

"Did not!" Gorman pointed his finger at his friend. "Well, I told you to bring Juliana to these men. You're the one who led her the other way."

"You'll not blame that on me," Halton said.

"Will to."

"Will not."

Thomas looked at Hugh. The sprights continued to bicker back and forth. When it appeared that they wouldn't stop, he interrupted them by asking, "What do you know about our sister?"

"We kept her from going to King Lucien's palace," Gorman said. "Hey, you want to let him down? He's looking a wee bit purple."

Thomas lowered Halton back into the pack. As soon as the spright was in, Gorman hit him, knocking him down, and said, "Did not and will to!"

They started wrestling. Thomas flipped the top over them and shook his head.

"Let's keep riding," Hugh said.

"Nay, wait!" A small hand came out of the pack. Thomas again looked in. "We have to go north to King Ean."

"Why?" Thomas asked.

"The muse came to me last night in a dream," Halton said. "She told me that a war was starting and we need to get to Tegwen. King Ean is the only one who can get you close enough to the Black Palace to see your sister. Without his magic you'll never get through the front gate."

"Not to mention his trolls," Gorman said.

"Oh, aye, the trolls." Halton nodded.

"And the goblins." Gorman rubbed his chin.

"Aye, and the goblins," Halton agreed.

"And the—"

"We understand," Thomas interrupted Gorman. He turned to Hugh. "What do you think?"

"William said Rees' kind was loyal. Juliana mentioned these two leading her in circles," Hugh said. "They could've been trying to protect her from King Lucien."

196

"Aye, that we were," Halton said.

"As sure as the sun is shining in the fiery heavens, we—"

"King Ean has blessed your family," Nicholas said quietly, cutting Gorman off. The sprights huffed, frowning at him. Both brothers turned to him, surprised he wasn't demanding they storm the Black Palace. "Perhaps it would be wise to seek his council before attacking his brother."

Thomas glanced at Hugh.

"Juliana is alive," Nicholas explained. "I would have her remain alive. She is what is most important in this. When she is safe, we will avenge my father. That is the way it should be."

Hugh nodded in agreement before looking down into Thomas' saddle pack. "You know the quickest way to Tegwen?"

"Aye," Halton said, nodding emphatically.

"Then you ride with me." Hugh reached in and grabbed him, setting him on the front of his horse. "But if you're lying to us, I'll hang you by your toes and leave you to rot."

<hr />

"My queen," Lady Roslyn said, flying high above the valley to join Tania on a branch. In their smaller bodies they could easily sit within the limbs of the trees, overlooking the great distance. "The birds tell me the humans travel north toward King Ean's army. The two sprights lead them."

Tania took a deep breath. She could still feel Hugh's kiss on her mouth. "Make sure the sprights find their way. It won't do to have them lost in the forest."

Roslyn nodded. "And Lord Bellemare? Shall we drug him and bring him back to you so he may finish the ceremony? Shall we let the others finish the journey for him?"

"Nay, you heard him as well as I." Tania smiled, touching her lips. "He will come back for me when his duty is finished."

Hugh shifted uncomfortably on his mount. All he could think about was Queen Tania. He had the strongest urge to go back and wring her pretty little neck. When he threatened to come back and finish things between them, he hadn't been joking. Only, he was torn between going back to make love to the teasing wench and the need to strangle her. Darkly, he mumbled, "Mayhap I will do both."

"Both of what?" Halton asked, breaking in his loud song.

Hugh shook his head, refusing to explain himself. That he could think at all above Halton's horrible singing and Gorman's incessant talking was a miracle in and of itself. The forest path was clear, the day perfect for travel and they made good time through the forest. Halton started singing again, louder this time.

"Hey, we're close!" Gorman yelled from the front of Thomas' steed. "See there. It is the yellow bird of Tegwen. It flies northeast."

"That's northwest," Halton argued, leaning over to the side. Hugh bent forward, keeping him from seeing the other spright. Every time the two talked it ended in a fight. Halton settled. "Follow the bird, my lord, and you will find Tegwen."

"And if the bird flies away from home?" Gorman yelled.

"Not again!" Hugh bellowed. "The next person to speak will find themselves ran through with my sword."

The two sprights were instantly quiet. Halton raised a finger to get his attention.

"What?" Hugh asked, irritated beyond measure. The fact that his sexual desires had yet to be relieved didn't help his dark mood. He hated the fact that he thought about Tania.

"You're really going to run yourself through with your own sword?" Halton asked, laughing.

"Ah, good one," Gorman called.

Hugh sighed heavily, not saying another word. What was the point?

Juliana wandered through the main hall, taking the door closest to the throne that Merrick always came from. For some reason, she'd been hesitant to go there. Seeing it was just a long passageway, she frowned in confusion. Well, Merrick had said to make herself at home in the palace and he never told her not to go wandering about.

The narrow hall was plain, except for the decorative arches overhead. From the pointed lancet windows in other parts of the palace, she could see the ominous landscape. The castle settled between the mountains and the great forest. But here, the view was of a path of dark stone leading to a walled courtyard. Even though it was day, moonlight cast outside over the path.

That morning, Merrick had let her pick her own clothes. She chose something from home, a conservative gown of soft blue linen. He quirked a brow at her request, but let her have what she wanted.

As she walked along the hall, she saw a door leading to the path. A small round window with the silhouetted head of a dragon was on top of it. Glancing down the hall to make sure she was alone, she reached for the door.

"Where do you think you're going?" Merrick said behind her.

Juliana gasped. Covering her heart, she said, "You startled me."

"You cannot go out there," Merrick said. "At least, not alone."

"Why? What's out there? A pet dragon?" Juliana asked, curious. She went back to the window, craning her neck for a better view.

"A garden."

She frowned. Her tone dry, she asked, "I can't go out into a garden without you?"

"This garden is very special," he said, stepping close. He touched her cheek, running his fingers along her jaw. His nails brushed over her skin, the longer length caressing her. "All may pass into its gates, but only I can find my way to the center and back out. If you were to go in there alone, I cannot guarantee I would find you again. The walls would keep you trapped within the never-ending maze."

"And what is in the center?" she asked.

"A divining basin," he answered, his voice dropping seductively.

"Like the bowl you showed me in my bedchamber?" Juliana willed his gaze from her mouth. She couldn't think when he looked at her like that.

"More powerful. All seeing. It can show the future, the past, the present."

"You can see the future? Will you show me?" she asked, excited.

"The past and present can be clear enough, even though you might not see all of the picture. But the future is a haze that is forever changing. The images are often unclear. Trust me on this. Knowing pieces of what is to come will only drive you mad."

Merrick's gaze dipped down over her body. She shivered at his intent look. "Now?"

He chuckled. "Always."

Juliana took a step back. She looked down the hall. "Here?"

"Why not?" He moved to follow her as she retreated.

"Will someone come by?"

He grinned. "Does it matter?"

"Didn't you say Lord Kalen was coming to discuss your war?" Juliana asked, almost desperately. He'd already made love to her once that morning. Though her body was more than willing to succumb to him, the idea of Lord Kalen and his Berserks walking in on them didn't appeal to her.

Merrick sighed and stopped walking. He nodded once. Gesturing that she was to follow, he turned to the main hall. "You're right, my lady. They come to the hall even now to dine. Come. Join us. I desire to have you by my side."

Lucien glanced around the great forest, before turning to where Gregor knelt on the ground before him. "You've done well, Commander Gregor."

"Thank you, my king," Gregor said, rising to his feet. "King Ean marches on Valdis. The war has begun. Now, I will have what you promised me."

"Soon enough," Lucien laughed. He gestured his hand to the side, not touching the light elf. "King Merrick will be within your grasp soon enough. That I promise you."

"I can't wait to see him choking on his own blood," Gregor spat, a look of impatience mixed with infinite pleasure on his face. "You cannot know how long I've waited for the day I would see him dead."

"You do realize that if you kill him, you will become him, don't you?" Lucien grinned.

"Aye." The lust in Gregor's eyes was unmistakable—lust for blood and power. It was for these weaknesses that Lucien had sought him out. A man driven by such greed was easy to manipulate. Gregor also wanted revenge against Merrick for some imagined hurt. That made him twice as vulnerable to Lucien's temptations.

Lucien turned his back on the elf and studied the forest. "Lord Bellemare is close."

"I thought he was on his way to Valdis," Gregor said.

"No matter," Lucien answered. He turned back to the elf. "Make the humans welcome at your fires. He will get you close to King Merrick."

"You're certain?"

Lucien frowned, letting the black depths show in his eyes. Gregor pulled away from him, stepping several paces back. Lying, Lucien said, "It has been seen."

Gregor nodded, not daring to question the King of the Damned again. He hurried away, disappearing into the forest.

"Hum," Lucien chuckled. It was almost too easy.

"His burden is great for he is the cruel side of pleasure and happiness," Lord Kalen said, twirling his wine in his goblet with a look of boredom on his face.

"Excuse me, my lord?" Juliana asked, shaken from her thoughts. They were alone in the hall, except for Volos snoring loudly in the corner. Merrick had left to answer the call of a goblin begging entrance into the palace. It had been only somewhat disturbing to watch him dissolve into smoke and drift quickly away from her.

"Merrick. His burden is great," Kalen said, looking up at her.

Juliana nodded once and looked away. Kalen said a great many things and though she understood the words, she didn't understand what he meant by them.

"The blessed have it easy for they are blessed. The damned are damned, but Merrick is neither blessed nor damned. He is unblessed, hated for the things he must do and for the mischief of his subjects. He is linked to his subjects. We bring winter to the mortal world and he is cursed for it because winter brings death. But death is as necessary as birth. It isn't his place to choose what happens, only his burden to bear it. We unblessed bring misfortune and suffering and bad luck. Without which you would not have fortune and prosperity. He is hated because his tasks are unpleasant. He is sworn against and feared because he is forever unknown."

"Why do you tell me this?" Juliana took a deep breath. She grew weary of trying to decipher who told her the truth and who tried to trick her. Her jaw tightened as she clenched her teeth.

"As far as the mortal realm is concerned, Merrick is not murderous, just mischievous, like trolls and goblins in your folklore," Kalen continued, as if he didn't hear her question. "Occasionally, their impishness results in death, like the tommyknockers misguiding those lost in a cave, but death is rare and never intentional. They bring bad luck so that people appreciate the good. Knowing this, you can reason that Merrick will not go out of his way to hurt others without just cause."

"I have cause to believe otherwise. You are his friend. Perhaps there are things you do not wish to see," Juliana said.

"There are many things, my lady, which I do not wish to see." Kalen lifted his goblet and drank slowly as he stared over the hall. The snoring troll snorted and wheezed, tossing on the floor before settling once more. Finally, the elf lord turned his eyes back to her. "Within his garden there is a basin. Look into it. See your answers for yourself."

"Whoever goes there will not come out," Juliana said.

"It is true that none but Merrick has entered the garden and returned, but that is not to say they could not return if they were to try. You must ask yourself, is the chance to know the truth worth the risk?" Kalen asked. "For I know Merrick will not tell you what you would know. His burden is great and he cannot see past it. He's watched everything around him die with his presence. Besides, he knows you wouldn't believe him if he was to speak of it. Can you see why he wouldn't even try?"

"Like the plants?" Her voice was soft. "They die when he is near."

"Aye, like the plants." Kalen nodded, as if she finally understood. "He's alone and he must bear the harsh deeds of others until his death."

"But, he's immortal," Juliana reasoned. "Doesn't that mean he cannot die?"

"Aye, should fate favor it, he will live forever. But that doesn't mean he cannot be killed. All things can end, my lady. Nothing is definite, least of all our futures."

Juliana nodded, but could say nothing.

"We can all see how you look at him. You fear him, even as you are drawn to his bed."

Juliana gasped. Instantly, she tried to deny it, "Nay, I—"

Kalen's rich laughter cut her off. He tipped his head back, letting the sound echo over the hall. "Do not deny it. You reek of him, my lady. His claim is all over you."

Stunned, Juliana tried to smell herself without being too obvious.

"Ah, perhaps reek is not the right word. You are marked by him. Immortals can smell it well enough. Do not worry, my lady, the smell is not unpleasant, just there."

Juliana stood, mortified the truth was so known and angry that Lord Kalen would be so ungentlemanly as to say it aloud. She tried to stomp off, but his words gave her pause.

"His power comes from fear. If you don't fear him, he can't have power over you." Kalen waited for her to turn before continuing. "He can be frightening, though, if you should tempt him. He can make you see things that never leave you."

Juliana stalked back to the head table, glaring at Kalen. "He is your friend. Why tell me all this? What do you get out of it?"

Kalen only smiled.

"Why would you help me?" she demanded, trembling violent. How was it possible she'd get angry at Kalen's help? It didn't make sense, for what he said would only benefit her. Still, her hands shook with fury. "What do you get out of it, my lord?"

Very straightforwardly, he leaned forward and whispered, "Merrick was never meant to rule our kind alone."

"And you think to help him?"

Kalen smiled. "Aye, I help him."

"You betray him."

Kalen looked upset. His jaw tightened in anger, but his voice was calm. "My army marches for him. He calls, I come. Do not speak to me of betrayal, human."

"He is your king. You are bound by duty to serve him." Juliana's whole body shook.

Kalen relaxed, the tension leaving him as quickly as it came. He stood. "Ah, mortals. You can never see things how they are."

"I'm tired of you people acting as if my mortality makes me stupid," Juliana growled. "I understand just fine."

Stepping around the table, Kalen came to her. He touched her cheek, stroking it. She refused to back down. His eyes flashed as it was the warrior who spoke, not the man. "Then don't be foolish. Use the knowledge I have given you."

Someone cleared his throat. Kalen and Juliana turned to Merrick. The king stared at them. Kalen slowly lowered his hand from her face. He looked unconcerned.

"My lady." Kalen bowed to her before walking toward Merrick.

Merrick watched Kalen leave Juliana. His gut was tight with anger and distrust, but he refused to show emotion. When Kalen neared, he said, "Gather your men. We ride into battle. Ean's soldiers have been seen marching toward Valdis' borders. They mean to attack."

"And the lady?" Kalen asked, not sparing Juliana a glance.

"She'll ride as well," Merrick said.

"Is that wise? A mortal on the battlefield?"

Merrick fisted his hands. "I can protect her. Do you doubt me?"

"Nay, my king, I do not." Kalen lifted a hand and placed it on Merrick's shoulder.

Merrick glared at him, still seeing the man's hand on Juliana's cheek in his mind's eye.

"But," Kalen continued, "she is a distraction. Besides, her brothers search for her. Ean wants her. Why bring them their prize? Leave her here where she will remain untouched."

"You have seen something?"

"If you bring her to the battlefield you will lose her forever," Kalen said.

Merrick stared at him, wondering if the man was telling the truth. He'd never been suspicious of Kalen before. His gut tightened. He was suspicious now.

"If you are worried, I will leave one of my men to guard her." Kalen gave a small smile.

Merrick tensed. "Nay. All of your men ride."

"As you wish, my king." Kalen bowed his head. He left the hall.

"Majesty?" Juliana called when he didn't move. Merrick closed his eyes. "Merrick?"

"Aye?"

"What did that goblin have to say?" she asked, coming closer to him.

"King Ean's army marches." He knew his words were clipped, but he couldn't help it. He was trying to rein in his jealousy. When he looked at her face he tried to read her emotions. He couldn't. "We will ride to meet him."

"You would truly fight your own brother? Your blood?"

"I would fight my enemy, the King of the Blessed. He is no longer my brother." Merrick took a deep breath. She stepped closer, studying his face. Her eyes searched his. He kept a passionless expression.

"He is your blood, Merrick. No matter what happens, he is your brother."

"Much has happened you do not know," Merrick said. "There are things which I will most likely never tell you."

"What can I do to make this stop?" She rested her head lightly to his chest. He felt her tremble. "What pledge would you have of me to end this? To never battle again? Is this really worth dying over?"

Merrick hesitated before lifting his hand to stroke her hair. The length was soft beneath his fingers. "You are the excuse, not the reason, Juliana. Just like the land, all things must renew. The season of peace must fall to the season of war. Peace has reigned for far too long and now there must be war. It is time. War is a necessity of peace. Without one there is no other. Immortals will die so more may be born."

Merrick ran his hand to her lower back, stroking lightly, thinking of his child growing inside her. He had no idea if the baby was there already or if he'd have to wait a thousand years to get her pregnant. Perhaps fate would be cruel and take the dream of a family away from him. Kalen's visions were only pieces of the future—bigger pieces than most, but pieces nonetheless.

Merrick had gone to the divining basin, staring at it. He asked to see the future, to see his son, in hopes of gleaning when it might be. All he got was the image of Juliana screaming, tears falling over her pale cheeks. Then he saw his own hands covered in blood.

"If I am to die, then so be it." Merrick wanted to ask her if she would mourn him, but refrained, unsure if he would like the answer.

He hugged her so tight that Juliana hit his arm to be let go. "Merrick, stop, you're hurting me." When he released her, she pressed a hand over her heart and gasped for air.

"I ride with Lord Kalen and his men," he told her.

"Nay, you…" Juliana bit her lip, not meeting his eyes. A wave of fear washed over him from her, feeding him. "I do not trust Lord Kalen."

"What proof have you of this fear?"

"None," she said, her voice small. "Just…do not turn your back on him."

"I trust him." Merrick pulled her forward into his arms once more. A soft music played and the stones of the hall shifted, lifting them a few feet as he danced with her.

"What are you doing?" Juliana looked at him as if he were mad. Perhaps he was.

"Dancing."

"On the eve of battle?"

"Aye. I felt like dancing." Wherever they stepped stones grew to support them and when they stepped away the stone disappeared.

"I don't understand you, Merrick," she said, even as she settled into his arms. "And it is clear to me I don't understand much of your world."

He twirled her around, enjoying the simple pleasure of her skirt brushing his legs, of her hair tickling his chin as she leaned her head to his chest.

"I want to go home." Juliana pulled back to look at him. "Please. I beg you."

"You are home."

"I want to go home to Bellemare. I want to be with my family. I want to see my brothers. I want…" She sniffed, a tear rolling over her cheek. "I want the magic to stop. I was a fool to dream of your world. I don't belong in this realm. I'm lost. I don't understand it."

"You would give up all I offer you to go home to Bellemare? Immortality? Power?"

"I have no power," she said. "I am your prisoner."

"Then ask me for what power you would have."

"I have never sought power. Such things are the pursuit of men. I long for a feeling. The type of contentment you get from laying on your back in a soft field, bathed by sunlight, knowing there is nothing better to do with your time. Those are the simple pleasures I long for."

She said the words and he longed for it too. It had been so long since he'd been free of responsibility. But where he wandered in the immortal realm, life did not blossom. The sun did not shine as bright as it had for him at Tegwen so long ago.

"Nay, my lady, your heart longed for adventure when I met you. You may not know it, but it longs for it still." Merrick kept dancing.

"Merrick…" She said no more.

"I must go." The music abruptly stopped as Merrick set her on the floor. His tone hardened. "I have a war to fight. You will remain here at the palace."

Juliana gasped as he strode away from her. He did not turn back.

Hugh eyed the elfin king, Ean's, encampment. They rode in without incident. It was as if the men had been waiting for them. The blessed soldiers stared as they passed, admiring the Bellemare horses more than studying the humans. Only one tent was set up in the clearing in the forest. Its white gossamer material fluttered in the breeze, looking to have threads of gold within its silky white. Through the tent walls, Hugh made out a lone figure on the ground. The man lay on his back, unmoving.

Hugh swung off his horse. Instantly a man was at his side, holding his hand out toward the stallion. Hugh placed the reins in the soldier's hand. The soldier dropped the reins and led the horse away without touching the animal, his hand uplifted under the horse's nose. After taking a few steps back, he stopped. Others gathered around the stallion, admiring it. They murmured amongst themselves, moving their hands to indicate the darker eel stripe over the horse's chestnut coat. Hugh didn't understand their language, but knew well the nods of appreciation the animal received. The horse didn't move. Hugh was amazed. His stallion was usually a spirited animal who didn't take to strangers.

The elfin soldiers were as tall and varied as humans, though they all appeared youthful and strong. There wasn't an old warrior amongst them. The only marked difference was their extremely long hair and the slight point to the tops of their ears. Most of the soldiers wore bright red tunics that hung long over their legs. They slit up the side to allow movement. Their dark breeches were plain and they wore boots, not so unlike those worn in the mortal realm.

Hugh heard Thomas and Nicholas dismount behind him. He glanced over his shoulder to see their horses led away in the same manner, only to be inspected. Nodding once to his companions, he moved to the tent opening.

"Come, Lord Bellemare" the man inside said. "I've been waiting for you."

Hugh brushed aside the gossamer flap and stepped inside. Instantly the noise from outside stopped, though he could see out of the transparent walls just fine. Thomas and Nicholas were on the outside, running their hands over the opening, unable to get in. Thomas narrowed his eyes in question.

His mouth moved but there was no sound. Hugh made a motion to wait. Thomas nodded and turned to Nicholas.

"I assure you, you are safe," the man on the floor said. His blue eyes opened to look up from the ground, where he lay on a soft bed of material. Long blond hair spilled over his shoulders. His tunic was similar in style to the red warriors, but the material was light blue with threads of gold. There was something familiar to the man, a feeling more than a recognition. It was the same feeling he got seconds after winning at tournament, a brief fleeting sensation that coursed in his blood after battle. Only now it was stronger, as if it emanated off the man before him.

Instantly understanding, Hugh kneeled on one knee, bowing his head. "King Ean."

Ean sat up. He crossed his legs, staying on the ground. "You know me?"

"Aye," Hugh said. He again stood to his feet. "By feeling."

Ean motioned that Hugh should join him on the ground. "You come to this realm for Lady Juliana?"

"Aye."

"I do not have her," Ean said. "Why come to me now?"

"King Merrick has my sister. I'm told you march against him. I would join your army in battle to win her back."

"My father truly blessed you, didn't he." It wasn't a question. Ean smiled slightly. "It is all over you and your brother. But, this other man. He is your knight?"

Hugh glanced at Nicholas. "He is a friend."

"And he seeks revenge." Ean nodded. "A cloud surrounds him."

"His father, Juliana's intended, was murdered."

"Mm, that would explain the darkness." Ean closed his eyes briefly, nodding in thought. The king smiled politely. "According to the scrolls, the Bellemare line has continued to earn the blessing we have given it."

Hugh watched the elfin king carefully. He had a likable manner to him. The tent was cool, as a breeze fluttered the tent walls.

"And William? He is a wizard apprentice."

"Aye. He is."

"You don't approve of this?" Ean gave a knowing look.

"I did not know of this," Hugh admitted. He got the impression he was being tested.

"I see by your clothes you've been to Feia." Ean chuckled as Hugh tensed. "I see by your face you did not partake of the pleasures of the faeries."

"Queen Tania imprisoned me and sent my sister to King Merrick." Hugh gritted his teeth, embarrassed to have been held captive by a woman.

"Meddling woman. She's still angry with me for denying Lady Lily and Lady Roslyn of her court. They both wished to be my bride. Because of their scheming, I cast them from my bed. Faeries are a flighty, vindictive lot, but their selfishness makes them predictable. Will you take revenge against the faeries for detaining you?"

"I am angry," Hugh said, "and will not make that decision today. I will wait until my temper has cooled and I can think on it logically."

"You're honest and fair." Ean stood and reached out his hand, fingers up. Hugh rose to his feet and hesitated before copying the movement. Ean pressed his palm forward. "You may ride with us, Lord Bellemare."

"Thank you, your majesty," Hugh said, bowing. When he pulled up the tent was gone.

"He has passed!" Ean announced. The warriors cheered. Ean clapped Hugh on the shoulder. "Come."

"I have passed what, your majesty?" Hugh asked.

"The place of truth. If you were to lie to me, it would have collapsed upon us." Ean shrugged. "An honest man will have honest pursuits. Now, come, let us eat. For tomorrow we fight." Then, throwing back his head, he laughed, "And do not worry. We have no women with which to torture you. Tonight, there will be no faeries."

Chapter Twelve

Gregor ran through the dark forest, light on his feet as he jumped over fallen logs. The path he chose was rough, but he dare not take the trail. Once between the two armies, he stopped, unable to see either side. Drawing back his longbow, he held his breath, firing a flaming arrow at first Merrick's and then Ean's camps. Then, without pause, he ran back to camp just in time to hear the guards call out the first warnings. He blended easily into the busy encampment completely unsuspected of foul deeds, as King Ean's men readied for war. No one would ever know who started the war, for Gregor had shot both a golden arrow and a black.

The first blows of battle struck the earth at dawn, just as stretches of pink light spread over the forest. Lucien watched it all from his perch high above, grinning widely at that which he'd brought about. Flitting over the forest, he saw everything but did not interfere.

King Merrick raised his sword high. He yelled, leading his men toward Ean's army. Lord Kalen and his Berserks were right behind him, their hideous curses calling over the battlefield. The noise accompanied the sound of breaking bones, as trolls joined Merrick's attack. The ugly creatures swung their giant clubs to crush the enemy. Goblins hid in trees, jumping down to distract the light elves as Merrick and his dark elves gained the upper hand.

King Ean, no less brave, met his brother's men head on. The forest echoed with the sound of war, metal clashing against metal. Screams pitched against dying screams as immortal lives ended early. Fires were set by two meddlesome sprights with a powerful wand, blazing the trees with a sudden fierceness like giant bonfires against the morning. As the battle between blessed and unblessed raged, gnomes, faeries and pixies worked to put out the fires before they spread.

Lucien threw back his head and laughed. The fruition of his plans was well upon him. Soon he would rule not only the mortal and immortal realms, he'd be a god amongst them all.

Lord Bellemare, Sir Thomas and Sir Nicholas fought bravely from atop their steeds, breaking through the lines to pass near King Merrick's encampment with a group of Ean's guards. There they found nothing but the trampled grounds and discarded tents. Juliana was nowhere to be seen. Having no choice, they fought back through the lines to rejoin Ean's troops. The light elfin soldiers went their own route, taking on Merrick's army from behind.

"There!" Hugh yelled, pointing to an opening in the trees. He rode his horse through, hearing the thundering hooves of Thomas' and Nicholas' mounts behind him. Hugh glanced over his shoulder as he made a small clearing. Nicholas was pinned on the other side of the opening, blocked by two large trolls. A third, pockmarked troll lumbered from the trees, coming up behind Thomas. "Thomas! Left!"

Hugh jerked the reins, turning his horse sharply to ride back toward his brother. Thomas swung, his sword cracking against the troll's club. The weapon splintered, throwing Thomas from his horse. The troll clubbed the horse, sending it flying through the air. Hugh dodged the animal, hearing it thud and skid behind him. Nicholas managed to break through to join them.

Hugh rode hard for Thomas, reaching out his hand. Thomas latched onto Hugh's wrist and swung up behind him.

The pockmarked troll swung again, striking Thomas in the back, sliding him hard into Hugh. They were pushed off the steed. The stallion kept running as a nearby tree burst into flames. Its neigh of panic echoed over the small clearing.

Hugh pushed up from the ground, rolling Thomas off his back. Nicholas fought the troll, screaming at it as he swung his sword. The other two had disappeared. Slime spat from the pockmarked troll's large mouth as he yelled back. Suddenly, the creature stopped, his eyes widening. Without obvious reason, the fierce creature turned and ran away.

"Thomas," Hugh cried, wiping the blood trailing from his brother's mouth. Thomas' eyes stared up at the sky, unmoving. His body was twisted at a strange angle and his chest quivered with each shallow breath. "Nicholas, help me!"

Instantly, Nicholas was at his side. He stared down at Thomas' broken body. The fallen man coughed, spewing blood out of his mouth. His breath became a long hiss.

"Thomas?" Hugh said, feeling helpless. He reached to touch him, only to draw his hands back. Thomas' hand twitched and Hugh grabbed it, squeezing. "Thomas."

"Hugh, we cannot leave him to suffer like this," Nicholas said. "I would not want to be left in such a manner."

"Argh!" Hugh's whole body jerked as he yelled. A tear trailed down his face. Shaking, he nodded. Nicholas lifted his sword up into the air, blade down. He trembled as he aimed the weapon over Thomas' heart. Hugh grabbed hold of the sword's hilt. "He is my brother. I will do it."

Nicholas relinquished the sword, nodding once. He jutted his chin bravely into the air. His chest rose with heavy pants. Quietly, he swore, "You will be avenged, my friend."

"You've lived well, my brother," Hugh whispered. He lifted the sword. "May you be greeted by pretty women and stout mead on the other side."

Juliana grew tired of pacing the castle. Merrick and his men had gone. Even most of the goblins had left with him, leaving her with Iago. She couldn't believe it. Merrick had walked out on her with no real farewell. Every second since, she'd feared that she might not see him again. In the moments the fear was at its worst, she'd think of a hundred things she'd want to say to him if she ever got the chance. Then, she'd remember all the reasons she'd never say them. She was held captive by him. He never denied killing Eadward and his reasons for keeping her were vague. Or maybe it was that she didn't want to admit he had no real reason for keeping her, that his reason wasn't because he had any feelings for her.

Merrick was so different than the men she had known. Least of which was the way he made her heart race and the thoughts drain from her head when he was near. Just thinking about him made her dizzy. There was so much about the immortal realm she didn't understand. She was so confused.

When she wasn't thinking of King Merrick, her thoughts turned to Thomas and Hugh. As the days passed and they did not come for her, she began to worry they would never come. Were they at Feia? Had something happened to them? Juliana knew they would never willingly leave her behind. She swallowed, nervous, praying they were far away from the battle this day. They were mortals in a world of magic.

The uncertainty of not knowing what was happening was too much. Tears of worry pooled in her eyes, but she did not cry out. Fear ate at her until she was sick to her stomach and just the mere thought of eating made her nauseous. It didn't help her appetite that Iago gleefully swallowed live slugs before her.

She thought of Kalen's words. Is the chance to know the truth worth the risk?

There was one chance to discover all she wanted to know. But did she dare go to the garden? Did she trust Merrick to find her if she didn't make it out? Could he find her? Did he trick her about the garden as he'd tricked her about other things? Juliana closed her eyes. She had to know what was going on. What she imagined had to be much worse.

Evading Iago was easy. The goblin was asleep before the fire, curled into a ball on the stone floor, his leg twitching like a dog. She went to the hall leading to the garden. The castle seemed abnormally quiet as she made her way to the door. Stopping, she looked out of the window at the path. The shadowed black stone and tall walls didn't look that frightening. Her hands shook and she didn't move for a long time.

"I have to know," she told herself. Juliana pushed the door. Moonlight streamed down from above. The moon was bright in the sky, though it was day. Realizing it was the first time she'd walked out of the palace since her arrival, she turned, looking up. The castle loomed before her. The hooked spires curled into the moonlit sky, frighteningly twisted against the cloudy heavens. A slight breeze hit her as she stepped backward, stirring her tunic gown about her legs. The clouds rolled across the sky and the spires seemed to shift and move in the breeze.

Holding her breath, she glanced around. A side yard extended from both sides of the black cobblestone. A dark wall encased the area, making it impossible to see out. She stepped to the edge of the path, trying to see into the corner where the castle met the wall. Her toe kicked a rock. Instead of bouncing into the cut grass, it disappeared. She gasped, her legs shaking as she fell down on the pathway. She sat on her knees, trying to catch her breath. Her heart raced out of control. Taking a stone, she threw it against the far wall. It bounced off the stone with a clink before it too fell through the yard.

"A glamour," Juliana whispered, somehow comforted to hear her own voice in the silent night. She reached out, dipping her hand down into the yard. It fell through. She jerked it back. "I can't do this."

Juliana tried to edge back, but when she glanced over her shoulder, the door to the palace was gone. She was trapped. The pointed lancet windows gave off a soft orange glow from within, helping to light her way. It was too late to turn back. She had but one choice. She had to go forward.

She crawled a few paces over the path before getting the nerve to stand. The arched entryway to the garden didn't change as she stepped carefully through it. The path veered off in several directions. Knowing she needed to get to the center, she went straight. The plants along the walls were withered and neglected. She lightly touched the vines, only to quickly draw her hand back. Thorns as sharp as blades edged the vines. Every few feet the path would offer her another direction. She kept forward. Then, the path stopped. When she turned around, the way was blocked. The maze had changed.

Juliana bit her lip, listening. The night was quiet. She could not hear the stones shift and move. She took another route, trying to work her way toward the center. It was no use. Every turn was a dead end. When she tried to backtrack, the maze was different. She was truly lost.

In a panic, she ran faster, trying to beat the changing walls. The thorns snagged her gown and she tore it away, screaming in frustration. The gown snagged on the other side and was stuck. She jerked it wildly to free it. After several pulls it gave loose. She fell back against the thorns, slicing her upper arm.

Juliana squeezed her eyes shut against the pain. She felt warmth dripping on her hand and had to look. Blood ran down her arm, covering the back of her hand and dripping onto the stone floor. Jerking at her skirt, she tore off a long strip.

This time when the stone moved, she heard it. Juliana glanced up. Where her blood splattered on the vines, crimson flowers bloomed. They were the color of her blood, looking almost liquid in the moonlight. The path opened around the flowers, pulling apart. Shaking, she stood and stepped through. Her arm still dripped and flowers bloomed up from the path where the droplets fell.

The wall parted again for her, opening up to let her pass. Her arm throbbed and she tied the wound with the strip of material. Each time she stepped forward, a new wall would part and open. Behind her, the walls closed. She kept going until she was in the center of the maze.

The center garden was a large enclosed circle, the ground covered in stone. It was plain, with a bench and empty vases along the thorny edges. Looking around, she saw that there was no way out. In the middle of the center garden was a platform. A giant basin sat on top of a long column. She went to it, ignoring the ache in her arm. Horrible creatures were carved into the base with human victims held within their hideous grasps.

Stepping on the platform, Juliana looked into the shallow pool of water. Her features reflected back to her in the moonlight. She glanced up at the dark sky. The big moon was directly overhead.

Glancing back down, she touched her cheek. She looked thin, pale. Blood smudged her forehead. She rubbed at it, but it did no good.

"Hello?" she said to the water. "I would like to see King Merrick, please."

The water didn't move. Remembering Merrick with the bowl of water, she tapped her finger on the watery surface. It rippled her reflection, but nothing appeared.

"Maybe start with the past," Juliana whispered. "Show me who killed Lord Eadward."

The water didn't move. She sighed in frustration. She'd come too far not to get her answers. Juliana glanced down at her bloodied hand, remembering how the blood seemed to open the walls. She lifted it up, tapping the water with a bloody finger. Red clouded the clear water.

"Show me how Lord Eadward of Tyrshire died," Juliana said to the basin. "Who killed him?"

The water glimmered. A light shone from within. Juliana gasped, a weak noise leaving her throat as Eadward appeared. The image was a little fuzzy, undulating on the rippling surface, but she could see him well enough. He was sleeping. She could see his chest moving, his lips quivering with breath as he snored. Then his eyes opened and they seemed to look at her. He had nice eyes, a kind round face. She wouldn't have loved him, but it would have been a good marriage.

"Is he alive?" she asked, hopeful. Juliana touched the side of the bowl, gripping it with her good hand.

Eadward's image turned from her. She made out the garbled sound of his voice, but she couldn't understand the words or see who he was talking to. Still seeing his back, she watched as he leaned over to a small table to grab a goblet. He lifted the cup to drink.

"Eadward," Juliana sighed, hoping he would somehow hear her. She may not love the man, but she did not wish him harm.

As the word left her lips, a sword glistened in orange firelight. Juliana screamed as Eadward was struck. She couldn't see the attacker but for his hand on the sword. The basin's reflection of the event was too fuzzy to make out the details of the man's clothing.

The goblet slipped from Eadward's fingers as the man fell back, a look of stunned horror on his face. He reached out, grasping the bed as he pulled himself away from the swordsman. The blade struck again, stabbing him in the chest, hacking at him repeatedly. Juliana cried out, covering her eyes and shaking her head. Eadward's head jerked and bounced on his shoulders from the heavy blows, even after his eyes lifelessly stared out from his face.

Juliana needed to know. She had to see. Opening her eyes, she forced herself to look. Her hand covered her mouth as if it could somehow protect her from the horror. The hacking stopped by slow degrees, leaving Eadward's mutilated body almost unrecognizable. Stunned, Juliana's whole body shook. Her brothers said Eadward was murdered, but this was too much. Whoever did this not only killed the noble, but hated him. The feeling of rage overwhelmed her, seeming to radiate out of the basin.

"Who?" she cried, hitting the water with her palm.

The water splashed, waving around in its bowl. The image moved, as if looking from Eadward to the attacker. An arm appeared from the sword and then a face. She stared at it, waiting for the water to settle enough to make it out.

"Nay," she whispered, not wanting to believe her eyes. "Nicholas. How could you?"

Blood splattered Nicholas' face and his eyes burned in a way she'd never seen. Dazed, she watched him pull off his tunic and throw it in the fire. Then, he washed his hands and his face in a bowl before dumping the water on the floor and smashing the bowl into the flames.

Nicholas killed his father. That meant Merrick was innocent of the death. Why didn't he say so? Why let her believe? Then she knew. It was like Kalen said. If he denied it, she would never have believed him. Hope unfurled inside her at the thought. Merrick was innocent of the crime. She didn't love a murderer.

"I love Merrick." Juliana gasped. The realization of the depth of her feeling hit her hard, making her heart thunder even more. "I love Merrick."

But if Nicholas killed Eadward, then were Thomas and Hugh in danger?

"Show my brothers at this exact moment. Show me Hugh and Thomas," Juliana ordered, touching the water with her bloody hand. She was so numb she could no longer feel the pain in her arm. A white light burst and she saw Hugh and Nicholas flying through the air. They landed in the forest, unconscious. Hugh still gripped his sword and it was covered in blood. She knew that they were in battle. Hugh's chest rose in shallow breath. "And Thomas? Where is Thomas?"

Instead of Thomas, she saw Merrick. Her heart skipped. He was so handsome. She longed to touch him, to tell him she knew the truth and that she was sorry for believing the worst in him with no proof.

Merrick glanced around. His clothing was marred with blood and his face contorted in anger as he looked down. The image moved, letting her see what he saw.

"Thomas?" Juliana whispered, not wanting to believe her eyes. Thomas lay bloody and broken on the ground. His blue lips didn't move. "Thomas?"

Merrick stood, towering over the body of her brother. In the distance, she saw the trees at which Hugh and Nicholas had been thrown. They too didn't move. She stared at Hugh's chest, but couldn't see him breathe.

"Merrick, why? How could you take my brothers from me?" Juliana turned away, not wanting to see more. For a brief moment, knowing Merrick had not killed Eadward had made her heart soar. But him taking Thomas and Hugh was much worse. Her heart squeezed as she fell down on the ground, unable to see more. She gagged, trying to breathe over the pain in her chest. Between ragged breaths, she swore, "I will never forgive you for this."

Lucien pulled back his hand mirror, smiling as he saw what Lady Juliana saw. How she got into the garden, he'd never know, but it was fortunate she had. It was easy to see the conclusion to be wrought by Merrick standing over Thomas. If he was lucky, she'd act rashly and kill herself before Merrick got back. Or perhaps she'd flee. Either way, Lucien would make sure he was there when Merrick needed him most, when the Unblessed King's anger was at its peak.

The battle went as was to be expected. Neither side had really wanted to fight, but they felt they were left with no choice. Gregor had done his job well, convincing Ean that Merrick wished to be at war with him. Unfortunately for Gregor, he was of no more use to Lucien. The King of the Damned sat back in his tree, content to let the battle unfold as it would. It didn't matter to his plans who took the field this day. Smiling, he let the hand mirror disappear into a puff of smoke. He couldn't have planned it more perfectly.

By the time morning turned to afternoon, the warriors were physically exhausted with no clear victor and many dead. Wounded soldiers littered the forest and search parties were dispatched to find them. As was tradition, both sides' remaining leaders met in the middle of the battlefield. Merrick eyed his brother. They were both covered in blood.

"Are you satisfied?" Ean demanded, charging Merrick and striking him angrily in the chest.

Merrick threw him off. "The battle is over, but the war is just begun. You got what you wanted."

"What I wanted?" Ean spat. Merrick turned his back on him. He couldn't look at him, not right now. Every death that day he felt. It was his burden. Ean would feel the loss, but he would never feel the death. "Don't turn your back on me. Face me you coward. Let us end this now! Between us."

Gregor stepped forward from his place of hiding, watching the meeting of the kings after battle. Seeing a body, he knelt down and smeared blood on his face and clothes, marring the nearly untouched material. Then, running the fallen troll through with his blade, he bloodied that as well.

"Don't turn your back on me. Face me you coward. Let us end this now! Between us."

Gregor flinched at the anger in Ean's voice. There was nothing he could do about it. Merrick kept walking. Ean growled but turned the other way. The Blessed King could not kill the Unblessed. Gregor waited until Ean's body blurred as he ran off.

The commander was propelled into action. He jumped from the trees and ran after Merrick. This was his chance, his time for vengeance. He charged the Unblessed King, striking out with his sword. Merrick turned on reflex, blocking the man's blow. Swords clanged, but no one was hurt. They squared off.

"Turn away," Merrick ordered. "Draw back your sword. The battle is over. I've had enough death for one day."

"The battle is not yet over," Gregor growled, attacking full force. He charged Merrick, hatred burning in his heart. Merrick aptly dodged the man's blows. "I am not afraid. This is a battle I cannot lose."

"Don't tell me you fight me over her." Merrick said in disgust. "Will you never understand it? Shyra is a whore."

"Only because that is what you made her." Gregor switched direction, trying to catch Merrick off guard. Merrick somersaulted out of the way before lifting up to stab Gregor through the stomach. Gregor blinked in surprise, looking down at the blade in his gut. It wasn't possible. How could this have happened?

Merrick ripped his blade from him. Gregor fell to the ground, clutching his gut. Merrick leaned over him. "Foolish man. Don't you know I cannot be killed by the blade? Now you will die for your stupidity. That woman was never worth as much anger as you gave over her."

Merrick growled and stalked off into the forest. Gregor looked up at the tree limbs in bewilderment. His vision was shadowed as dark, sinister eyes leaned over him, blocking his view.

"Lucien," Gregor gasped, fighting against the pain. "Help me."

"Why?" Lucien's mouth curled up at the side in amusement.

"You promised I could kill him. I cannot die here." A shudder of pain racked him. "I have served you these many years. I have done all that you asked of me."

"Aye, you did."

"You promised to help me kill him. You promised to give me my Shyra back."

"I promised King Merrick would be within your grasp and he was. It is you who failed, not I. And don't worry. Your whore Shyra will meet her fate with my demons soon enough. It is up to you to find her in the afterlife."

Realization dawned on Gregor. He jerked, fighting his fate. "You lied. You did not keep your bargain. I demand that you help me."

"Very well." Lucien knelt on the ground. Reaching forward, he covered Gregor's mouth with his hand and pinched his nose. Gregor's eyes widened as he struggled for breath. His hand gripped Lucien's arm, but he was weak from blood loss. As he watched, Lucien's eyes darkened to black. Heat spread from the Damned King's fingers. Gregor tried to scream, but fire burst from Lucien's hand, incinerating his insides. Darkness surrounded him and he felt no more.

Hugh pushed up from the ground, blinking in confusion as he tried to get his bearings. Hearing a moan, he turned to Nicholas. The man was standing, holding his bloodied head.

"What?" Nicholas whispered, squinting at Hugh.

Hugh shot to his feet, as his memory flooded back to him in full force. He ran into the field. "Thomas!"

"Thomas?" Nicholas repeated softly, before shouting, "Thomas!"

Hugh found the grass where his brother's body had lain, still stained red with Thomas' blood. He looked around the clearing for a sign of him, but found none.

"Where is he?" Nicholas asked, spinning in circles in his confusion.

"Thomas," Hugh yelled, not caring if he brought the whole of King Merrick's army down on him. "Thomas!"

"Hugh, he's gone," Nicholas said, grabbing his arm. "King Merrick must have taken him."

Hugh grabbed Nicholas by the tunic and shook him. Rage poured out of him. First Juliana and now Thomas. "He will not have my family!"

Nicholas gripped him back. "He will pay for this. We will make him pay."

Hugh let go, nodding. "You are a good friend, Nicholas. I've given it much thought and I want you to take your father's place. If you'll have her, regardless of what has happened to her, I wish for you to wed Juliana."

"Shouldn't we ask Juliana what she wants?" Nicholas asked.

"She'll do her duty," Hugh said, assured of it. "And I would have her close to Bellemare always lest we are needed to protect her from this accursed realm. We will combine the lands you inherit from your father with Bellemare's. Together we will build a fortress the likes of which this realm has never seen. We'll hire priests to bless every corner. These immortals will never touch our families again."

"Aye. I will take your sister as wife. Let us agree on it." Nicholas nodded, grasping Hugh's wrist in his palm and holding it firmly.

"It is done," Hugh said.

Juliana didn't know how long she lay on the hard stone before pulling herself back up to the basin. Again her image stared back at her from the water's smooth surface. Her eyes were red and puffy, her hair frizzed about her head where she had pulled at it. She did not recognize the pale, drawn features that reflected back at her.

"Show me the future," she said, dipping her fingers. "Show me my brothers."

The basin remained unchanged. Maybe there was no future to see. She looked at her hand. The blood had dried. Finding a single crimson flower on the wall, she walked toward it. Her head pounded violently, causing a horrible ache behind her eyes. The wall gradually parted to let her pass, the stone moving slower than before. Juliana didn't pay attention to her surroundings as she numbly staggered through the maze. She reached the black path, walking across without so much as a glance to the side yards.

"I wondered when you'd get back. I've been waiting a long time to meet you."

Juliana gasped, looking around the torch lit passageway. The voice startled her from her misery.

"Such a nasty cut. Would you like me to get that for you?"

Juliana spun around. Black eyes stared at her from a dark face and she swore she saw flecks of red dancing within their depths, the crimson color too deep to have come from the soft torch light. The man dressed like Merrick, in darker clothing. The material matched his long black hair. He smiled, giving her a sinister look as he toyed with a ball of fire in his palm.

"Are you a wizard?" Juliana asked, watching him control the flames.

"I've come to help you, my lady," the man answered.

"I don't need your help." Juliana backed away from him. There was something about the man's eyes, something hidden and dark, death and pain. Every fiber in her being told her to run, that this man was evil.

He twisted his hand, pointing his index finger upward. The fire trailed to the tip. With a quick strike of his arm, he drew the finger over her wound. The fire seared the cut shut and she cried out at the sudden twinge. When he pulled back, the wound was sealed, but ached terribly. She grabbed her arm, breathing raggedly against the renewed pain.

"Better." The man smiled.

"Who are you? What do you want?"

"Lucien," he answered. "I've come to help."

"I know who you are. You're the King of the Damned." Juliana continued to back away. "I don't need your help."

"And you're a king's whore," he spat, rolling his eyes heavenward. "Please, let us not dwell on titles. I do not judge you for your sins. I embrace you for them."

"I ask you again. What do you want?" Juliana's back hit the door leading to the hall. It was closed. Reaching her hand to the handle, she pulled. It wouldn't open. Lucien loomed closer.

"And I answer again. I come to help you." Lucien smirked.

"I don't need your help, nor do I want it. Leave this place at once. King Merrick—"

"You aren't curious as to my offer?" He affected a small pout, the very look mocking her fear of him.

"Nay."

"Even if it's to avenge your brother's death?" he asked, tilting his head to the side knowingly.

Juliana felt as if he'd slapped her. She couldn't move. Her hand dropped from the handle to stare at him. In that moment, she'd listen to anything.

Lucien stepped closer, leaning over to whisper against her ear. His hand cupped her face, as gentle as a lover's caress. He rubbed his smooth cheek to hers. "Mm, you know Merrick killed him, don't you? Your beloved Thomas is dead."

Juliana's mouth trembled, but no sound came out. She couldn't speak. Tears ran down her face and Lucien caressed them, rubbing his thumb over her cheek to smear the moisture around.

"I can give you the power to avenge Thomas." Lucien pushed his fingers into her hair. Pulling back, he studied her face. His voice was soft, sweet, tempting.

"Is Hugh…?" Juliana trembled, thinking of him lying on the ground, unmoving.

"Aye. He's dying. There is nothing to be done for it. Go see it for yourself out in the garden if you don't believe me. I hear Merrick has a divining basin within the center."

Juliana cried harder, silent, heartbroken tears. It was as she feared. Remembering Thomas' broken body, she trembled and whispered, "I saw it."

"It is left to you, Juliana," Lucien whispered. "Only you can avenge them."

"What is your price of this revenge? My soul?"

Lucien licked her lips, running the tip of his tongue over the seam. The hand in her hair kept her from backing away. Her mouth trembled, trying to block out his taste. She didn't want him touching her, didn't want his lips kissing her. His touch repulsed her. "Would you give me your soul for this?"

Juliana tried to think straight. So much had happened. Hugh and Thomas' faces flashed before her eyes. She wished she was dead too, right along with them. Dead, she would never have to make this decision. Was there even a decision to make? She knew her brothers wouldn't want her to give up her soul to avenge them. "Nay."

"Ah, but would you give up your body? Would you come to my palace?" Lucien kissed her, thrusting his tongue just past her lips. She didn't move, didn't kiss him back. Juliana clamped her teeth together to keep him from probing further into the depths of her mouth. "Would you give yourself to me?"

Juliana knew her brothers wouldn't want her to give her body to Lucien for revenge any more than they'd want her trading her soul. She'd sinned with Merrick. Would God forgive her if she sinned again with Lucien? If she did it for honor? For duty? For revenge? "I want to go home."

"There is no home for you. Your brothers are dead."

"William," she whispered. "I have William."

"Not after Merrick gets to him," Lucien said, casting his eyes down. He let her go, stepping back. "He goes there even now."

"Help me to stop him," Juliana demanded. Her choice made, she said, "I'll give you what you want if you help me to stop him from hurting William."

Lucien closed his eyes. Slowly, he shook his head, gasping softly. "Ah, nay, it's too late. William is dead."

"Nay." Juliana didn't want to believe it. She pulled his shirt, shaking him. "Nay. Stop him. Stop it. I won't listen to you!"

"He kills your brothers knowing they will always come for you," Lucien spat, forcefully pushing his body into hers. "Now there is no one to come for you. You belong to Merrick. Forever."

"Nay. I belong to no man," Juliana said.

"Very well. Do what I ask of you and I will take you to Bellemare," he said. "Keep your soul and your body. Do this for me and that will be payment enough."

"Why are you helping me?"

"Does it matter?"

Juliana didn't answer.

"Take your dagger." Lucien lifted up his hand. In it was her jeweled dagger, the one her brothers had given her. She'd thought she'd lost it. There was blood on the blade. "Do not worry. The blood of the dragon will weaken him. Stab it into his heart."

Juliana stared at the blade. Could she do it? Could she stab Merrick? She shook her head in denial, unable to touch it.

"Take it!" Lucien ordered. Juliana jolted in surprise and quickly grabbed the hilt. "Good. Stab him in his heart to weaken him and then slit his throat to kill him. Think of Thomas and Hugh and William. Think of what Merrick took from you."

"I do this and you will send me to Bellemare?" Juliana asked.

"Aye, my lady." Lucien nodded. "If you kill King Merrick, I'll send you wherever you like."

Juliana didn't move. Her whole body shook with fear and anger and heartache. Everything she loved was dead or didn't exist in the first place. Lucien bowed low, his body bursting into flames leaving behind a puff of smoke as he disappeared. She was left alone in the hall.

It didn't matter that Nicholas killed Eadward, for she had seen his death with Hugh's. Merrick had killed the three things she had held dear above all others—her brothers. Even as she hated him, a part of her loved

Merrick, would always love him. Maybe that was his curse. She loved the part of him she saw in private. She loved the man, not the king. How could a man who touched her with such kindness be so cruel? How could she kill him? Then again, how could she not?

Mia looked up from her place lounging on the floor of Lucien's bedchamber. The fireplace surged and she knew Lucien was pleased with himself. That was never a good sign.

"I take it your war was bloody?" she asked, a little bitterly. She turned away, unable to look at him. How could she hate him so much and still love him?

"Mm, aye," Lucien grinned, "very bloody."

"Who won the battle?" Mia asked in dejection, knowing it didn't really matter.

"I did," Lucien said. He came to her, urging her to rise.

Mia obeyed, coming to her feet. "You fought?"

"Nay, I watched. Fate favors us this day, my nymph." Lucien grabbed her hand. Mia gasped as he pulled her into his arms and hugged her tight. "Everything is perfect. Soon Merrick and Lord Bellemare will belong to me. Either that or they'll be dead."

Mia closed her eyes. "Tell me what you have done, my love. Tell me everything."

Lucien pulled back, stroking her cheek. She knew he was studying her, trying to see her deceit. She leaned up on her toes and kissed him. Then, slapping his face, she watched desire flame in his eyes at the rough play.

Mia shot him a challenging glare. "I said tell me."

Lucien grinned. "Lay down on the bed and I will tell you everything you wish to know, my nymph."

Chapter Thirteen

Hugh bowed before King Ean. The image of Thomas' battered body was never far from his mind. How could it be, as only a day had passed spent collecting the bodies of the slain? Thomas' corpse had not been amongst them. Hugh was no fool as to believe Thomas lived. He'd seen the mangled body, heard the last of his breaths for himself. What Merrick wanted with his brother's corpse, he couldn't be sure, but the Unblessed King had taken the body with him.

"Rise, please, Lord Bellemare," Ean said. Hugh stood. They were still at camp within the forest. "My men have brought back Thomas' horse. It will be buried."

Hugh nodded. He wasn't about to argue over a dead horse. It seemed the elfin people had an affinity for animals and treated them with almost as much respect as they did their own kind. "Thank you, Majesty."

Ean nodded. "Our war is not over, but your part in it is."

Hugh opened his mouth to protest, but Ean held up his hand.

"I have consulted the wizards. You're not to fight with us anymore. Go to the Black Palace and do what you must to rescue your sister. I don't believe Merrick will harm her. I'll have two of my men show you the way, but they will not pass beyond the front gate." Ean motioned two of his guards forward.

"Thank you, Majesty." Hugh bowed low, his body stiff.

"You have proven yourself a good man, Lord Bellemare." Ean stood, walking down to clasp Hugh on the shoulder. He squeezed lightly before letting go. "The blessing on your home stands, so long as your family continues to maintain honorable lives. My advice to you is that you return to Bellemare and live out your days. Should you need my assistance, all you have to do is ask."

"And I, King Ean, am at your service." Hugh bowed again. He turned to Nicholas and motioned him to follow. Swinging up on his horse, he waited for their guides to show them the way.

"Wait, my lord," Gorman yelled, hopping down from the trees onto Nicholas' horse.

"We're coming, fresh from the fight," Halton added, jumping in front of Hugh. Hugh frowned at him as he blinked his wide blue eyes.

"Hold, my lord, where's the other one?" Gorman asked.

"Aye, we like him," Halton added. "Where's Sir Thomas?"

Hugh clenched his jaw. It was all he could do not to knock the spright from atop his horse. Instead, he kicked the horse in the flanks, sending it thundering off into the forest.

Halton gasped in surprise, flying off the horse and into a tree. He tumbled to the ground. Gorman jumped down after him as the horses galloped away. Rubbing his sore backside, Halton frowned. "He's in a fiery mood. Was it something you said?"

◈◈◈◈◈◈◈◈◈

Juliana heard footsteps coming into the hall of the Black Palace. As she looked up from her place on Merrick's throne, the sound stopped. Merrick stood before her, eyeing her curiously as she sat hunched in his chair. The goblins were quiet. They had been since she took the throne that morning.

"Juliana?" he asked, frowning. She continued to stare at him, feeling numb inside, watching as if she were in a cloud. Nothing had felt right in her since going to the garden. Merrick stepped closer. "Juliana? What goes on with you?"

Her breathing was loud in her ears, drowning out the sound of his voice until only a muffled thread of it remained. Grief pumped through her veins with every heartbeat until she could feel nothing else. She looked away from him to the arm of the throne chair. It hurt too much to see his face for she loved him still, even as she hated him. Her hand was still covered in dried blood. A bath had materialized for her in the bedchamber, but she didn't use it, nor had she changed to the gown that still lay over the end of the bed.

There was nothing left for her. Nothing but a mortal life without those she held most dear. She felt the knife against her hip and knew what she had to do. But to kill Merrick would be to kill the last thing she cared for. Not to kill him would be to betray her family's memory.

"Juliana!" he demanded, louder, storming up to her. She slowly turned her eyes back to him and stood. Her body was stiff, jerking with each movement. Her chin lowered, she stared up through her lashes. A slight breeze blew and the banners over the fireplaces turned red. They dripped with blood, thick trails of it running down the walls. The fires grew in the fireplace, surging forth only to temper back down. Borc cried out in pain as he caught afire. Neither one of them turned to the goblin as he put himself out by rolling in the blood.

Juliana felt air entering her lungs. She felt the slight sting in her arm, the irritating brush of her clothing against her skin. But the sensations didn't register in her detached mind.

The sound of stone grating against stone echoed over the hall. The goblins murmured to themselves as a giant black angel grew from the hall floor. She had long hair carved over her naked back. Her stone wings wrapped around her body, hiding her arms, and her eyes glared at Merrick's back. Merrick glanced over his shoulder. His frown had deepened when he looked back at Juliana.

"Juliana?" he asked. "What goes on here?"

Juliana opened her mouth, but no sound came out. Blood ran from beneath the angel's wings at his words, pooling on the floor. It crept toward his feet. Merrick leaned over, touching it. When he lifted his hand it was crimson. He turned and the angel spread her wings. Thin red trails dripped from her eyes, nose, ears, mouth.

Merrick stepped toward Juliana, reaching for her. She lifted her bloodstained hand, mimicking him as she slowly walked forward. Her skirts dragged in the blood. She didn't care, even as her feet were swallowed up in the liquid warmth. When she reached Merrick's side, she said, "You have killed me, Merrick."

Merrick reached for her, but his hand went through her body, unable to touch her.

Juliana sat up in bed gasping. The fog was gone. Pain rolled over her full force as nausea rose in her throat. She scrambled off the bed, falling hard onto the stone floor. Finding a basin, she dry-heaved into it.

When she finished, she weakly sat back against the leg of the bed, staying on the floor. What a strange dream. It had felt so real. Slowly she stood. She turned to the bed and froze. Fresh blood stained the coverlet, trailing to her feet. She looked down, gasping. The hem of her gown was stained. Her slippers were covered.

"But it was a dream," she whispered, shaking her head. Tears streamed down her face. It was too much. She couldn't do it. On the floor was her knife. She picked it up and thought of her brothers. "My heart betrays them."

***

Merrick watched Juliana disappear. His hall righted itself. The angel disappeared, taking the blood with it except for that on his clothing and hand. The banners waved, becoming black. Something wasn't right and not just with the fact that Juliana had been on his throne. Or in the way she looked at him, her eyes passionless, dead. The blood had not been his doing, nor had the angel. They came from Juliana.

"Iago," Merrick bellowed.

Iago's short legs pumped as he ran to the king.

"What happened while I was gone?" Merrick demanded.

Iago cringed, holding his stubby fingers up over his face. His gruff voice echoed over the silent hall as he spoke. "I know not, my king. Lady Juliana has not been herself since before the battle. She paces the halls, mumbling, always mumbling. She goes mad, my king."

"You were supposed to be protecting her! Where did she get the power to move about the castle at will?" Merrick growled. The goblin made a weak noise and curled into a ball. Merrick slashed his hand through the air. He should have left a Berserk with her for protection. He'd just been so jealous over seeing her with Kalen that he couldn't see straight. "Iago. Fetch me Lord Kalen."

"Aye, my king, aye," Iago rasped, bowing profusely as he backed away.

"And mind you don't disappoint me again," Merrick warned.

"Aye. Aye, my king," Iago said. He ran from the hall as fast as his little legs would carry him. Merrick took a deep breath. His eyes turned up to the bedchamber. He sensed Juliana was there. He wanted to go to her, but had something he had to do first.

His body dissolved into a fine mist as he drifted down into the bowels of his castle—a place so dark even he stayed away from it. The dungeons were near empty since he began his reign, though a few of the truly evil who had transgressed against the past Unblessed King were locked up behind iron doors to wither away their eternities. The curved ceilings were low and Merrick had to duck his head under the arched doorways to pass through. This was a place he did not dare rearrange with his magic, lest something slip out from a cell and escape. The only way in or out was a small crack in the floor. Merrick could bring prisoners in and out with magic, but no other could pass through.

Coming to the end of the hall, he knocked on a metal door. It creaked on its hinges as an old, blind witch stuck her head out of the door. Her eyes were missing from her head. A band of white material covered the sockets, pulling tight to her short white hair. Still, in her blindness, she saw many things. The hem of her linen gown was tattered from years of wear.

The woman did not move out of the way as she pointed her face at Merrick. When she spoke, her low words were enunciated and raw. "What you ask of me is to defy the King of the Damned. His demons guard the gates and do not let souls pass without a heavy price. You cannot bring him back without risking one of them attaching to his soul. It is better to leave him where he is. One does not see the other side without becoming tainted by it, good or bad."

"What price? Name it," Merrick said softly. He folded his hands in front of his waist. He knew the risk.

She considered his words and then nodded, opening the small door to let him pass. The witch had lived beneath the castle for centuries, surviving in her little round room of magic. The large brick walls were overgrown with moss. Broken bottles littered the hearth. A stone ledge wound around the walls, filled with jars of herbs and vials of other mystical concoctions.

In the center, on a cot, lay Thomas' corpse. His face had turned a ghastly shade of bluish grey. The mangled limbs had been straightened and healed. Merrick looked down at the dead man. "Can you bring him back?"

"Aye," the witch answered, as if it was an everyday request that she reverse death. Then, cackling with laughter, she added, "But it will cost you, my king."

"Name your price, witch," Merrick demanded. He knew Juliana cared for her brothers deeply. If she knew Thomas had died in a war she believed to be Merrick's doing, she would never forgive him. Her grief alone would torment him, not to mention her hatred if she believed him responsible.

"I demand three things from you, King Merrick," the witch said. She touched Thomas' cheeks before running her wrinkled fingers down over his neck. Lifting his head, she cracked it one way and then the other. A loud, popping noise echoed in the room.

"The first?" Merrick prompted, studying his fingernail.

"A new gown," the witch said. She gave a toothless smile, motioning down over her tattered clothing.

Merrick sighed. Moving his hand, he gave her a new gown, just like the one she wore, only it was new and without holes. The witch felt down over the skirt and nodded in approval. Merrick again looked at Thomas, knowing they didn't have much time before it was too late. "The second?"

"A vial of your blood, my king," the witch said, grinning evilly. With a vial of his blood she'd be able to do much mischief.

"Two drops," Merrick said. "That is more than generous of an offer for this task."

The witch frowned and mumbled under her breath.

"The third?" Merrick asked.

The witch began to laugh. "That lady of yours, my king. She's going to ask you if you love her. Your answer will greatly affect her actions."

Merrick's breath caught. Juliana? She wished to know if he loved her? Did that mean...? Did she? Could she? He looked up toward his bedchamber where she still hid. Could Juliana love him?

"You're to tell her nay," the witch said, laughing harshly, "regardless of what may happen."

Merrick watched her closely. "Why would this concern you?"

"It doesn't," the witch laughed harder, cackling. She pointed in Merrick's direction, wiggling her finger at him. "But I love to see misery."

"It matters not to me. Just do it, witch," Merrick ordered. He turned to go.

"Ah, the blood," she said, breathing erratically in anticipation. She licked her chapped lips, moaning softly. "First the blood."

Merrick materialized a knife and poked the tip into his fingers. He let two drops fall onto the stone ledge. A vial grew around the drops, holding them in. "You have your blood, witch. Now bring that man back to life. No tricks."

"I am bound by my word, my king. Leave me now." The witch ran her fingers over Thomas' stomach and hips, feeling down his legs.

Merrick watched for a brief moment before taking a deep breath. He again dissolved into mist, leaving Thomas alone with the witch. There was nothing more he could do for the man.

❦

Juliana paced the bedchamber. Her clothes had dissolved to be replaced by a clean gown of tight, black elfin silk. The revealing bodice reminded her of the corset top she wore her first day in the Black Palace. The kohl lined her eyes and wrapped around her arm. The tight, straight skirt and high boots made it harder to walk back and forth, but she didn't stop. Clutching her blade, her hands shook violently. It was time.

❦

Lucien watched Mia kiss his chest. He didn't move, enjoying the pleasure of her tongue as she flicked it against his nipple. Everything was working out as planned. He smiled as she moved lower over his body. Suddenly, a nagging feeling ate at him and he sat up, knocking Mia aside.

"What is it?" she asked, clearly shocked by his abrupt action.

"Lord Bellemare rides close to the Black Palace. He should be with Ean's armies, not so close to the palace gates."

Mia reached for him. "You, yourself, said nothing can ruin your plans. Come back to bed. Let whatever happens, happen."

Lucien glared at her. In his irritation, he flung his hand through the air. Mia was tossed to the head of the bed, knocking lightly against it. She gasped, her eyes round with surprise. Then, growling, he turned and stormed from the chamber.

❦

Hugh glanced at Nicholas, reining in his stallion as he stopped to look at the Black Palace. A long stone bridge led up to the front gate. The spires curled like gnarled fingertips in the heavens, black against the grey night. Clouds drifted past the moon, shadowing the already dark earth.

"Whatever happens, if one of us can get out with Juliana, we go," Hugh said.

"Aye," Nicholas agreed.

Hugh was a seasoned fighter, but his gut tightened in apprehension as he urged his horse slowly over the abandoned bridge. Mountains rose up over the distance as they came out of the forest and to the rock. The horses' hooves clopped on the hard stone, punctuating the silence with their steps. Nearing the front gate, Hugh stopped. There was no guard along the wall, no way to get in.

"Look around," Hugh ordered Nicholas, pointing along the wall. "There has to be a way inside. We'll climb the walls if we have to."

Hugh dismounted, joining Nicholas as they tried to find a way inside.

࿇࿇࿇࿇࿇

Juliana found herself in the main hall. She thought of it and somehow she was just there. Such things had been happening a lot lately. Though in her grief it was possible she just walked the distance, too preoccupied to remember doing it. Aside from the abnormally quiet goblins, the hall was empty. She drew the knife behind her back, holding it out of sight of the throne.

"Merrick," Juliana whispered, staring at his throne. "Show yourself to me."

Almost immediately he appeared, materializing as mist trailing on the floor as he went to his throne. When he solidified, his legs lounged over the side as his body draped lazily across the seat. Tight black breeches molded to his legs, matching the loose linen shirt. His blond hair spilled over his chest. Dark eyes met her from across the hall. Slowly, she stepped forward, crossing the distance until she was before him.

"I went to the garden beyond the maze," Juliana said quietly, never once looking away.

Merrick quirked a brow. "How did you make it through?"

"I didn't at first. Then I cut my arm. My blood parted the stone and I was able to pass."

Merrick instantly sat up, his eyes widening. He looked her over, questioningly, as if he sought to find some answer by doing so. His hand reached out as if to touch her. Whispering, he sounded stunned, as he said, "Juliana?"

Juliana wondered at his strange reaction to her words. "I saw the basin, Merrick."

The king's eyes again roamed over her. His fingers shook. Then, drawing his hand back, he balled the fingers into a fist, rested his chin on it. He didn't move, didn't speak.

"I saw you kill him," Juliana stated.

His head tilted to the side. "Who? Gregor?"

Juliana stepped closer. She felt like crying, but she held back, instead forcing herself to remember her brothers. "I know what you did. Why?"

"Juli—"

"I asked why?" she screeched, interrupting his soft tone. Her breath came in hard gasps as she stepped closer. "I begged you not to start a war. I begged you to send me back to Bellemare and end it. Your vanity has brought us to this place, Merrick."

"I told you, I cannot release you," he answered. "It is truer now more than ever. You are bound to this place as much as I."

"You broke your promise to me."

"What promise?"

"You have killed me with what you've done to me. You promised not to hurt them if I bound myself to you." Juliana felt empty, hollow. "All I would know is why. Why, Merrick? You could've left me at Bellemare.

You could've let me have my foolish dreams of this place, never knowing the immortal realm was real."

Merrick stood. He looked at the ground for a long moment before stepping down the platform. Coming before her, he asked, "Is that what you would have? Truly? Your mortal life at Bellemare?"

Juliana looked at him, searching his face. Before she could answer, she heard footsteps behind her.

"I cannot give you the past, Juliana, but I will let you have the future. So be it. I can no longer fight you on it." Merrick glanced over her shoulder. "I release you. You're free of me."

"Juliana?" It was Hugh's voice. The knife fell from her hand. Merrick glanced down in question. When he looked up, realization dawned in his eyes. He took a step back from her, knowing that she'd meant to kill him. Juliana opened her mouth to speak, but Hugh's voice again broke into her thoughts. "Juliana, is that you?"

"Hugh?" Juliana turned. She stared at Hugh. He was alive. Feeling returned to her numbed heart.

Hugh rushed forward, Nicholas more cautiously behind him. Their eyes roamed over her strange attire and she knew she must look strange in the dark elfin gown. Grabbing her in his arms, Hugh hugged her to his side, keeping her close as he pointed his sword at Merrick. "Step back. I'm taking her with me."

Juliana glanced at Merrick. He ignored Hugh and the sword as he stared at her. Merrick bowed his head. He was truly letting her go. Her chest tightened. She didn't want to be free. Turning back to her brother, Juliana pulled his sword arm down. Tears streamed her cheeks as she said, "Methought you were dead. I saw you laying in the forest and methought you dead."

Hugh's body was still tense, but he reached his hand to cup her face, keeping his sword lifted cautiously toward Merrick. Juliana saw Nicholas and hugged her brother tighter.

"And Thomas? Where is Thomas?" she demanded, looking past Nicholas

"Juliana," Nicholas began. She shrank away from him, remembering his face as he hacked into his father.

"Hugh?" Juliana demanded, shaking violently. "Where is Thomas?"

Hugh didn't answer. He closed his eyes briefly, shaking his head. When he again opened his eyes, he was glaring at Merrick. Juliana followed her brother's gaze. Merrick sat on his throne, unmoving. He wouldn't look at them as he stared into the fireplace.

"Ask King Merrick where Thomas is," Hugh spat.

"Hugh, come," Nicholas urged. "We've gotten what we've come for. Take her and leave. I will finish this."

"Nay," Juliana shouted. She pulled away from Nicholas. Then, desperately, she said to Hugh, "I saw things in the water... I... You must listen to me..."

"Juliana?" Hugh questioned.

"Juliana?" Nicholas repeated, reaching to touch her. "Come. We will discuss this—"

"Lord Eadward—" Juliana tried to speak.

"Do not worry. You will be safe," Hugh soothed, looking at her as if she'd gone mad. "Nicholas will take care of you. Go with him. I will be right behind you, but first I must finish this."

"Nay," Juliana shook. She looked at all three men before gripping Hugh's arm tighter. "I saw him. I saw what he's done."

"Thomas?" Hugh asked.

"Eadward," Juliana corrected. She looked at Nicholas. "I saw you." She cried harder. "I saw what you did."

Nicholas paled and backed away. Weakly, he asked, "What madness is this? What has he told you? It's a lie, Juliana."

Juliana pulled from Hugh, backing away from all three men, keeping them in her sights. Hugh was confused, angry, hurt. Nicholas was pale and shaking violently. Merrick was calm, watching the flames with a look of dispassion on his handsome face.

"I saw you kill your father, Nicholas. You took your sword and massacred him in his bed." Juliana stared him down. "You made us believe it was Merrick, but it was you." Juliana shivered. As she said the words, she saw the truth on his pale face, even as he tried to shake his head in denial.

"Nicholas?" Hugh demanded. "What is she talking about?"

"He was too old for her," Nicholas whispered. His eyes pleaded with Juliana, even as he spoke to Hugh. "He knew I loved her. He knew and still he planned to take her as his wife. I couldn't let him take her from me. I only wanted to love her. I've only ever wanted to love her, but she wouldn't even look at me. I didn't mean to kill him. The voice…the voice told me to. It took over. It whispered in my ear, telling me to do it."

A trail of fire appeared, growing in the stone beside Merrick. The flames formed and soon King Lucien was standing in the hall, looking at the mortals with disdain. No one moved.

"Lucien," Merrick said, frowning, "these affairs do not concern you."

Lucien laughed. Stepping down from the platform, he didn't answer Merrick as he looked at Nicholas. Passing Juliana's knife, he stopped and picked it up. "I'm very disappointed in you Nicholas. The demon I gave you shows so much promise and yet you confess to the murder like a whining child."

"I never asked for this," Nicholas said.

"Then you should have taken more care with what you say." Lucien's face contorted. He lifted his hand. Nicholas screamed, falling to his knees before the Demon King. Juliana couldn't move. Fire burned in Nicholas' eyes. He clutched his chest, falling over on his side.

"Let him go!" Hugh demanded.

"Hugh, nay!" Juliana said, running around Lucien to stop Hugh from attacking. If Hugh went up against the powerful king, he'd never survive. When he'd touched her, she'd seen the death in Lucien. As she passed by Lucien's back, he spun around and grabbed her arm.

"And you, my lady," the King of the Damned spat.

"Unhand her, Lucien," Merrick ordered. Nicholas continued to scream. Hugh surged forward to stop Lucien. The Demon King flung his power out at him, throwing him across the main hall. Juliana screamed, kicking and scratching at Lucien to be set free.

"Stay back, Merrick," Lucien warned. He drew the blade to Juliana's stomach, pointing the tip at her. "Dragon's blood covers this blade. I don't have to tell you what that can do."

Merrick froze. Lucien motioned his hand. Shackles grew from the floor, binding Merrick's hands and tugging him down to the stone so he knelt beside his throne. Juliana knew Merrick could've stopped it, but he didn't. His dark eyes looked up at her, giving nothing away. Nicholas screamed again, writhing in agony.

"Ugh, enough bellowing," Lucien growled. He flicked his hand at Nicholas, twisting his fingers. Nicholas went up in flames, almost instantly burning into a pile of ash. Juliana screamed, fighting Lucien's hold. Her heart went out to Nicholas in pity. "Quiet! I grow weary of this game. It is time to end it."

Juliana stiffened. Merrick strained against his ties, but didn't get free. Lucien lifted his fingers as Hugh ran forward from the back of the hall. Reaching out his hand to stop him, Lucien lifted Hugh up into the air, suspending him.

"You have a choice, Juliana," Lucien whispered into her ear. "Kill the man who killed Thomas or watch another one of your brothers die."

Juliana looked from Hugh to Merrick. She didn't know what to believe anymore. Lucien was a liar. He'd told her Hugh was dead. Maybe Thomas was safe. Nothing in this realm was as it seemed. Isn't that what everyone kept telling her? That things were not as they appeared, to look beyond what she saw with her eyes. Maybe it was time to go with how she felt.

'Ah, mortals. You can never see things how they are.' Kalen had told her that when he urged her to go to the garden. She thought of the basin. She didn't see Merrick kill Thomas, only saw him above his unmoving

body. Maybe there was more to the story which she wasn't being told. Was it possible the basin hadn't shown her the whole picture, just a fragment that she misinterpreted?

"My patience wanes, my lady," Lucien warned. He lifted the knife, offering her the hilt. His eyes flashed with the color of flames before turning completely black.

Juliana took the knife. She looked at Merrick, shaking. He lifted his chin, proud, giving nothing away—not begging, not pleading. She heard his words in her head. *'That's the problem with mortals. You can't see beyond the rational. You can't feel into your dreams. With your kind, everything is literal, logical, either right or wrong, good or evil.'*

"Decide," Lucien hissed into her ear. "Your brother or the man who killed Thomas."

Juliana nodded at Lucien. He let her go with a shove. She stumbled toward Merrick, gripping the blade. "I have a question for you, Merrick. According to the deal we made at Bellemare I have the right to ask you a question at the end of the journey. I would say this is the end."

Merrick nodded once. He didn't try to defend himself as she came to him, not that he could have trapped to the floor. His face was hard, yet so handsome. She ached to comfort him, but didn't know how. "Ask your question of me."

Juliana closed her eyes.

"Ask him to send us home," Hugh yelled, still in the air at Lucien's will. "Free yourself! Get far away from here!"

"Quiet!" Lucien yelled, slamming Hugh onto the floor.

"I ask you, Merrick, will...?" Juliana looked deep into his unreadable eyes. "Do you...? Could you ever love me?"

Without flinching, he said, "Nay."

Lucien laughed, the sound echoed over the hall.

"Juliana, nay!" Hugh yelled trying to push weakly from the floor.

Juliana gripped the knife. She stepped closer. Again, Merrick's words drifted through her thoughts, 'You mortals look with your eyes and hear with your ears, but you are blind and deaf. All I ask is that you see me for what I am, hear me.'

"Do it," Merrick whispered, looking at the blade. She felt sadness— his sadness. It passed through her. "You've made your choice."

Merrick knew that if she were to stab him, she would not kill him. It would take more than the blade to end his reign. But it would weaken him, make it possible for Lucien to finish the job. But Lucien would not be king of both. The crown would be his to appoint. Either that, or Lucien would keep him alive, just on the border of death and use him for all eternity as his slave.

Merrick watched Juliana, his face hard and unmoving. She always believed the worst in him and why not? He had wronged her in many ways. Even if he couldn't help himself, even if bringing her to his palace was the will of fate, he could've fought to stop it. Truth was, he didn't want to stop it. He wanted her here, wanted her from that first moment. Even as she hated him, he wanted her. Her face, not so innocent as before but far from jaded, was the one piece of heaven in his hell. As he studied her, her body thin, her face pale, he realized what was happening. She was like the flowers of the immortal realm. To be with him would mean her death. He would slowly suck the life out of her as he did all things. He was her winter.

If she believed he was dead, believed she'd done the right thing, then maybe he could give her a small measure of peace. Ean blessed Bellemare and would be watching it more closely now. Lucien could not cross over into the mortal world. She would be safe, of that he had no doubt. Her brothers could love her, protect her. She'd be blessed. All Merrick had to offer her was a curse.

Merrick glanced at her stomach, wondering if she would raise the child and knowing automatically that she would love the boy. He knew the moment she said her blood let her into the garden that she was pregnant. Now, more than ever, he knew he had to let her go—for their son, for her life. He had to force her hand. Regardless of what happened to him, she had to be free of him. His eternity no longer mattered. What mattered was his family, even if he couldn't be with them. And, maybe someday, he'd be able to see his boy from afar.

"You cannot do it, can you, Juliana?" he taunted, laughing cruelly, even as it killed a piece of him to say the words. "I kidnap you to start a war. I take your innocence. I bring you here—lie to you, trick you, torture you—and still you are too weak to strike back."

Juliana gasped, looking as if he slapped her. It took all his concentration to remain calm, to keep the mocking expression on his face. Her fingers shook, gripping the blade so firmly that her knuckles were white.

"I've made my decision," she snarled, glaring at Merrick. The Unblessed King closed his eyes, waiting for the first strike of her blade. He heard her move and looked just in time to see her spin around. She threw the blade at Lucien. It struck the Demon King in the stomach. Lucien groaned in surprise, leaning over to pull at the blade. Growling, she said to Lucien, "My brothers taught me how to throw a blade as good as any man. I will not be manipulated by you. Begone at once from my sight!"

Lucien's hold weakened. Merrick's arms were freed from the shackles. He stood, throwing his arms forward. Lucien yelled in anger as Merrick's power struck him to force him from the hall. The Demon King's body blurred, fading into the wind as he blew from the Black Palace. Merrick used all his power to lock the man out.

Juliana's knife clanged to the floor. She looked at it before rushing around the fallen blade to help Hugh to his feet. Merrick stood, not moving to follow her. He kept his body stiff, his face impassable. It was for the best. He would give her no reason to stay.

"Hugh, are you…?" she began, shaking terribly.

"Aye, I'm fine," he assured her.

She helped her brother to his feet. Looking at Merrick, she asked, "Is Lucien dead?"

"Nay, but he will be too weak to come back. Your way home is safe. Take your brothers and leave. I have my war. I'm done with you. Ean blesses you and Lucien cannot enter the mortal realm. You will be free of us."

"Brothers? You said brothers?" Juliana asked. The door behind the throne opened. Thomas limped out, looking dazed. He stumbled before stopping and looking around. "Thomas?"

"Thomas?" Hugh repeated, bewildered. "How? I saw you. You were dead."

Juliana ran to him, wrapping Thomas in her arms. He moaned and she instantly pulled off. He coughed weakly as he swayed on his feet. Hugh joined them. All three looked at Merrick.

"Go," Merrick said, his voice dark. He forced a bored expression to his face as he crossed over to his throne. He lounged over the side, closing his eyes. It was easier than watching her walk out of his life. "Before I change my mind and kill you all off. I'm tired of this game."

"How?" Hugh asked.

"Your journey begins as any other." Merrick motioned his hand for them to leave the hall. "By walking out the front gate of the castle."

Chapter Fourteen

Juliana glanced at Merrick, not moving. He stared back at them and frowned, shaking his head as he turned his eyes toward the nearest fireplace, refusing to look at her again. His head rested against his throne and his knee was hooked over the arm of the chair, his foot swinging lightly back and forth.

Hugh cleared his throat to get her attention. Juliana helped him support Thomas as they walked from the hall. When they reached the front gate, the land was no longer a forest but a long field. The horses of Nicholas and Hugh grazed right on the edge. In the far distance she saw Bellemare castle. It was a welcome sight, one that would always be in her heart.

Juliana touched Hugh's face, kissing his cheek. Then, kissing Thomas', she said, "I love you both."

"Juliana?" Thomas questioned. He glanced toward home.

Juliana shook her head. "Nay. I'm staying. Give my love to William. Take care of each other and I promise I shall see you all again."

"Why?" Hugh demanded. "You heard him. He doesn't love you. He's let you go. He doesn't want you here. Whatever his reason, he's freed you from this game of his. It's over. Leave the immortals to their realm. We do not belong here."

"Nicholas wants to marry you—" Thomas began, his eyes pleading.

"Thomas, nay." Hugh shook his head, giving his brother a meaningful look. Thomas paled, which was a feat considering his already white pallor. To his sister, Hugh asked, "Why do this, Juliana?"

"Because he was never meant to rule his kind alone," she said simply. "And I love him."

"But he doesn't return your love. I cannot allow this," Hugh said. The days of stress and worry were on his face as he looked at her. She was sorry for it, but she could do nothing else. "You have a duty to your family, to Bellemare. It is my duty to protect you, to do what is right. I forbid you from staying."

"He does love me, in his way," Juliana said. "You just have to hear with more than your ears. It's not perfect, but it's what I want."

"I forbid it, you're not married," Hugh said. His hand rose in frustration. "This place is not for us. This realm is not for us. Come home where I can protect you."

"I love you both," Juliana said, as she lifted her hand taking a step back.

Hugh narrowed his eyes in warning. "Don't do this, Juliana. Don't make me take you by force back to Bellemare. I will. I will lock you in a tower if I must, but I will keep you safe."

"Take care of each other," she said.

"Juliana!" Hugh yelled. He faded from her sight and Bellemare was replaced by trees. Juliana wiped a tear from her cheek, not completely sure she made the right decision. However, she knew she made her decision. This was what she wanted.

Slowly she turned and walked back into the palace. A great roar sounded. Goblins came running from the hall. Juliana moved past them, rushing to see what happened. Merrick stood in the hall, yelling in anger. She stopped, watching him. "Merrick?"

He turned to her, a look of disbelief on his face. His eyes were almost completely black. She shivered, her body shaking as she took a step for him.

"What are you still doing here?" he spat. "I told you to leave."

"I'm sorry I blamed you for Eadward," she said softly. "I'm sorry I was blind."

"I don't need your forgiveness or your apologies. I said go. Now." He didn't move as he glared at her.

Juliana took a deep breath, slowly edging forward. "I've made many assumptions about you, Merrick. I've been wrong, but you haven't made it easy either. You could've tried to tell me the truth."

"For what reason?" Merrick frowned, but his eyes lightened by a small degree. "If you believe the worst in me, you will never believe anything I say."

"Possibly," she said. "Still, you could have tried."

"Leave, Juliana," he said, shaking his head. "I'll reopen the portal, but you must go. Go home to your beloved Bellemare. Go home to your brothers. Have you not begged me for that very thing since we first met? That is where you long to be. That is where you belong."

"I made a deal with you, Merrick. I belong here. I would keep my word." Juliana was scared, not of Merrick or what he would do, but of herself, her feelings, of the idea of never seeing him again.

"Go or I'll kill you." Merrick pointed at the door, taking a threatening step for her. He was terrifying to behold. Still, she didn't allow herself to be scared.

"No, you won't."

"My life draws from yours. See how pale you are? How thin? You will soon wither like a flower of this realm. I will kill you whether I wish to or not."

"Your power comes from fear. I may fear things, but I don't fear you, not anymore." Juliana closed the distance between them. She touched his face. "Your presence cannot hurt me, Merrick. You cannot hurt me. If I am pale, it is because I am tired and if I am thin, it's because I am hungry."

"Don't be so sure," he warned.

"I love you, Merrick," she said, ignoring his gruff voice and his irritated sighs. "Whether you like it or not, want it or not, I love you. Freely. Completely. Forever. And I'm staying by your side. You cannot be rid of me."

A breeze fluttered over the hall. Merrick's black banners were replaced with lighter blue, a cheerier color. He glanced around the hall. Juliana's dark gown changed. The kohl faded from her eyes and arms. Her tight black dress was replaced with a blue tunic gown.

"I didn't do that," he whispered in awe.

"I did," she said.

"How?"

"I have absolutely no idea," she laughed softly, looking around. All she knew is that she desired it and it happened. "You have lived in darkness for too long and you have ruled it alone. Not anymore."

He didn't speak.

"Tell me you love me," she demanded, smiling insecurely.

Merrick hesitated. She knew he was scared, felt that he was. Slowly, he nodded. "Aye."

Juliana grinned, knowing he wouldn't say the words aloud, and pulled at his neck. She forced his body to hers as she kissed him. Pouring all her passion and feelings into the embrace, she couldn't stop smiling.

Finally, pulling back, Merrick stroked her hair, "I should force you to leave."

"I won't go."

"The things I said to you earlier about kidnapping you to start a war," he explained.

"Were done to get me to leave," Juliana said. "You can't trick me anymore, Merrick."

He smiled. "It will not be easy."

"The best adventures never are."

Merrick looked down at her stomach. Lightly he touched her. She stiffened, following his eyes down. "I should tell you something. Kalen saw—"

"—too much," Kalen's voice sounded behind her. "You send Iago to the borderlands to retrieve me from my post only to make me watch this?"

Juliana turned. Kalen strode into the hall frowning. The man shook his head, giving a wry smile.

"Go away, Kalen," Merrick said, grinning. "You are no longer needed."

"Wait," Juliana ordered. She eyed both men. "Kalen saw what?"

"Many things, my queen, many things." Kalen winked.

"Hum," Juliana began to question further when she froze. "Did he just call me queen?"

"Well, aye, you are," Kalen said, as if it was no big deal.

"Married?" Juliana looked from one man to the other.

"For sometime now, my queen," Kalen answered, grinning widely. "I told you we smelled him on you. We've been waiting for the announcement for quite a long while. Oh, and another celebration. If not for this damned war, I would have enjoyed the company of a dark mermaid temptress last time."

Juliana quirked a brow at Merrick. "I am your queen and you were just going to let me walk out the door?"

"I didn't know," Merrick said, looking just as stunned as she.

"Well, I didn't want to ruin it. You seem so happy when you're fighting." Kalen turned to leave, before stopping and saying, "Oh, and if you think that news shocks, wait until that baby is born. You're in for a great surprise."

Juliana gasped. "Merrick?"

"I was trying to tell you. Your powers, the reason you were able to get through the garden."

"A baby?" Juliana looked down, shocked.

"A family," he whispered, capturing her face and kissing her gently. Then, kneeling before her, he pulled her hips, resting his cheek on her stomach. Juliana smiled, stroking his hair. "I won't let anything happen to you. I swear it."

"And I will protect you as well, my love," Juliana said, stroking his blond hair. "Your burden is no longer your own."

Lucien gripped his stomach, growling in anger as he glared into the little cell beneath his palace. Three men hung before him in chains. They didn't move, didn't moan in pain. Trapped in their minds, they were in a suspended state of horror and pain.

"Welcome home, Sir Nicholas," Lucien said darkly, eyeing the newest member to his prison. Nicholas opened his eyes and instantly screamed in agony. He looked around in confusion. Lucien merely chuckled, knowing the man didn't completely understand what was happening to him. "Don't worry. I'm leaving you with some very prestigious company."

Nicholas stopped screaming as Lucien lessoned his pain. The man turned to the two elves hanging motionless by his side.

"Meet Ladon and Wolfe, once princes of Tegwen, two of my most treasured possessions." Lucien laughed. "Like you, no one knows that they live. You disappointed me today, Nicholas, but you show so much promise, so much rage, that I hate to let you out of our bargain so quickly. I have a feeling I may need you someday soon."

Nicholas breathed hard, glaring at Lucien, unable to speak. The King of the Damned laughed, waving his hand in the air. Nicholas again fell into the hellish world of his dreams, reliving the crimes which he committed over and over again.

Lucien was angry his plans had gone awry. Merrick would no longer trust him. Lord Bellemare wasn't his to control. Lady Juliana was obviously in love with Merrick—a fact that would make him even more on the side of the blessed than of the damned. The only bright spot in his failed plotting was that Tegwen and Valdis were still at war. Gregor had done his job well and with his death, none would ever know the truth of it. The kingdoms would fight and Lucien would wait. Someday, he would find a way to try again. Someday, he would rule all.

Letting the flames consume him, he went to Mia to release his frustrations. This news would bring her happiness, no doubt. And, whereas her happiness weakened his strength, it also pleased a small part of the man left inside him.

"My queen," Lady Roslyn said, bowing low before Tania in the Silver Palace's hall. "It is done. The whispers say King Merrick has accepted Lady Juliana. She is his queen."

"What news of my lord?" Tania demanded. Her heart fluttered, mimicking the rapid beat of her wings as she hovered over the throne. All knew the war had started between the blessed and unblessed. Many would stay out of it until they were forced to take sides, letting the two kingdoms fight. Tania knew she would have to choose Tegwen, but faeries were no good with war and it was unlikely they would call upon her people.

"Lord Bellemare lives, my queen," Roslyn said, her blue wings fluttering. She glanced over to her sister Lily. Lily looked down at the floor, her wings turned down, as she hid her face behind her long blonde hair. "The rumors say he fought bravely."

"Then he will come soon," Tania said, smiling slightly. She tried not to let her pleasure show, but it was hard when her body practically sparkled with just the thought of Hugh.

Roslyn and Lily both looked up at her. They weren't smiling.

"What is it?" Tania demanded, flying to stand before them. She lowered her voice. "Tell me."

"I don't think he's coming, my queen," Lily said quietly.

"He's gone back to the mortal realm. He's at Bellemare even as we speak," Roslyn added.

"He did not come for you as he promised," Lily said.

Tania's skin darkened. She shook, not liking the bad feelings forming inside her. Hugh did not come for her. He forgot her already. "It cannot be. He will come. He will take care of Bellemare and he will come back."

"Yes, my queen," Lily and Roslyn said in unison, backing away from her.

Tania breathed hard, her face contorting in anger. Screeching loudly, she repeated, "He will come back."

***

"I christen you, Commander Adal, leader of the Tegwen armies," Ean said, placing his hand on Adal's dark head. The man's bronzed skin glistened with oils from his preparation for this night. He was a big elf, a strong, true warrior, quite capable of leading the men to battle. All were surprised Ean picked the man over all others, over those who'd served closest to the fallen Commander Gregor. King Ean was surprised himself. Something told him, as he was about to name Talan the new commander, to pick Adal instead. He followed his instincts. Talan was not happy with the choice, but could not fight it. As king, Ean's word was law. "Rise, Commander Adal."

Those gathered in the hall cheered. Musicians struck up a song and couples instantly spread out over the floor to dance. Faeries brought out trays of food and pitchers of mead. It was going to be a great celebration. Ean put his hand out, fingers up, pressing his palm to Adal's.

"Enjoy your night, Adal," Ean said. "Tomorrow afternoon we will talk."

Adal smiled. "Thank you, my king."

Ean moved to leave. He needed to be alone to think.

"My king?"

Ean turned to Adal.

"Pardon me, but may I walk with you? Just for a moment?" Adal asked.

"Aye," Ean said, as he unhurriedly made his way to his private chambers. "And speak freely."

"Not that I question your judgment, my king, but why choose me over Talan?" Adal glanced over his shoulder.

"It's what fate wanted," Ean answered without further explanation.

Adal nodded. "I will not let you down."

Ean clasped the man's shoulder. "I know."

"There is one more thing, my king. Rumor has it that King Merrick has taken a queen," Adal said.

"I have heard this. Lady Juliana. It would seem she was truly Merrick's mate. You will be told all you need to know of her on the morrow," Ean assured the man.

"Aye," Adal nodded. "But King Merrick is Unblessed. He shouldn't have a true mate. And there is more. I have also been told that Lady Juliana carries the heir to the Valdis throne."

Ean stiffened, stunned by the words. "If it is true, the baby cannot be his. It's hard enough for us to beget heirs, but for the Unblessed King to find such a match, even with a mate, to reproduce without spells or black magic. It...it can't be."

"Merrick was like you once, my king. Perhaps that lingers," Adal persisted.

"If she carries a child, it cannot be Merrick's," Ean said. Adal opened his mouth, but the king held up his hand. "There is plenty of time for this, commander. Now I order you to go. Find a woman or two to warm your bed and celebrate this night as it should be celebrated. I have to go contemplate a war."

"Aye, my king," Adal said, grinning. "I will gladly obey a command such as that."

Ean watched the man leave before climbing the stairs. Merrick, a father? It was impossible. It was too bad that Merrick didn't choose Juliana as his bride from the beginning. If he had, perhaps the whole war could have been avoided. Once started, it was hard to undo.

Regardless, Merrick's army shot the arrow. It was clear his brother wanted this war, Queen Juliana or no. Ean had no choice but to fight it.

*

"Oh, aye, of course I knew!" Gorman boasted, puffing his chest out with pride. He glanced around the forest at his fellow sprights. The small village was lifted into the trees. Small rope handrails worked along the tree limbs, joining the small houses. The onlookers stared at them with rapt attention, treating them like heroes as they brought them leaves filled with nuts and berries. "I mean, Lady Juliana is obviously blessed. Anyone could see it with just one look at her."

"Obviously," Halton added. "And we're to be moving to the Black Palace to protect her. We tried to resist, but it was her wish and we are now bound to serve her."

"When a queen calls, you must listen," Gorman added. "She wants us to be her protection against damned forces."

"Protect a queen," someone said in awe.

"Aye," Gorman said smartly.

"Tell us about the war," a young boy said. "Is it true you fought alongside Tegwen?"

"Nay, we fought for both sides," Halton bragged. "The Blessed King wanted us and Lady Juliana, being the future unblessed queen wanted us, so we helped both sides win the battle."

"Aye, that's never been done before," Gorman added. "Now, we have to go to Valdis to be with Queen Juliana. She demands it. Naturally, I'll be in the castle. I'm her favorite."

"What?" Halton demanded. "You know I'm her favorite. I'll be sleeping in the same room as she and King Merrick."

"Will not!"

"Will so!"

"Will not!"

Halton leapt up from his chair, tackling Gorman to the ground. Dust flew up around them. "Will so!"

Hugh sat on the end of Thomas' bed, his feet kicked up as he leaned against a poster. Thomas was recovering slowly, but his injuries had brought him so close to death that Hugh was still worried for him. William sat beside Thomas on the bed. The youngest brother agreed to stay at Bellemare, helping Thomas and Hugh to understand the immortal realm better. None could make sense of Juliana's decision and Hugh was not sure he could make peace with it either.

No one spoke of Nicholas and they did not spread news of his deeds. Nicholas was dead. There was no reason to dwell on it. The man had been like a brother to them and they could not make sense of Eadward's murder.

"I cannot believe you kissed Queen Tania," William said, laughing to break the silence. "I'll bet she was livid."

"Aye," Thomas said, his soft laughter joining William's. "You should have seen her face."

Hugh frowned. "I don't wish to discuss it."

"Aye, he's still sore because he didn't get to bed the pretty ladies," Thomas said, grinning weakly. His skin was pale, but it was good to see him smiling.

"Perhaps he's not sore," William snickered, "and that's the problem."

Hugh grumbled. "I don't want to hear any more about that woman or her faeries. She's a menace and I'm glad to be rid of her."

His brothers laughed harder. Hugh shook his head, giving nothing away. Truthfully, his body still burned for Tania. He would never admit to it and he knew going back to slake his lust wasn't wise. It was better to leave things as they were. He didn't belong in that world any more than she belonged in his. Besides, the last thing he needed was that aggravating pain in the neck as his lover. He'd be as likely to strangle her as to make love to

her. No, his duty was to Bellemare. This is where he would stay and here he
would find another lover. So long as her body was soft and her arms
willing, any woman would do.

"The only reason I would ever go back to the immortal realm is if
Juliana needed us," Hugh said.

"Aye," Thomas whispered. He stared down at the blanket.

"Aye," William added. He too became quiet with contemplation.

The brothers didn't say a word as the room again fell to silence.

Juliana wrapped her arm around Merrick's waist and sighed. The
garden walls parted as they moved toward the divining basin. The stone
didn't make a sound. Soft moonlight caressed them from above and crimson
flowers bloomed as they walked, rippling like a wave over the dark stone.

There were no more secrets. They'd talked for a long time about what
was between them. Merrick told her everything she asked to know.
However, just because they didn't have secrets didn't change the fact that
they were still at war with Tegwen. Juliana came to understand that war was
just as necessary as peace. And, hate it as she did, she would dream of a day
when peace could again have its turn.

"Can't we just send a missive and tell Ean we don't want to fight?"
Juliana asked. "Can't we just hate each other for awhile, play some pranks
and then call a truce?"

"It doesn't work like that, my queen," Merrick answered, kissing her
temple. "I told you. Peace has ruled and now is the time for war. It is the
way things must be." He slipped his hand over the small swell in her
stomach. "Those must die so others can be reborn."

She covered his hand with hers.

"Do you regret staying with me?" Merrick asked. "The curse of what
we are will only get harder with time. The things you've been seeing,
feeling, they only get worse."

"So long as we have each other," Juliana said softly, caressing his chest, "we will be fine. No burden is too great."

"Aye." Merrick kissed her softly, continuing to walk. "May you always feel that way."

"I will," she assured him. "Together we can get through anything. I love you. Nothing can change that."

"And I you," he said, never saying the actual words. Juliana didn't care. She knew he feared what would happen if he admitted his feelings aloud. How could she blame him? He was King of the Unblessed after all.

They reached the center garden. As the wall closed, blocking them in, the flowers spread, filling up the garden with crimson life. Merrick led her to the basin of water.

"Are you sure we have to do this?" she asked.

"Aye." Merrick looked at the water.

"But we will no longer be able to see the future and past. What if we need to someday?" Juliana asked.

"This basin was from Lucien. I will not give him access to my home." Merrick let go of her, knocking the basin of water over. The pedestal fell. The basin cracked. The demonic figures slowly faded and turned to dust, blowing away in the wind.

"How will I see my brothers? A bowl of water?" Juliana asked softly.

"That power was tied to the basin," he said, motioning to the broken stone. "I'm sorry, but I can't show you like that."

"Then how will I know all is well with them?"

"In time you can visit Bellemare. I will take you there with our son. Just not now." He gave her stomach a meaningful pat. Juliana smiled. "Not until it is safe."

Slowly, he walked her back toward the Black Palace, her new home. It wasn't perfect, but it was what she wanted.

Michelle M. Pillow

To learn more about Michelle M Pillow or the Realm Immortal series, please visit her website at www.michellepillow.com. Send an email to Michelle at michelle_pillow@yahoo.com or join her Yahoo! Group to learn of upcoming and current releases! http://groups.yahoo.com/group/michellempillow/join

Now available in print!

Stud Finders Incorporated
By Alexis Fleming
1-59998-042-8

Wanted -- An Orgasm... and the chance to fulfill all her sexual fantasies.

Madison believes she's frigid. Her ex told her so and maybe it's true, because there's one thing she's never experienced. An orgasm! Now she wants it all. So when her mother rings Stud Finders Incorporated and hires a stud for her to practice on, why look a gift horse in the mouth?

Jake's ex-lover said he was boring, both in bed and out. So when sexy Madison asks him to teach her to have an orgasm, he jumps at the chance to prove his manhood. Even if it means hiding the fact that the purpose of Stud Finders Incorporated is to find the studs behind the wallboards of a building so the owner can safely hang his paintings.

Warning: This book contains hot, explicit sex between two people explained in graphic language.

Now available in print!

Loup Garou
By Mandy M. Roth
1-59998-043-6

Lindsay Willows craves a simple life. One where she can make a difference without drawing too much attention to herself. As the daughter of both a vampire and a fay, the cards were already stacked against her. Finding out she's the supposed mate of a dark fay prince doesn't help matters. Especially when there are those who will stop at nothing to prevent her from mating with a prince she's never even met.

When Exavier Kedmen, the incredibly sexy front man for a world-famous band, shows up wanting her to go back to a field she left three years ago, she can't explain the strong feelings that surface for a man she barely knows. Lindsay finds herself confronting demons from her past, coming to terms with the ones in the present and finally looking forward to a future with the man she was created for. And she discovers evil doesn't care who it hurts to obtain its goals but even the evilest of things fear something, or in the case of Exavier, someone.

Warning: This book contains hot, explicit sex and violence explained with contemporary, graphic language.

Now available in print!

Forever Again
By Shannon Stacey
1-59998-044-4

Fifteen years ago, Gena Taylor and Travis Ryan were forced into a marriage neither wanted, the price they paid after one night of passion. But what he believed to be a lie forced Travis to walk out of her life shortly thereafter, crushing Gena's dreams of a happily ever after with the only man she'd ever loved.

Fifteen years later, Travis and Gena meet again. Only now, she owns the inn he's considering for his wedding—to another woman. And this time, she's guarding her heart carefully. She's not going to allow him to hurt her—or their daughter.

Despite their resolve to keep things impersonal, the past comes rushing back and feelings they both thought long dead rise from the ashes. But there arc other lives at stake now, including that of the child Travis once thought was a lie.

Now available in print!

The Gripping Beast
By Charlene Teglia
1-59998-055-X

The wild magic that brought them together is nothing compared to what they find in each other's arms.

Lorelei Michaels, flamboyant lead vocalist of the all-female rock band The Sirens, has a passion for myths and legends. She just never expected to find herself actually living one.

While touring with the band, a Viking armband with an interesting history and a design known as the gripping beast throws her into a time warp—full of Norsemen, macho attitudes and a lamentable lack of modern amenities.

Upon seeing the strange, beautiful woman being auctioned off, Erik Thorolfsson was mesmerized. Until the slave trader put his hands on her. With a roar of rage and sword drawn, he charged forward to take that which he wanted for his own. But he discovers owning her isn't enough, he has to make her his—for all time

Samhain Publishing, Ltd.

It's all about the story...

Action/Adventure
Fantasy
Historical
Horror
Mainstream
Mystery/Suspense
Non-Fiction
Paranormal
Romance
Science Fiction
Western
Young Adult

http://www.samhainpublishing.com

Printed in the United States
56275LVS00002B/155